OTHER BOOKS by KASSANDRA LAMB

The Kate Huntington Mystery Series:

MULTIPLE MOTIVES
ILL-TIMED ENTANGLEMENTS
FAMILY FALLACIES
CELEBRITY STATUS
COLLATERAL CASUALTIES
ZERO HERO
FATAL FORTY-EIGHT
SUICIDAL SUSPICIONS
ANXIETY ATTACK
POLICE PROTECTION

The Kate on Vacation Novellas:

An Unsaintly Season in St. Augustine
Cruel Capers on the Caribbean
Ten-Gallon Tensions in Texas
Missing on Maui

The Marcia Banks and Buddy Mysteries:

To Kill A Labrador
Arsenic and Young Lacy
The Call of the Woof
A Mayfair Christmas Carol
Patches in the Rye
The Legend of Sleepy Mayfair
The Sound and the Furry
A Star-Spangled Mayfair
(coming Summer, 2019)

Unintended Consequences
Romantic Suspense Stories:
(written under the pen name, Jessica Dale)

Payback
Backlash
Backfire
(coming 2019)

THE SOUND AND THE FURRY
A Marcia Banks and Buddy Mystery

Kassandra Lamb

author of the Kate Huntington Mysteries

a misterio press publication

Published by *misterio press LLC*

Cover art by Melinda VanLone, Book Cover Corner

Photo credits: silhouette of woman and dog by Majivecka, foliage by Venus Kaewyoo, golden retriever by Ruibo Wang

(The right to use above photos purchased through Dreamstime.com; these images and the cover image of this book are copyrighted. They cannot be used without express permission.)

The Sound and the Furry is a work of fiction. All names, characters, events and most places are products of the author's imagination. Any resemblance to actual events or people, living or dead, is entirely coincidental. Some real places may be used fictitiously. The towns of Mayfair, Florida, and Dahlia, Florida are fictitious.

The publisher does not have control over and does not assume any responsibility for third-party websites and their content.

ISBN-13: 978-1-947287-11-2

CHAPTER ONE

It seemed like a good idea at the time. A great idea, the more I'd thought about it.

But my fiancé didn't seem to agree with me. The brow of Will's rugged face furrowed. "Two whole weeks?"

"Look, I have to train Ellie Burke anyway, and yeah, normally I'd do it a few days at a time and come home in between, but that would run into December and might end up conflicting with our trip north to my mom's."

"You could wait until after Christmas to train the woman." Will got up from the kitchen table and went to the coffee maker on the counter. "Want some more?"

I shook my head, both to the coffee and the idea of postponement. "I don't get paid until I deliver the dog. I need to buy Christmas presents."

"I could float you a loan."

That was a nonstarter and he knew it. I was fiercely independent when it came to money. I was even a little uncomfortable with letting him pay for the twenty-by-forty-foot "extension" being built to attach our two bungalows together. I always thought of it in quotation marks, because the new section was almost as big as my entire house.

Which brought me to the other, more compelling issue. "I can't stand the noise anymore, and I can't train with all the racket and disruption. It's too upsetting for the dogs." I glanced over at Buddy. He was currently lying on top of his bed, his big black head resting on his paws. But the bed was scrunched up in the middle, where he'd taken to burrowing under it when the jackhammers started each morning, as the workers demolished the cement-block wall separating my house from the new section. And next week, it would get worse when they attacked the wall in Will's kitchen, next to where we were currently sitting.

Oops, *our* kitchen.

"I'm not sure they'll be finished with the drywall in two weeks," Will said.

In other words, the hammering might not be over by the time we got back.

Then we'll stay away longer, Ms. Snark said inside my head. I mentally slapped a hand over her mouth. I did not need her weighing in and turning this discussion into a full-blown argument.

Will sat back down at the table. He wrapped his big hands around his coffee mug, as if seeking its warmth, even though it was a mild November day. We had the kitchen door sitting open, with a soft breeze drifting in through the screen.

I took a deep breath of the fresh air. I love the long autumns in central Florida, when the intense heat and humidity have let up, but most days, it's still tee-shirt weather.

I was secretly looking forward to staying with Ellie Burke and her husband on their private island, thinking of it as a mini-vacation, even though I would be training for part of each day. Ellie said the island had some wonderful beaches.

I had been staring at Will's hands. Now he lifted one to scratch the stubble on his chin. He'd taken to not shaving on the weekends. I kind of liked the look.

He smiled and his sexy dimples made an appearance. Certain parts of my body began to tingle.

"I've got an idea," he said. "Can you take the weekend off in the middle? We could meet somewhere and stay at a B&B."

The tingling parts voted yes, but my brain was still sufficiently engaged to be cautious.

"I like that plan, but can we wait until Wednesday to make it final? I should know by then if we're to the point in the training where I can leave Nugget with Ellie for the weekend."

"Shouldn't be a problem getting a room on short notice this time of year. I'll research places that allow dogs. You are taking Buddy with you, right?"

"Of course, and Bonbon is going to Stephie's for the two weeks." My assistant—in training to eventually be a trainer herself—would keep the chocolate Labrador from backsliding.

Will raised an eyebrow and frowned again. "So, you had this planned out already?"

Was he really unhappy or just teasing me?

"Well, if she hadn't been okay with taking Bonbon, that would've been a deal breaker."

Will pushed up from his chair and walked around the table. His belt-less jeans rode low on his hips, and his tee-shirt was snug enough to show off his muscular chest.

Lots more tingling now.

His baby-blue eyes softened as he looked down at me, and his mouth twitched on the ends. "So what would've happened if *I'd* objected more strongly?" He took my hand and pulled me to a stand. "Would that have been a deal breaker?"

I relaxed into his warmth, wrapping my arms around his waist. "Of course." I crossed my fingers behind his back.

"Are you crossing your fingers when you say that?" he asked, while burying his face in my thick auburn hair.

"Um, no." I crossed the fingers on the other hand as well, to cover the second fib.

He laughed, his chest vibrating under my cheek. I lifted my head and rubbed that cheek against his scratchy chin to distract him.

It worked. He leaned back a little in the circle of my arms and lowered his face to kiss me.

A phone buzzed on the counter.

Crapola!

Will had gone very still. "Please tell me that's your phone."

"Uh, mine's in my purse in the bedroom."

He muttered something under his breath that I couldn't hear. Probably intentional, since it was no doubt a string of curse words. Bless him for his restraint and respect for my dislike of swearing.

He broke away and walked to the counter, as the phone buzzed again. He read the text, then his fingers flew over the screen. "It's Joe. We've got a case."

Several emotions danced around in my chest and fluttered in my stomach. The hollow feeling of disappointment that our leisurely Saturday was ending so abruptly… but also some relief, and then guilt for feeling relieved. He wouldn't be around much for the next few days anyway—he worked ridiculously long hours when he and his partner were on a new homicide case, only coming home to sleep and change clothes. My being away really wouldn't matter that much.

The fluttering in my stomach I recognized as the ever-present anxiety whenever he was working. I wouldn't say I was used to it, but it only half registered most days now.

It's part of the package when you love a law enforcement officer.

∽

I got my first surprise when I spotted the small green sign that read *Dahlia Park*.

This was it? A gravel parking lot and a few wooden picnic tables. No sign of any buildings.

My GPS piped up, "Arriving at 2045 S. Joshua Drive on your left."

I slowed my car to a crawl. Another even smaller sign declared *No Overnight Camping*. Was overnight parking the same as camping? I'd already had concerns about leaving my car in a park for days on end.

I came to the entranceway and turned in, expecting it to curve around through the trees and foliage and take me to the park building. I'd just go in and check with whoever was on duty.

But the road didn't go anywhere. About thirty feet in, it faded into a wide expanse of gravel and sand that stretched down to water. Nothing to the right but palmetto bushes, some Southern pines and the occasional palm tree. The greenery ran all the way to the river's edge. To the left was a grassy area, also dotted with palm trees and a couple of rather scraggly looking live oaks, dripping with Spanish moss.

I pulled into the patchy shade under one of the oaks. "Be right back," I said to the dogs, then got out to look around. A few cars and trucks were scattered under the trees, a couple with empty boat trailers attached.

I scanned the area for some sign of a road I had missed. Nope, this was it.

I took out my cell phone and pulled up Ellie's text again. I had the address right, and she had specifically said Dahlia Park.

Not to be confused with Dahlia Community Park on the other side of town, the text read.

I was trying to decide what to do next when the puttering of a small motor penetrated my consciousness. A small fishing skiff rounded the palmettos to the right of the park. Gray metal with a blunted bow and a steering wheel halfway back, it didn't look all that sturdy.

A man stood behind the wheel. He turned away. The engine's

puttering stopped, and he brought its prop up out of the water. Pointing the boat toward the shore, he let it drift up onto the sand and gravel.

I walked toward the spot where he would end up. Since he was the only human being in sight, I figured he was my best bet for figuring out if I was in the right place.

He was slightly below average height with a lean build and coppery brown skin. African-American, I assumed, until the boat drifted closer, and I got a better look at his face. It was narrow and weathered, with a long thin nose. A bit of gray was sprinkled through collar-length straight black hair.

Native American?

He raised a hand and gave me a small wave. The sleeve of his white tee shirt rode up, exposing somewhat lighter skin.

He obviously spent a lot of time outdoors.

He jumped over the side of the boat. Bare feet splashed in the shallow water, spraying droplets up onto knee-length cargo shorts. He dragged the skiff farther onto the beach.

He walked toward me, his gait steady, unfazed by the gravel and shells in the sand. "You Ms. Banks?"

"Yes."

He handed me a folded piece of paper. "Ellie said to give that to ya." His Florida Cracker accent was slight.

I unfolded the paper. *This is Jack Denson. His bark is worse than his bite. He'll bring you over to the island. See you soon. Ellie*

I smiled. The note read the way Ellie talked—light and breezy, as if she were always on the verge of laughing.

I knew from her file that the Air Force lieutenant and aeronautic engineer had PTSD, related to watching one of the pilots in her unit die in a plane crash during a test flight. But you'd never know she was dealing with such emotional distress based on her surface personality.

"You got a bag?"

"Yeah, sure. Um, nice to meet you, Jack. I'm Marcia."

He nodded briskly and marched toward my car.

I scrambled to keep up. He stopped by my trunk.

"How'd you know this was mine?" I hit the button on my key fob to open the trunk.

"Only one I don't recognize." He pulled out the duffel bag on top and slung it over one shoulder. "This it?"

"Um, no." I pointed to another larger duffel. "That's the dogs' stuff. Let me get them out."

I opened the back door and unhooked the dogs' safety straps. First Buddy climbed out, then Ellie's dog, Nugget, a golden-retriever-and-something-else mix.

Jack's arched eyebrows suggested that no one had warned him about the size of the dogs.

"Bruce said no worries about your car bein' here. He told the deputy about it."

"Deputy?"

Jack looked at me like I was simple. "Sheriff's deputy. He's the law in town."

"Oh, okay."

What town? The only signs of civilization I'd seen so far were just that, signs—and they weren't overly informative.

Jack steadied the skiff while I climbed aboard. The dogs looked skeptical, but when I called their names they bounded into the boat.

"Sit on down," Jack said.

I took the only seat, a board bench in front of the wheel. He tossed my bag to me.

I eyed the thin layer of fishy-smelling water on the floor of the skiff and wrinkled my nose. But there was no alternative. I signaled the dogs by holding my hand out parallel to the floor and lowering it. They laid down at my feet.

Keeping my bag on my lap, I awkwardly pulled off my sandals, before they got saturated. Hmm, maybe sandals and white capri pants weren't a great choice for today.

Along one side of the floor, safely out of the water, were three fishing poles, one slightly shorter than the others, and a green plastic, make-believe one with *Fisher Price®* stamped on the handle.

I smiled at the sight of the big yellow plastic hook on the end of its sturdy line. I'd had a similar toy as a young child.

The heavier duffel of dog supplies still over his shoulder, Jack shoved the boat back into the water and jumped aboard, rocking us side to side. He took up his position at the wheel.

I glanced back at my car. In Florida, even in the fall and spring, one goes for shade, the sun is so intense. Should I have forfeited shade for a lower risk of a dead limb crashing down on my car? "Those live oaks back there don't look too healthy."

"Water's kind of salty," Jack said. "Their roots might not like it."

"Brackish," I said, showing off my familiarity with the concept, from growing up near the Chesapeake Bay.

It was as if I hadn't spoken.

Jack pulled the cord on the motor and it spluttered to life. "They get a beatin' too, when the wind's high," he raised his voice to be heard over the noise.

"What's the river's name?" I called back over my shoulder.

"Salt River."

Of course.

After that, I gave up on making conversation and enjoyed the cool air blowing on my face. It had a slight tang to it... you guessed it, of salt.

My second surprise of the day—more like a shock, really—came when we arrived about twenty minutes later at a narrow pier sticking out from a heavily wooded island. I couldn't make out any buildings.

Ellie Burke was seated on a lawn chair in a crescent of sunshine, just past the point where the pier joined the land.

Jack dropped the engine down to an idle.

Ellie spread her arms wide, a big smile on her face. "Welcome to Haasi Key, Marcia," she called out.

She was thinner and paler than my memory of her from six months ago, when I'd brought Nugget to meet her, to make sure the two were a good fit. Her blonde hair was up in a ponytail, but a few loose strands floated around her face in the light breeze off the river.

Then I got a better look at her chair, and my mouth fell open. It wasn't a lawn chair.

Ellie was sitting in a wheelchair.

CHAPTER TWO

I clamped my mouth shut and plastered on a smile, but inside I was doing a slow burn.

I'd met with Ellie twice before and there'd been no sign of a physical disability, nor was any mentioned in her file. If I'd known about whatever injury or ailment now had her in a wheelchair, I could have trained Nugget accordingly.

Jack killed the engine and let the skiff drift toward the narrow beach near the pier. "Can the dogs get a little wet?" he asked.

Now he asks, Ms. Snark commented, *after they've been lying in brine.*

I kept the fake smile in place. "No problem. Buddy loves water."

My boy was already standing, peering down at the water and quivering all over.

"Go on," I said.

Buddy jumped out of the boat and splashed to shore. Nugget and I waited until the bottom scraped sand, then we followed at a more sedate pace, my sandals dangling from my fingers. Jack brought up the rear, with the duffel bags.

I stopped to slip my sandals on. Buddy shook all over and trotted over to me. I swear he was grinning.

As we approached Ellie, a movement in the shadowy woods behind her startled me. An older woman stood back several feet, a sour expression on her face.

Despite my fake smile, Ellie must have picked up on my displeasure. She struggled to a stand. "I only use this occasionally." She pointed to the chair.

The older woman stepped forward. "Ellie?" Her tone was half questioning, half censoring.

Ellie waved a hand in the air, then winced. "I feel much better than I did this morning, really." But her smile seemed forced. "Hi, Nugget."

The dog looked up at me. Even though she wasn't on duty, I gave the release signal. Her red-gold tail waved in the air, and she bounded over to her new owner.

Ellie leaned down, her movements stiff. She scratched behind the dog's ears and crooned softly to her. Nugget ate it up, her whole back end wiggling.

I watched indulgently, stroking Buddy's head as he sat beside me.

"Come on up to the house." My hostess turned and wobbled a bit.

"Might as well ride, Ellie." Jack's tone seemed slightly impatient. "I gotta wheel the chair up there anyway."

"You need to take it easy," the older woman said, with a slight accent I couldn't place. The words were solicitous, but her expression belied that. She looked like she sucked on rotten lemons on a regular basis and enjoyed it.

Ellie sank into the wheelchair. "This is Greta, our housekeeper."

Jack dropped the smaller of my duffels in her lap. With the heavier one slung over his shoulder, he stepped behind the chair. He shoved it none too gently toward the house, which I could see, now that I knew it was there.

Its facade was mostly hidden behind several ancient live oaks, but I got an impression of rough wood siding—cypress, maybe—painted a medium gray with white trim, and a slightly lighter gray metal roof.

And as Ellie had said, when trying to convince me to stay with them, it was huge. Three stories, with a wide porch on the first floor and several sets of French doors along the second and third, each with its own small balcony. It was positioned at a slight angle, so that both the front and one side had a river view through the trees.

It was a handsome house, but also a little creepy looking.

That's your imagination, Banks, I told myself.

Still, a slight chill ran down my spine as we entered the shaded area around the house, and I gazed up at its massive facade.

The house was elevated about five feet off the ground, resting on a cement block foundation that I doubted was part of the original construction.

Ellie turned her head, following my gaze. "It used to be on stilts, in case of flooding, but my father-in-law added the blocks years ago, to keep the wind from getting under the house in a hurricane."

"Do you get many of those hitting here?" I said, mostly to make conversation.

"Five, in the history of the house, but none a direct hit. It was built in 1919. My husband's great grandfather had made a fortune manufacturing parts used in the early automobiles."

We'd stopped at the base of the porch steps as Ellie gave her spiel. Jack lifted my bag from her lap.

"Then he fell prey to a con man who sold him a 'glorious island,'" she made air quotes, "that could easily be converted into a luxury resort for the wealthy who liked to winter in Florida. He had visions of an elegant hotel, similar to the Ponce De Leon in St. Augustine. But when he arrived in Dahlia, the last few miles traveled on dirt roads at the time, he discovered that, one, the town had a grand total of eighty residents, mostly fishermen, and two, his island was one of the outermost of the Nature Coast Keys, with no way to access it except by boat."

She paused and grinned. "I wish I'd known the old man. Instead of bemoaning his fate or filing a lawsuit, he built himself this house and declared that it was his objective all along to retire to a beautiful and secluded island."

I smiled my first genuine smile since landing on Haasi Key. "If life hands you lemons, make lemonade."

"Exactly." Ellie pushed herself out of the chair and grabbed the wrought-iron railing.

We all watched, me with bated breath, as she hauled herself up the steps on shaky legs. She stopped at the top, breathing heavily.

I let out air.

Jack carried the wheelchair up, and Ellie sank into it. She smiled back over her shoulder. "Lunch is in an hour. Greta will show you your room so you can get settled."

"Okay, um, I'd like to do some training after lunch." Considering her weak condition, I felt almost guilty bringing it up, but it *was* why I was here.

"Sure." Ellie said, then she and Jack disappeared into the house.

Greta made a harumphing sound in the back of her throat. "Wait here while I get some towels." She walked briskly away, around the side of the house.

She returned after a minute and helped me dry the dogs off. Then she climbed the porch steps. The dogs and I followed. She led the way into the house.

The front door opened into a large living area that reminded me of a hunting lodge. A half-dozen seating arrangements around the room were furnished with sofas, loveseats and overstuffed armchairs, of varying vintages.

Greta kept moving toward a wide stairway that rose up from the center of the room. Its steps were covered with soft burgundy carpet, its railing polished mahogany. The second-floor hallway was the width of a medium-sized room, with glistening wooden floors partially covered by

Persian area rugs.

Greta started up another less elegant set of stairs. It led to the third floor and a narrower hallway with a bare oak floor. It was also polished to a high gleam, however.

She turned to the left and opened a door at the end of the hall, then stepped back to let me go in first. The dogs pushed past her, unwilling to be separated from me in a strange environment. Greta scowled.

I held out my hand and lowered my palm toward the floor. Both dogs dropped to their bellies.

Greta's expression became somewhat less sour. I think I might have impressed her, but couldn't be sure.

The room was really more of a mini suite, with a sitting area as you first entered and a queen-sized bed over by the French doors. The furniture was vintage, most of the pieces probably worth more today as antiques than they originally cost. Bric-a-brac was scattered on a small set of shelves against one wall and on a polished end table.

Next to one end of the settee—its velvet upholstery the ugliest shade of eggplant purple I'd ever seen—sat a plastic and metal mesh contraption, posing as another end table.

Good. Ellie had remembered to purchase a dog crate.

I sat in the chair that was the same purple as the settee. Despite the unfortunate color scheme, it was a comfortable room. I let out a sigh as I pulled my phone out of my pocket.

Greta fussed around, plumping pillows on the bed and checking the attached bathroom.

I texted Will. The message didn't go through. I frowned at the phone.

"Cell service is not very reliable, I'm afraid," Greta said.

"Do you all have internet?"

She nodded. "*Ya,* Bruce had a satellite dish installed."

German. That was her accent.

"Good enough. I'll email folks to let them know I've arrived safely."

Jack entered through the open door, dropped both duffels on the floor and left again without saying a word.

"Let me know if you need anything, Miss Banks." Greta lowered her head, a cross between a nod and a bow. I wouldn't have been surprised if she'd clicked her heels.

"Please, call me Marcia."

She lowered her head again and left the room.

I got my laptop case out of my duffel bag and booted it up. The wi-fi network needed no password. Of course not. Who was going to steal their service way out here—the seagulls?

I chuckled to myself and sent off three quick messages to my mother, my best friend Becky, and my neighbor Sherie Wells. She would spread the word around our small town of Mayfair that their prodigal daughter was safe and sound.

Then I wrote a longer message to Will. I reported my surprise that Ellie was in a wheelchair and described the house and the staff.

I've yet to meet Ellie's husband, but I wouldn't be too surprised if he turned out to be Herman Munster… LOL. I feel like I've been dropped into a Gothic novel.

I added a smiley face and a heart and hit *Send*.

The distant tinkling of a bell summoned me to the dining room for lunch. Ellie was standing at the antique walnut sideboard, plucking items from various dishes lined up buffet-style.

The wheelchair was shoved into a corner.

"So, you're, um, feeling better?" I said.

She glanced my way and gave me a smile. "Yes."

If anything, she looked even thinner, more waif-like, than she had earlier. I realized it was because the breeze was no longer billowing her too-loose white tunic out to the sides.

"Help yourself." She stepped back and waved a hand at the buffet.

My stomach growled as I grabbed a plate from a small pile on the end of the sideboard. I loaded food onto it—crustless sandwiches, a green salad with cherry tomatoes, fruit salad, and mac and cheese.

Yum, one of my favorites, although this version seemed to be made from white cheddar. Not my preference but still... I couldn't wait to dig in.

Don't be a pig. My mother's voice inside my head.

I mentally stuck out my tongue at my inner Mom. I was starving.

Once Ellie and I were seated, her at the end of the table and me to her left, she pointed to the wheelchair. "Might as well address the elephant in the room."

I could only nod, since I'd just stuffed one of the sandwiches into my mouth, a triangle of whole-grain bread with no crust and something rich and slightly fishy inside. It was delicious.

I chewed and swallowed, as she took a small bite of fruit salad. Then she put her fork down. "This...," she waved a hand along the length of her body, "...started about four months ago. The doctors say it's sarcopenia."

"What's that?" I stole a glance at my heaped plate. My stomach rumbled unhappily, but it seemed rude to eat while Ellie discussed her illness.

"Muscle atrophy," she said, her tone matter-of-fact. "It's rare and usually only seen in the elderly, often related to old injuries. I was a competitive jumper in my youth."

My mind produced an image of a younger Ellie vaulting over a series of hurdles and sprinting toward a finish line.

"I fell off my horse a lot."

Oops, wrong type of jumping.

Ellie grimaced. "But the doctors are still baffled that it's happening in someone so young."

She reached for the salt shaker in front of her, and I took the opportunity to shovel some mac and cheese into my mouth.

"You sure you don't want some salt on that?" She was liberally dousing her own small pile of creamy noodles. "My husband's a bit of a health nut, insists on no salt in the food, but I add some at the table. Otherwise, most things are pretty tasteless."

I tried not to let my dismay show on my face. The mac had an unusual flavor, and the cheese tasted more like yogurt.

I took the proffered shaker and sprinkled salt on it. Only a slight improvement.

"Greta makes the noodles herself, from rice flour."

I resisted the urge to curl my lip.

Ellie pushed her glass away. "Bruce also insists on everyone drinking grapefruit juice, because it's high in vitamin C and antioxidants."

There were two glasses in front of my place. One of water, and one of what did indeed look like grapefruit juice. I nudged the water glass her way. "You want my water. I'm fine with the juice."

Another big smile. "Thanks. I used to like grapefruit juice, but you can only drink so much of it before..." She trailed off, stabbed a cherry tomato from her plate and popped it in her mouth.

We ate in companionable silence for a few minutes. Ignoring the mac and cheese, or whatever the heck it was, I gobbled down more sandwich triangles and some fruit salad. Finally, my hunger was somewhat appeased and I slowed my pace.

We both started talking at once. "Did you leave the dogs–"

"I'd like to do some–"

Her cheeks turned a little pink. It actually improved her appearance, not so pale and wan.

"You left the dogs upstairs," she said.

"They're kind of rattled by the strange environment. But I would like to do some training this afternoon. And I wish you had told me about the sarco..."

"Sarcopenia."

"I could have taught Nugget some tasks that would've helped you, such as picking up dropped items."

Ellie heaved a sigh. "Up until a few days ago, I was convinced I would get better. But my doctor finally broke through my denial at my last visit. This isn't going away." She opened her mouth to say more, than clamped it shut again.

"Well, Nugget's a very bright dog. I may be able to teach her some things while I'm here."

"So, where's the best place to work?" Ellie asked.

"Outside is best when the weather's agreeable. Gives us lots of room."

"The lanai out back then, whenever you're ready."

An hour later, I had shown Ellie all the things Nugget could do, and I'd had her practice one of the simpler tasks, the *Cover* command. Simple for the human partner, that is. It was one of the most complicated tasks to teach the dog. But all the human had to do was remember to pay attention to the dog's tail and ears when they were standing still, with the dog facing behind the person, literally watching their back. The dog would twitch their ears and a give a small tail thump to indicate that someone was approaching.

Folks with PTSD tend to be hypervigilant and startle easily if taken by surprise. So knowing the dogs would alert them, if someone was coming up from behind, gave them more confidence out in public.

Ellie's shoulders were sagging. She was tiring.

I gestured toward the wheelchair. "Have a seat for a minute. Lemme show you just how bright your dog is." I slapped my thigh. "Buddy, come here."

He'd been snoozing under a tree. Now he bounded over.

I laid down on the ground on my side, my torso propped up on one arm. "Here, boy." Buddy came over and stood next to me.

Nugget watched us, her head tilted to one side. She knew the drill. If I was about to do something with Buddy, I would be asking her to do it next.

"Brace, Buddy." The dog lined himself up right next to me and stiffened his legs.

I placed a hand on his back. Since I'm able-bodied, I didn't put much weight on him, but pretended to as I pushed myself up to my feet.

Nugget wasn't quite as big and muscular as Buddy, but then Ellie was a slight woman. The golden retriever should be able to handle some of her weight.

After demonstrating twice with Buddy, I called Nugget over.

The first time, she laid down when I put my hand on her back. I took my hand away and told her to stand. Then I manually moved her feet so her legs were spread out a bit. "Brace."

I put my hand on her back, but didn't go any farther. She stayed standing. I gave her a treat from the fanny pack at my waist and praised her.

I repeated that three times. The fourth time, I pushed myself to a stand without putting any weight on her. I gave her a treat.

I ran through the whole process two more times, still not putting any weight on her back. She stood still, although she turned her head once to look at me, as if she was trying to figure out what this was all about.

"That's enough for today." I turned toward Ellie, who was watching with a rapt expression on her face. "I'll do that again tonight, and several times each day, adding a little more weight as we go. I think she'll have it down by the time I leave."

Ellie nodded vigorously, her blonde ponytail bouncing. "It's amazing, watching how you do that."

I shrugged. "Not all that hard. You just have to break it down into little steps and reward each step."

I patted my thigh, the non-verbal signal to Nugget to follow me, and walked over to where Ellie sat under the tree. Then I gave the dogs the release signal. Buddy flopped at my feet, while Nugget went to Ellie looking for some pets.

She got some. Ellie was grinning from ear to ear. "I hope Bruce loves you as much as I already do," she crooned to the dog.

"Speaking of Bruce, will I meet him at dinner?"

Ellie shook her head. "He'll be home tomorrow morning sometime. He's on a fishing trip with a friend, on our boat. That's why Jack had to come get you in his skiff. Sorry for the tight fit."

"Hey, we made it okay. Do you want me to get Jack to wheel you inside?" I wasn't at all sure I could push the wheelchair in the sandy soil, and I didn't want to end up dumping her on her face.

"No, I can walk." She pushed herself to a stand.

I clipped Nugget's leash to her service vest and handed it to Ellie. "Hold out your hand like I showed you."

Ellie did so, palm down, and Nugget touched it with her nose.

"Now she's back on duty."

Buddy and I gave the two ladies a head start.

Ellie was moving slow, but it seemed to me her shoulders were straighter.

Too bad that darn sarco-whatever was.... What was it doing? It sounded, from the description, like it was eating her body from within.

I shuddered as Buddy and I walked to the house.

That night, I kept Nugget in my room with Buddy and myself. It would be a few days before I transferred her over to Ellie's care. And I wanted to work some more on the *Brace* command.

By bedtime, Nugget was getting the hang of it, and I had started putting a little bit of weight on her back when I rose.

I washed up and put on my jammies, then opened my laptop.

Everyone had acknowledged my emails, with comments to stay safe from Mom and Sherie Wells, and to have fun from Becky. Will's response wasn't a whole lot longer than the others but his ended with, *Miss you already.*

Smiling, I closed the computer and turned out the light. Normally I don't sleep all that well the first night in a strange bed, but it had been a long day.

Heart pounding, I opened my eyes to total blackness. *Where am I?*

Oh, yeah. I was at Ellie Burke's house, on its own little island in the Gulf of Mexico.

But what had happened to the ambient light that had been filtering through the thin curtains over the French doors? Had the moon gone behind a cloud?

A low rumble from the floor next to my bed. That's what had woken me, Buddy growling, deep in his throat.

"What is it, boy?" I whispered, as I fumbled for the lamp on the night-stand. The light revealed an empty room. No intruders and the French doors were closed up tight.

But something had set Buddy off. And Nugget was standing up in her crate, whining softly. Whatever it was that literally had Buddy's hackles up, she had heard it too.

Territorialism and protectiveness are intentionally trained out of service dogs, since they must stay on task in public around strangers. But when Buddy had started "breaking training," at times when I needed some defending, I'd made a conscious choice to let it go. He was a mentor dog now, so it was less critical that he not bark or growl at strangers, and he still behaved himself when he had his vest on. Will and I had even been trying to teach him some new tasks, modifications of some of those used by police dog handlers.

I swung my legs over the side of the bed.

Buddy growled again.

I slid my feet into my slippers and walked toward the door, the dog right by my knee. I put my ear against the old wood. A faint rustling on the other side.

I leaned down and held my finger to my lips. It was the signal that Buddy was now *not* supposed to growl or bark. Then I held my hand parallel to the ground and lowered it.

Both dogs laid down, although Buddy seemed reluctant.

I listened at the door again. No rustling sound now.

Slowly I turned the knob and cracked the door open just enough to peek out. A thin wedge of light knifed down the hallway, ending against blackness. The rustling noise and a flash of something red in the shadows.

I jerked, accidentally opening the door wider. The blackness receded from me, and then was gone. I was staring at the third-floor hallway, empty of anything that could possible move.

It was possible I'd imagined something black moving away from me, but not the rustling sound. The dogs had heard that too, and had interpreted it as menacing.

So probably something more than mice behind the walls.

I looked down at Buddy, who was now sitting quietly next to my knee, giving me his patented what's-up look.

"Got me, boy. I'll check it out in the morning."

I went back to bed, but not before leaving the light on in the bathroom.

It took me awhile to get back to sleep.

CHAPTER THREE

I stepped out onto my balcony the next morning and breathed in the tangy air. My room was on the side of the house, but if I turned slightly to my left, I could see the river through the trees. The rising sun sparkled on the water. A soft breeze tugged a few strands of hair loose from my ponytail.

Okay, Ellie's mobility issues might make the training a little more challenging, but I was determined to relax and enjoy my stay here.

I took another deep breath of the tropical air and smiled. Yes, this little getaway was just the thing to restore my sanity after the construction chaos at home.

Ah, the naïvety of the optimist, Ms. Snark commented.

Well, good morning to you too, I countered.

Today, I wasn't going to let even her deflate my mood.

Ellie and I had settled at the big table in the dining room, plates in front of us—mine full, hers bearing only some fruit and a piece of toast—when a cough came from the doorway. Ellie jumped.

I turned my head, a forkful of food halfway to my mouth.

A tall, lanky man strode into the room. He had dark wavy hair, hazel eyes, and stubble on his face that was a day or two past fashionable.

"Oh, hey," Ellie said, trying not to look like she'd just jumped out of her skin. "When did you get in?"

His gaze still on me, the man said, "You must be Marsha. Glad to finally meet you." He extended his hand.

I gave it a quick shake. "Good to meet you. Bruce, I assume. And my name is pronounced Mar-see-a."

"Sorry. Yes, I'm Bruce. Welcome to our home." He flung his arms wide.

Ellie flinched and ducked, even though his arm hadn't come all that close to her head.

Bruce didn't seem to notice that he was triggering his wife's PTSD all over the place.

"Sit down, dear, before you break something." Ellie's words sounded casual enough, but the chuckle that accompanied them seemed forced.

Bruce flashed a smile at me, while Ellie, behind him, tensed her shoulders and winced. She was obviously in pain.

I gritted my teeth behind closed lips.

He turned toward her. "You look tired, my love. Bad night?"

She nodded. "Nightmares," she said softly.

I noticed for the first time the dark circles under her eyes.

Sheez, Banks. Here I was thinking ill of her husband for not noticing her flinching or answering her questions, and I hadn't even noticed that she was paler than usual and obviously sleep-deprived.

She asked her question again. "When'd you get in?"

"Wee hours of the morning." He walked to the sideboard and grabbed a plate. "I slept in my study. Didn't want to disturb you."

"Well, Greta must have known you were here, based on the amount of eggs and fruit she laid out."

Bruce came to the table and sat across from me, his plate heaped with food. "I left her a note on the kitchen table."

"How thoughtful of you."

Was it my imagination or was there an edge to Ellie's words?

Up until this moment, I had thought this staying-with-Ellie idea was a good one. Now, I wasn't so sure. I really didn't want to bear witness to their marital stresses.

I took a bite of the omelet on my plate. It was tasteless—all egg white, with some dark green specks I assumed were spinach. That was it, no cheese and no flavor.

Ellie took a bite of dry wheat toast.

Bruce scooped up a big chunk of omelet and chewed with gusto.

I added some salt but still found mine hard to choke down. I nudged the eggs aside on my plate and, like Ellie, focused on my toast. Even without butter or margarine, it was quite good. I was pretty sure the bread was homemade.

I glanced at Bruce's plate. No toast.

"I don't do wheat," he commented.

I felt my cheeks heat, embarrassed that he'd caught me checking out his food.

"Where are the dogs?" Ellie asked, her voice sounding a bit strained. "You know, it really is okay to bring them down with you. Nugget will certainly have the run of the house later."

Bruce shot her a quick, unreadable look.

What does that mean? Ms. Snark asked internally.

I found myself telling a fib. "I wasn't sure when your... when Bruce was coming home." I quickly crossed my fingers under the table. "I didn't want to create a chaotic situation."

Actually, Buddy had seemed sluggish this morning, when I'd taken the dogs for their morning walk. Wondering if he'd stayed awake all night guarding me, I'd left both dogs upstairs to grab some extra sleep.

"Oh, I love dogs," Bruce said, "Looking forward to having one around the house again."

That was a relief to hear. Ellie had expressed some concern to me that Bruce might find having a dog painful. The family pet, an elderly Labrador, had died shortly before they'd married five years ago. Bruce had taken it hard and hadn't wanted a dog since.

I ate some fruit, then said, "Is your study on the third floor, by any chance?"

Bruce's eyebrows went up. "No, it's on the second floor. Why do you ask?"

"Um, something woke me up last night, a rustling noise, and when I opened my door, I thought I saw movement in the hall." I was sorry I'd brought it up. Maybe the whole thing had been my imagination.

But Buddy had heard the noise first, sensed something was wrong.

Ellie and Bruce exchanged a look, their faces tight.

"Black cape, red kerchief?" Ellie asked.

My stomach suddenly felt queasy. I nodded, glad that I hadn't eaten much yet.

"Are you afraid of ghosts?" Bruce asked.

Not *do you believe in them*, but *are you afraid of them*. My stomach clenched a bit more.

"Not particularly."

"We have two," Ellie said. "One came with the island, a teenage girl. She's benign. The story goes that she came here, years before the house was built, to meet a lover. He never showed up, and she wandered through the forest in despair and ended up falling off the cliffs on the north end of the island."

"Cliffs?" Florida is a fairly flat state. Cliffs are rare.

"There's an old sinkhole over there," Bruce said. "She might've jumped off. I've heard that version of the legend as well. She's a wispy thing, sometimes cries at night."

Somehow, I didn't think she was the presence in the upstairs hallway last night. "And the other one?"

Ellie grimaced. "I bought some supposed Spanish doubloons at a flea market. I thought Bruce would get a kick out of them. Shortly after that, this pirate ghost showed up. He'd root through drawers and closets. We figured he was searching for the coins–"

"So I got rid of them," Bruce said, his expression smug. "Sold them to a business associate I don't particularly like."

"But the ghost didn't go away." Ellie shuddered a little. "Instead, he started coming into my room and acting like he was going to climb into bed with me. One night, I woke up with him on top of me. He even growled, 'Hold still, wench.'"

I realized my mouth was hanging open and closed it. "What happened?"

"I screamed, and he jumped up and ran out."

"I still think you might've dreamed that," Bruce said.

Ellie shrugged. "I do have nightmares about the pirate now. It's hard to tell sometimes, what I've dreamt and what really happened."

Crapola. As if this woman didn't have enough to be freaked out about.

"But we've had house guests since acquiring this ghost," Bruce said, "and he's never bothered anyone but us. We can move you to the second floor though, closer to our rooms, if you want? It won't be as big a room though."

"No, we're okay upstairs. Um, Buddy woke me up with his growling, so I don't think the ghost will take me by surprise."

"Wow, I didn't know dogs could sense ghosts," Ellie said.

I gave her a small smile. "Me either, but Buddy is pretty talented."

"Speaking of the dogs," Ellie said. "Shall we work some this morning? Then I may need a nap before lunch."

Bruce shoveled the last bite of his second omelet into his mouth and jumped up to get her wheelchair.

~

Out on the lanai behind the house, we worked on Ellie keeping the dog on task and resistant to distractions. Despite being in the chair, her stamina wasn't great. After an hour, her body was sagging.

"A few more minutes," I said, "and we'll stop for this morning."

I pushed the wheelchair, Nugget walking alongside on a loose leash. A squirrel ran across the other end of the lanai. Nugget ignored it.

"Good girl," Ellie murmured and held out her hand for Nugget to touch her palm, the on-duty, pay-attention signal.

"Very good," I said.

A few seconds later, Ellie laid a hand on the dog's head. Nugget turned and nosed the woman's knee, her tail wagging.

I stopped the chair and walked around in front, squatting down so I was at Ellie's eye level.

"You don't want to be affectionate with her when she's on duty, unless it's part of rewarding her for a specific desired behavior."

Actually, Nugget had probably assumed that Ellie was seeking comfort because she was upset, but we hadn't covered that yet. And I wanted to make the point about not distracting the dog from her tasks.

Her eyes had gone a little wide. "Why not?"

"Did you see how she turned to you, looking for more affection. She was no longer paying attention to the environment, watching for people approaching and such. You were the distraction this time."

Those big blue eyes grew shiny. "You mean I can't be affectionate with her?"

"You can, as much as you want, when she is off duty. You want to create and maintain a clear distinction between the two states."

Ellie nodded. "When should she be on duty?"

"Always in public, and she should have her vest on then, to show others she's a service dog and they shouldn't pet her. At home, well, you'll figure out when you need her on duty and when not, but be clear with your signals."

Another nod. "But what if someone asks to pet her?"

"I wouldn't let them, unless it's here at the house and she is off duty. In public, it may confuse her, even if you give the release signal first."

A frown now. "Some people in Dahlia already think of me as a foreign intruder. They'll be offended if I don't let them pet her."

My knees were screaming at me that this crouching thing wasn't the best idea. I gave Ellie a smile I wasn't really feeling. "You'll need to come up with a spiel to give when people try to pet her. I'll help you with it, if you want." I stood up, my knees making soft popping noises. "For now, I want to do one more thing before we quit for this morning. I'm going to have Buddy intentionally create the biggest distraction of all. Be ready to keep Nugget on task."

Normally I didn't warn my human trainees of what was coming, but Ellie seemed so fragile today, I didn't want to upset her.

I returned to the back of the chair and started pushing. "Buddy." I held a finger up and twirled it around in a circle.

He lifted his head from where he'd been napping beside a picnic table. Then he was on his feet and running, barking, toward Nugget.

She ignored him, as I knew she would. I was more concerned about what Ellie would do. I kept pushing the chair, as Buddy cavorted off to one side, playacting a dog eager for some romping with another.

It was somewhat belated, but Ellie put out her hand, palm down. Nugget nosed it and we kept moving.

"Stop, Buddy. Good boy."

He instantly stopped his bouncing around and trotted back to his spot by the table.

"That's amazing," Ellie said. "How'd you teach him that?"

"It wasn't hard. He's a bright boy."

His nose came up and his ears perked.

Ellie laughed. "And he knows we're talking about him."

I chuckled. Best to end our session now, on that happy note. "Give Nugget the release signal."

Greta came out as we approached the back door. She helped Ellie up the three steps to the door, while I backed the empty wheelchair up behind them.

Buddy was right there, but when I glanced up, no Nugget.

I looked around. She was sniffing at some leaves beyond the far edge of the lanai. "Nugget, come here, girl."

She came to me, dragging her leash behind her.

Finding myself at loose ends while Ellie took a nap, I tried to call Will. Only one little tiny bar on my phone.

Crapola. I could email him of course, but I really wanted to hear his voice.

Leaving Nugget in her crate, enjoying a much deserved snooze, Buddy and I went outside. We walked around the house and toward the pier. I checked the bars on my phone as we went. A second little bar lit up, then went away again when I took another step onto the pier.

I stood still. The two bars came back. I moved the phone toward my ear and watched in my peripheral vision. The second one disappeared again.

Putting the phone on speaker, I held it out in front of me and punched the speed dial number for Will. It rang, and I prayed he wasn't busy chasing some criminal.

"Hey there," he said, sounding far away.

I smiled. "Hey yourself. How are things on the mainland?"

"Not bad. The builder ran into a snag while..." A bunch of static, ending with, "...confident he can take care of it."

I opted not to ask for a repeat of the middle part. One of the few advantages to being on this island, far away from him, was that I was also far away from the stresses of our building project.

"How are things there?" he asked.

"Okay, but a bit slower going than I'd hoped." I told him about Ellie's muscle disorder and how quickly she tired. He made appropriate sympathetic noises.

"Oh, and remember my comment about being dropped into the middle of a Gothic novel? Well, we've got ghosts here, two of them, but Ellie and her husband say they're benign."

"Are they sure?" Will's voice now sounded worried.

"Yes." Best not to mention that the pirate ghost had tried to assault Ellie. I was confident Buddy would warn me of either ghost's approach.

"I wish..." More static, then, "...with this storm coming."

I shifted my feet slightly to one side, and for a second I had three bars. "What storm?"

Technically, we were still in hurricane season, but just barely. November storms in the Atlantic were quite rare, but the Gulf of Mexico's waters were still warm enough to sometimes spawn them.

"It's only tropical strength now," Will said, clear as a bell. "None of the models have it hitting anywhere near where you are. One has it veering north toward the panhandle and the other has it going east toward Cuba."

I held perfectly still so as not to disrupt the phone's reception. "Okay. We'll keep an eye on it. When's landfall?"

"Not until late Friday. Gotta go, but it sure was good hearing your voice. Love you."

"Same here. Love–"

And that quickly the call and all the beautiful bars were gone.

Inside the house, I went in search of either a television or a human being who could tell me where one was. I found neither.

I ended up in the kitchen.

Greta was busy making sandwiches for lunch, spreading a thin layer of some kind of paté over multiple slices of wheat bread. A platter of darker triangles with white filling—pumpernickel and creamed cheese, maybe—was already off to one side, covered with plastic wrap.

"Hi, Greta."

She startled and whirled around toward me, the sharp knife in her hand menacing. I blinked, and she was simply Greta again, formidable but not dangerous.

Indeed, her eyes were wide and her cheeks puffed out. She worked her mouth quickly, then swallowed hard.

Wondering what had her so jumpy, I told her about the storm. "I was looking for a TV, but I'm not finding one."

"*Ya*, Bruce doesn't believe in them."

I assumed she meant TVs, since storms were not something you could or could not believe in. They would blow your house down regardless of your opinions.

"But he has a weather radio." Greta pointed to a big black box on the end of one counter. Then she returned to her work, flopping a second slice of bread on top of one of the wheat sandwiches. "He is following the storm, no doubt." She wacked the crusts off with four swift blows.

The thwack of the knife made me shiver a little. "Good. Thank you." I turned toward the door, but caught sight of something in my peripheral vision. I swiveled my head around. A small plate had been pushed to the back of the counter, a corner of dark bread on it and a brown smear. And something green—the end of a pickle?

With Bruce's aversion to salt, I doubted pickles were approved fare for the household. Did Greta have some of her own food stashed somewhere?

Unfortunately, I had forgotten to pack my e-reader. With Buddy snoozing on the rug next to my bed, I sat on top of the comforter cross-legged, trying to figure out how to download an app onto my laptop, so I could read some of my books floating in the cloud.

As if on cue, a fluffy white cloud drifted across the blue sky outside my French doors. Hard to believe there was a tropical storm out there somewhere.

The impulse hit me to research Ellie's muscle disease. I spelled it wrong, but Google helpfully corrected me. Sarcopenia's symptoms included muscle pain in the shoulders, thighs, and lower back, and weakness in the arms and legs.

As Elie had said, it was a rare disease, usually found in the elderly. And it could be exacerbated by certain medications, especially those for cholesterol.

Duh, I don't need a TV. I could look up the storm online. I went to the Weather Channel's website. Sure enough, Tropical Storm Pierre had formed off the Yucatan peninsula. And he was expected to become at least a Category-1 hurricane, with sustained winds of seventy-four to ninety-five miles per hour, before either veering due north or teetering off to Cuba.

A warm breeze breathed the scent of wisteria against my face. I glanced at the French doors. I could've sworn they were closed a minute ago, but now they were open.

The breeze felt good, so I left them that way.

Suddenly sleepy, I laid back against the pillows, shoving my computer off to one side of the bed. I'd just close my eyes for a moment…

A rustling sound. My eyes slowly opened. My face was turned toward the balcony. A thin teenage girl stepped past the gauzy curtains blowing in the breeze. The wisteria fragrance was stronger. She raised a stick-like arm, wisps of a thin fabric hanging down, and pointed toward the room's door.

"The pirate," she whispered.

I bolted up in the bed and jerked my head around. There was nothing near the door but an old-fashioned floor lamp next to the armchair.

I whirled my head back around. "Where's the pir–"

The girl was gone.

And the balcony doors were closed.

Shivering, I grabbed my laptop and looked up wisteria in Florida.

It bloomed in the spring and early summer, not in November.

CHAPTER FOUR

I'd intended to leave the dogs upstairs, to emphasize to Ellie that these are working animals, not pets.

But after my disturbing dream—it had to be a dream, right?—I couldn't bring myself to go downstairs for lunch without Buddy. We left Nugget in her crate, happily gnawing on a chew stick.

We were the first ones in the dining room. I pointed to one corner, and Buddy went over and laid down. The buffet of sandwiches and salads was already spread across the sideboard, but I felt funny helping myself.

After a couple of minutes, Greta pushed Ellie's wheelchair through the extra wide doorway from the living area. Greta tried to take her employer's arm to help her over to the dining room chair.

Ellie shook her off. "I'm fine. You can go."

When Greta was well out of the room, Ellie stood up and smoothed the front of her sky-blue tee shirt over denim capris. It was not the same outfit she'd been wearing earlier. She flopped down into the chair at the head of the table.

"Would you like me to get you a plate?" I asked.

She waved a hand in the air. "Nah, I'll get it myself in a minute." Her eyebrows went up as she looked at Buddy, snoozing in the corner. "That's not... Where's Nugget?"

"Upstairs in her crate. Once you've clearly established the boundaries between on duty and off duty, you can integrate her more into your family life, like I have with Buddy. But until then..."

"Until then, my dog gets to be locked up in a cage." She waved her hand again. "Never mind. We're going to work with her after lunch, right?"

"Yes." I got up and went to the sideboard. I was starving. "You sure you don't want me to get you a plate?"

By way of an answer, she pushed herself to a stand and took a few wobbly steps, then grabbed for the back of a chair to steady herself. Her body was definitely shaky, but her spirit seemed more... Determined? Independent? I wasn't sure what the right word was, but it seemed like movement in the right direction.

I made room for her at the buffet. She clung to the edge of its top with one hand, while putting food onto her plate with the other. Her selections were a bit different today, leaning more toward the sandwiches than the salads.

Was that why Greta put out such a spread of food for two or three people, so that Ellie would eat whatever struck her fancy? The young woman definitely needed to gain some weight.

Where's Bruce? I wondered.

Ellie managed to get herself and her plate back to the table. She sank into her chair again, with a slight grimace.

"What did you do with yourself this morning?" she asked.

"I talked to my fiancé. He told me there's a tropical storm in the Gulf."

Ellie again waved a dismissive hand. "Yeah, Greta's all in a dither about it. But they never hit here. Oh, we might get some wind and rain, but it's like we have a protective bubble or something around us." She laughed. "The Burkes' pact with the devil, I like to call it."

Okaaay. I wasn't touching that.

"So, how much do you know about how I ended up with this lame PTSD diagnosis?"

"Um, all I was told was that you witnessed a plane crash about a year and a half ago." I knew more than that but didn't want to upset her.

"It wasn't any old plane." She wolfed down her second triangle of sandwich and grabbed up a third. "It was the first test flight of a fighter plane we helped design."

I stuffed half of a pumpernickel triangle into my mouth, partly so I could avoid saying anything—and almost choked. The stuff in the middle had the texture and taste of congealed library paste, with a little spinach thrown in.

A crafty smile spread across Ellie's face. "It's some yogurt concoction. More of Brucey's crazy eating." She crammed another wheat triangle in her mouth. "These are made with tuna," she said around it, "not half bad."

Greta entered the room balancing a tray with three glasses on it. She set two in front of me and one by Ellie's plate. Mine seemed to be water and grapefruit juice again. I thanked the housekeeper.

Ellie turned her head and stuck her tongue out at Greta's back as she left the room.

"Here." She held up her glass. "Pour this on that plant over there, would you?"

I followed her line of vision. A rubber plant in a big pot in the corner didn't look all that healthy. Apparently, this wasn't the first glass of grapefruit juice it had been blessed with.

I murmured an apology to it as I poured the liquid onto the dirt in its pot.

As I resumed my seat, I picked up my own juice and downed half of it to kill the aftertaste of that sandwich.

The pasta salad was palatable, with a healthy dose of salt. At this rate,

I'd lose some weight during this gig. Not a totally bad thing since my hips tended to be a whole clothing size bigger than the rest of me.

Although Will didn't seem to mind.

"So, what else did they tell you?" Ellie's question yanked me out of my reverie about Will's admiration for my hips.

"About what?"

"The crash."

"Um, that the pilot died."

"And?" Her tone was slightly angry now, like I was holding out on her.

"And he was a friend of yours."

She snorted. "That's one way of puttin' it. Hey, grab me a couple more sandwiches, would you?"

"The tuna?" I stood.

"Of course."

I brought the whole plate of tuna ones back with me. When I sat down again, I noticed my water glass was half empty.

I frowned. I would have happily given it to her if she'd asked, but it annoyed me that she'd helped herself.

I picked up two of the sandwich triangles from the plate and stood again. "I'll go get Nugget so we can get some work done."

"Great idea." Either she hadn't noticed my terse tone or she was ignoring it. "Meet you on the lanai in ten."

I called Buddy to me and we left the room.

"Greta!" Ellie bellowed from behind me.

She was sitting in her wheelchair on the lanai, Greta nowhere around, when I came down with the dogs.

I let go of Nugget's leash and she approached the wheelchair slowly, almost cautiously.

"Hey there, Gorgeous," Ellie crooned, holding out her hand, palm up.

"Palm down, not up," I said.

She flashed a confused look my way, then said, "Oh, yeah. Of course." She turned her hand over.

Nugget touched her palm and stood calmly beside the wheelchair. I decided her earlier hesitation was a figment of my imagination. Maybe the ghost dream had rattled my sense of reality more than I'd thought.

I started pushing the chair around the lanai. It was Tuesday, and I wanted to be able to confirm my weekend plans with Will by tomorrow night. That meant getting these two ready to go out in public by tomorrow. I wasn't leaving Nugget in Ellie's care until I was sure they were beginning to coalesce as a team.

It was time to intentionally distract Ellie to see if she lost control of the dog. "Can you tell Bruce or Jack or whoever that we need the boat tomorrow? We're going into town."

"Oh goody." Ellie clapped her hands.

Not the reaction I had expected, after her concerns this morning about the townspeople's reactions to her having a service dog.

Nugget was trotting along beside us, one ear cocked toward Ellie. I stopped the wheelchair. The dog immediately turned and sat down, facing me.

I snapped my fingers behind my back.

Buddy, in his favorite spot by the picnic table, raised his head. He hopped up and jogged over.

Nugget's ears twitched and her tail thumped against the stones of the lanai.

Ellie didn't react.

"She just signaled you that Buddy was approaching."

Ellie looked over her shoulder at me. "So?"

Grrr. What was with this woman today?

"So, if he had been a stranger approaching out in public, that might have triggered you."

Ellie snorted. "Not me."

Huh?

Confused, I took a treat from my fanny pack and held it over the woman's shoulder.

After a beat, she took it from my fingers and gave it to Nugget. "Good girl." She gave the dog a somewhat perfunctory pat on the head.

Stifling a growing sense of unease, I started us moving again.

Buddy trailed behind me. He should have gone back to his spot by the table, but maybe he sensed my discomfort.

Trying once again to distract Ellie, to see if she still kept the dog on task, I said, "I had the weirdest dream earlier, when I was napping before lunch. I dreamt that a teenage girl was standing just inside my balcony pointing toward the bedroom door, and she said 'The pirate'…" I trailed off as Ellie's shoulders began to shake.

Nugget trotted two steps forward and then turned to lay her head on the woman's knee.

I stopped the wheelchair to keep from running over the dog.

Nugget put a front paw up in Ellie's lap. The woman wrapped her arms around the dog's neck and cried harder.

I moved quickly around the wheelchair. Remembering my popping knees from earlier, I knelt in front of her.

Ellie shook her head. "I'm sorry. I've upset Nugget."

The dog licked her chin.

"No, no," I said gently, "she's doing what she's been trained to do. She's supposed to comfort and ground you when *you* get upset."

Ellie managed a strained smile through her tears. "Well then, good girl, Nugget." She patted the dog's head. Nugget licked her hand.

We worked for another half hour, Ellie being the model trainee, before I called for a break.

"You rest for a while. Nugget and I will come to your room later and show you how she will wake you up from nightmares."

That's when it dawned on me that Buddy hadn't woken me up when I'd dreamed about the ghost.

Had I not shown any signs of anxiety before I bolted upright in bed?

Or had it not been a dream?

Again leaving Nugget in her crate for a snooze, I grabbed a windbreaker jacket, and Buddy and I went down to the pier, in search of a better cell signal. From there, we followed the beach so we wouldn't get lost.

Slowly the water became bluer and more choppy. I figured we were now on the Gulf side of the island. The beach here was wider, and as we approached the water's edge, I suddenly had three bars.

Woohoo!

I called my mom but got her voicemail. "Hey Mom, just wanted to touch base. I'm still alive and well, on a lovely island on the Gulf Coast. Working with my client a few hours a day, and then the rest of the time is a mini-vacation." I kept my tone cheerful. Any hint of discontent in paradise and she would start worrying. "But phone reception is awful here, so don't be surprised if you can't get me. I'll call every few days."

There, that ought to keep my mother happy for awhile. Next, I called my bestie.

And got voicemail there as well. *Crapola.*

I left her a breezy message, repeating the "I feel like I've been dropped into the middle of a Gothic novel" line and telling her I'd email with all the details.

Disappointed, I considered calling Will, but I'd already disturbed him once today during work hours.

My calves were complaining about the exertion of walking through sand for the last twenty minutes. Buddy had flopped down beside me, his tongue lolling out, panting softly.

"Time for a break, boy." We trudged up to the tree line, and I found a big rock to perch on in the shade.

I was daydreaming about my upcoming weekend getaway with Will when a low rumbling sound registered. I glanced down at Buddy, lying beside my rock.

His head had come up and he was growling softly.

My heart rate ratcheted up several notches—had he spotted a gator? I followed his line of vision off to the left, toward the end of the beach where it curved around out of sight behind the trees. Was that movement?

Buddy stood up, his growl rumbling louder. I laid a hand on his head and he quieted.

A man came into view. No chance of seeing his features from this distance, but he had a lanky build and dark hair. Bruce, probably.

I patted my chest, willing my thumping heart to calm down.

Despite the cool-ish day, the man wore a tee shirt and cutoff jeans. He'd taken two steps along the water's edge when he suddenly turned back and stopped.

He opened his arms. Someone stepped into them and they embraced.

His body was blocking most of his companion's, but I caught sunshine glinting off of blonde hair.

Not wanting to be caught spying on his and Ellie's little tryst, I raised my hand and was about to call out when they broke apart and started walking along the beach.

Again, Bruce was between me and the woman, but his strides were long and sure on the wet sand at the water's edge. The woman didn't seem to have any trouble keeping up.

They stopped and turned, holding hands side by side, looking out at the shiny blue Gulf waters.

The woman was almost as tall as Bruce, wearing a sleeveless tank top and boy-style short shorts. She had to be a little chilly, with the breeze blowing off of the water.

She also had to be someone other than Ellie.

CHAPTER FIVE

The woman had broader shoulders and shorter hair, a darker shade of blonde.

The couple suddenly ran for the water and dove in.

I sucked in air. *Nope, definitely not Ellie.*

"Come on, boy," I whispered to Buddy. I rose and moved us carefully along the edge of the woods to our right. I didn't dare move on into the trees, not knowing what creatures might be hiding in the thick underbrush.

My gaze flitted back and forth between the stony, packed earth in front of us and the couple cavorting in the water. They seemed to remain oblivious to our presence.

At the far end of the beach, I glanced back over my shoulder one last time.

The couple was standing in hip-high water, kissing, the woman's long fair arms wrapped around Bruce's neck. Even from this distance, I could tell that those arms were thicker than Ellie's waif-like limbs.

Buddy and I scrambled around the curve in the beach.

～

This time, I left Buddy in my room and took Nugget down the stairs to the second floor, and encountered a half dozen closed doors. Which one was Ellie's? I had no idea, so I went on downstairs to find Greta.

When we walked into the kitchen, she took one look at my face and her own paled. "What's wrong? Did something happen to Ellie?"

"Nothing's wrong." But the heat creeping up my cheeks put the lie to that statement. One of the many reasons I have never used my master's degree in counseling psychology to actually do any counseling—I'm not very good at hiding my feelings. A necessary skill in that profession, so the client stays focused on their own feelings, not yours.

"I think she's resting upstairs," I said, "But it's time for another training session, and I don't know which room is hers."

"Turn left at the top of the stairs, then the second door on the right."

"Uh, Greta, where does Bruce go all day?"

She froze for a moment in the process of drying a pan. "He has an office in town. The manufacturing businesses—his father sold them years ago. But there is still real estate to be managed."

Real estate management, my foot, Ms. Snark commented inside my head. For once, I had to agree with her. Bruce wanted an excuse to stay away from the house for long periods so he could be with his lover.

"Thanks. Just curious." I went back upstairs.

"Come in," Ellie called out, in response to my light knock.

She was sitting up in bed, reading on an e-reader. She moved to throw the covers off her legs to get up.

"Stay," I said, holding my hand up. "This training is done in bed."

"What?" Her tone was more surprised than it should have been. I'd mentioned several times now that the dog would wake her up during nightmares.

It wasn't like she had to do anything during that task, but I liked to have my clients go through a dry-run a few times, so it wouldn't be startling the first time the dog woke them up at night.

"Which side of the bed is yours?" I asked.

Her cheeks turned pink. "Both. Bruce usually sleeps in his study."

Oops. I'd stepped right in the middle of that pile of goo. And I should have expected as much.

I didn't realize I was frowning until Ellie said, "Well, I mean we still get together, you know, but he thought I might sleep better without his 'big sweaty body' as he put it…" she made air quotes, "taking up more than half the bed."

If Bruce Burke had been standing in front of me in that moment, I might have strangled him with my bare hands. Not only was he having an affair, but he'd abandoned his fragile wife to her nightmares and an amorous ghost.

I shrugged and tried to plaster on a smile. "Okay then, which side do you usually get in and out on?"

She patted the mattress with her right hand.

I took Nugget around to that side, held out my palm for her to touch it with her nose, the *on-duty* signal, then gestured for her to lie down. "Now, I want you to lie back and pretend you are asleep, then pretend you're having a nightmare. Start thrashing around." I backed away from the bed and stood by her closed French doors.

Ellie did as instructed. She even pretended to snore. Then she began to whimper and flail around a bit.

Immediately, Nugget was on her feet. She woofed softly, put her front paws up on the side of the bed and nudged Ellie's arm.

Ellie laughed, opening her eyes, and threw her arms around Nugget's neck. Then she yanked them back again.

"No, this is one of those times when you can be affectionate with her while she's working. She'll stay there so you can pet her and calm down, until you give her the signal to get down."

"Which is?"

"Either the word *down* or this gesture." I held my hand out parallel to the floor and moved it downward.

Nugget wasn't focused on me, so she didn't respond. But when Ellie repeated the gesture, she dropped her front feet to the floor, her tail wagging slowly back and forth like a fluffy red-gold flag.

I nodded slightly, pleased that Nugget was starting to look to Ellie for instructions, rather than me.

"Say light switch," I whispered to Ellie.

"Light switch," she repeated.

Nugget ran to the door and jumped up, flipping the light switch up with her nose.

Ellie laughed, as the dog returned to the side of her bed, tongue hanging out, eyes on Ellie.

Yes. I did a mental fist pump.

I was reaching into my fanny pack for some treats, when a draft of air, scented with wisteria, brushed my cheek.

Ellie's head jerked around toward the closed doors.

I looked at the spot she was staring at.

"Do you see her?" Ellie whispered.

"No."

"Do you smell wisteria?"

"Yes."

Nugget's head swiveled back and forth from Ellie to me. She knew something was happening but wasn't sure what.

Neither am I, girl.

Ellie gasped and a hand flew to her mouth.

Nugget ran to the bed and put her paws on the edge, shoving her head into Ellie's lap.

"She's responding to your anxiety," I whispered.

Ellie swallowed hard, still staring toward the window, then she deflated. "She's gone." She absently stroked Nugget's ears.

"You saw the girl ghost?"

"Yes, she kept saying 'Bruce' and shaking her head." Ellie shook her own head. "She sometimes warns me when the pirate is coming." Turning toward me, her eyes wide. "Do you think she's trying to warn that something's going to happen to Bruce?"

More likely the teenage girl had become aware of Bruce's affair. But as much as I wanted to expose his sin, I knew it would devastate Ellie. I kept my mouth shut and prayed that the ghost would do the same.

Instead I said, "That's why you got upset earlier? When I described my dream about the girl ghost."

Ellie frowned. "I doubt it was a dream."

Now, so did I.

Dinner was close to being the most awkward event I'd ever endured. It almost beat out the last Baltimore Symphony reception I'd attended, after I'd found out my violinist husband was bonking a cello player, but I didn't know which one. I'd spent the evening in a corner, stress-eating *hors d'oeuvres* and dissecting Ted's every move as he worked the room.

Unfortunately, there wasn't much available for stress-eating tonight. Greta had served a white fish entree with brown rice and mixed vegetables. There was no sauce or butter on anything. But the freshly baked fragrance emanating from a big basket of wheat rolls made my stomach growl.

Ellie passed them to me without my having to ask. She had two on her plate.

"The girl ghost showed up today," she said to Bruce, trying to sound casual, but there was a definite strained undertone.

"Oh yeah." He gave his wife an indulgent smile. "What'd she have to say for herself?"

I so wanted to reach across the table and smack him.

"She kept repeating your name and shaking her head. I think…" Ellie glanced at him, then away again, "she might be trying to warn us of something."

Bruce waved a nonchalant hand in the air. "You probably dreamed the whole thing."

"I wasn't dreaming. I was wide awake."

"And I was there," I blurted out.

"Did you see or hear this ghost?"

What's with this guy? Ms. Snark commented. Again, I had to agree with her. What *was* with him? Before, he'd acted like he believed in the ghosts.

"No," I said, "but I smelled her."

He shook his head slightly. "Ah, that wisteria scent. It's part of the legend. The power of suggestion, no doubt."

Ms. Snark was making growling sounds inside my head, but I managed to keep them from coming out of my mouth. "I didn't *know* it had anything to do with the ghost, until after I smelled it. Twice. The ghost was in my room earlier too."

"Well, she's never been known to harm anyone." He stabbed a chunk of fish and forked it into his mouth. He chewed and swallowed. "Nothing to be worried about."

I clamped my mouth shut. Ellie slumped in her chair, her expression miserable.

We finished the meal in silence.

I had reached the second-floor hallway when I heard. "Marcia, wait up."

Bruce jogged up the wide steps. "Listen, I indulge my wife's flights of fancy about these ghosts, but I've never seen them." He'd reached the hallway. "And they never made an appearance when my parents were alive either."

He leaned toward me. "Ellie drinks, you know," he said in a confidential tone.

I gritted my teeth while struggling to keep my face neutral. "No, I didn't know that." And I didn't believe it.

"I find vodka bottles stashed all over the house. I mean, she doesn't get crazy or anything. She just takes a nip now and then. I mean, her life… She doesn't have much quality of life right now, so who am I to judge if that makes it easier to cope. But it can make her imagination get the better of her." He leaned even closer. "You know what I mean?"

I stepped back and pivoted toward the stairs to the third floor. "No, I'm not sure what you mean. Perhaps you think I was drunk too when I saw the pirate in the hallway the other night and smelled the wisteria today." And with that, I ran up the stairs, wanting to get far away from this man.

I didn't trust him as far as I could throw him.

But I paused at the top of the steps, smiling a little. That was one of my mother's many sayings. I could almost hear Will's low chuckle and his deep voice saying, "Another of your motherisms."

My chest ached. *Miss you so much, sweetheart.*

Huh, interesting. I almost never used endearments with Will, but that wasn't the interesting part. Calling him *sweetheart* without having my usual mini-panic attack—*that* was interesting.

Despite the fact that I'd requested the use of the boat at dinner last night, it was gone by the time I got up the next morning. As was Bruce.

But Jack was available to shuttle us to the mainland, when we'd finished our breakfast—which turned out to be whole wheat pancakes. There was no butter or syrup, but Greta had produced a jar of homemade strawberry jam.

My tummy happy for a change, I loaded the smaller duffel bag with the dogs' service vests, a travel water dish and a couple of bottles of water. Jack took me and the dogs to the little park in Dahlia.

I checked my car. It was fine.

Then I sat down at a picnic table to kill time until Jack brought Ellie to me. With the dogs napping in the shade under the table, I called Becky.

"Hey, girl," she answered, sounding cheerful.

"Hey, yourself. How are the rug rats?" Her infant twins were my godchildren, and I adored them.

"They're great. Winnie's gained back the weight he lost last month."

I swallowed hard, trying *not* to remember those harrowing hours when we weren't sure if her son would survive.

"I can't believe you've started using my nickname for him. You're gonna scar him for life. It was just supposed to be a secret name between him and me."

Becky laughed, and I pictured her in my mind's eye—dark curls bobbing around her heart-shaped face. "Don't worry. I only call him that when talking to you."

"In other words, you're jerking my chain."

"Exactly. Hey, are you keeping track of this storm?" she asked, her voice now serious. "It's up to a Cat-1 and it might go to a Cat-2."

I strained my brain to remember the wind speeds of the different categories. I was pretty sure Cat-2 meant sustained winds up to a hundred and ten, with gusts even higher.

Dang it, hurricane season was supposed to be close to over.

"My host is keeping an eye on good ole Pierre, or I should say an ear. No TVs on the island, but he has a weather radio." I paused. "Um, speaking of my host, you got a few minutes?"

"Until one or the other of my darlings wakes up, I do."

I took a deep breath and told her about seeing Bruce and his lover on the beach. "I'm not sure what to do, Beck."

"I don't know that you need to do anything. If you weren't living with the client at the moment, you wouldn't even know about it."

"True."

"Does he seem to care about Ellie?"

I had to stop and think about that. "Yes, I think he does, in a kind of condescending way. But he's not around much."

"The way I see it, this could be a case of a total jerk taking advantage of his wife's disability so he can screw around on the side. *Or* it could be a man staying loyal to his disabled wife, while trying to create some semblance of a life for himself. We really don't have enough information to judge which is reality."

"Well, coming down on the jerk side of things, he told me last night that Ellie drinks."

"And you don't believe him?"

I hadn't at the time... "I haven't seen any signs of her drinking." The words were no sooner out of my mouth than I flashed to yesterday's lunch. Ellie had been more animated, downright flamboyant at times. Could she have been a little drunk?

"Look, I know it's hard to do, when you're staying with them, and that detective part of you is no doubt vibrating by now."

I chuckled. "You know me too well."

"Just my take on it, but you probably ought to stay out of their business."

I sighed. "You're right, as usual."

She purred into the phone. "That's my preening-at-the-compliment noise."

I laughed out loud. "You are also a nut."

"Hazelnut."

"My favorite kind."

"Gotta go. The kiddies are stirring."

"Give them a hug and a kiss from me, and say hi to Andy for me."

"What? I can't give him a hug and a kiss?"

"Of course, but don't say they're from me."

The laughter in her voice as we signed off left me in a much better mood.

I vowed to take her advice and stay out of the Burkes' business.

Ms. Snark snorted. *We'll see how long that lasts.*

I wanted to argue with her, but decided not to bother.

I wasn't a buttinsky by nature, but I also hated seeing people getting hurt.

CHAPTER SIX

I was daydreaming about riding my horse Niña across the fields behind my house when the put-put of Jack's engine brought me back to reality. The fishing skiff rounded the curve of the river, passing the stand of palmettos and Southern pines at the far end of the small park.

Jack stood behind the wheel, and Ellie slumped on the small bench in front of him.

He beached the skiff on the gravel boat ramp and jumped out, his wet bare feet flashing in the mid-morning sun. Then he scooped Ellie up in his arms and carried her to my car.

Once the dogs were situated in the backseat and the wheelchair was in my trunk, Ellie said, "Bruce wants me to go to the post office to pick up a package while we're in town."

Ms. Snark popped out before I could stop her. "Hope it's not any bigger than a matchbook." My car's capacity was pretty much maxed out.

She ducked her head. "He said it was important, and he had to go to Inverness today and didn't have time to stop." Her voice was apologetic.

"Hey, it's not a problem. I was joking."

After a couple of minutes, I broke the semi-awkward silence. "So, where's the big boat?"

"Huh?"

"If Bruce took it to come ashore to go to Inverness, why wasn't it at the park?"

"Oh, his lawyer probably met him at the other park, farther up the coast a bit. It has a better pier, for tying up the boat."

Wonder if his lawyer is a leggy blonde, Ms. Snark commented inside my head.

The town was only about a mile up the road. I parallel parked the car on the main drag, which was basically the only drag. "Have you decided what you want to say when people ask why you have a service dog? Keep in mind that they're not supposed to ask what your diagnosis is, but they can ask what the dog does to help you."

"Do you think it would be horrible if I pretended I have her because of my physical disability?"

"Wouldn't bother me, but she isn't trained to do most of the things a service dog would normally do for someone in a wheelchair. The best I'll be able to accomplish is completing her training to brace, if you fall and need her help to get up." I'd been working with Nugget a couple of times a day on that command. She was getting the hang of it and was now holding still even when I put a good bit of my weight on her.

"You can honestly tell people about that," I said, "and that she turns the lights on and off for you. That should satisfy folks."

She nodded, and I got out to pull the wheelchair from the trunk.

When everyone was strapped into wheelchairs or service vests, respectively, we started down the sidewalk toward the post office.

A matronly woman in a tailored purple dress was coming our way.

"How are you doing, Ellie?" She stopped, blocking half the pavement and leaving us no choice but to stop as well. Both dogs immediately turned and sat, going into the cover position.

"A little better, Mrs. Warren. I have Nugget here now. She's helping a lot."

"A service dog. How wonderful. And she's such a pretty thing." The woman held out her hand for the dog to sniff. Appropriate etiquette for meeting a strange dog, but not for dealing with a service dog.

She took a step forward and leaned toward Nugget, trying to get the dog's attention.

I moved around the wheelchair and between her and the dog. "Um, service dogs shouldn't be treated like pets. When they're on duty, they shouldn't be petted."

I thought I was being fairly diplomatic, especially since *Do Not Pet* was stenciled length-wise across the top of Nugget's red vest. In big black letters, no less.

But Mrs. Warren gave me a sour look. "And who are you?"

"Marcia is Nugget's trainer," Ellie said, her cheerful tone sounding forced to my ears. "She's working with me, showing me the ropes of how to utilize a service dog."

"Mar-see-a. Wherever did you get a name like that?"

"From my mother," Ms. Snark said. I didn't even try all that hard to stop her. This woman was beginning to pluck my last nerve. And no, that isn't a motherism. That one I'd picked up from my octogenarian friend and neighbor, Edna Mayfair.

The woman stepped back as if I'd slapped her. "Well, I never–"

"Sorry, Mrs. Warren," Ellie said. "I know it might sound harsh, but a service dog…" She trailed off, apparently unsure how to end the sentence.

"Needs to stay on task," I said.

At that moment, Buddy's ears and tail twitched.

A second later, so did Nugget's, but Ellie was focused on the woman.

Mrs. Warren pursed her lips. "But she's not doing anything at the moment."

"Actually, she is," I said.

Both dogs thumped their tails and twitched their ears in unison, just as a man nudged around me on the sidewalk.

Ellie jumped a good inch in her wheelchair when he moved past her.

I suppressed the urge to snap at Mrs. Warren and plastered on what I hoped was a pleasant expression. "Nugget is watching for anyone approaching from behind, like that guy. When Ellie gets into the habit of noticing the dog's signals, she won't be surprised and startled, like she just was."

"Oh," the woman said. Whether truly mollified or she'd finally remembered her manners, she turned to Ellie. "Well, you take care, my dear." Ignoring me, she walked around us and went on down the sidewalk.

"I'm sorry, Marcia. Mrs. Warren can be a bit abrasive. I hope she didn't upset you."

I crouched down to Ellie's eye level. "It takes more than one old biddy to upset me, but you do need to learn to be, um, somewhat more assertive about stopping people who want to pet Nugget."

She ducked her head and shrank into herself. "I know. I'll try harder."

"I'm not scolding you, Ellie. I know it's hard. But it's important."

She nodded, her head still down, not making eye contact.

We made it to the post office without further issues. It was the smallest one I'd ever seen, no more than twenty feet square. Its front door was propped open, probably to catch the pleasant breeze blowing off the Gulf.

You might be a redneck, Ms. Snark quipped internally, *if your post office is smaller than a garden shed.*

I stifled a snort.

"Hey, you cain't bring them dogs in here." A woman's voice, with a creaky Florida accent.

I stopped the wheelchair in the doorway. Unfortunately, we were blocking a customer who was trying to leave, a youngish woman in a faded tee shirt with two preschoolers clinging to her jean-clad legs and a baby balanced on her hip. She clutched some envelopes in her other hand.

I nudged the chair on over the threshold to get out of her way, Nugget beside my knee and Buddy trailing behind.

"I said, you cain't bring them dogs in here." The speaker was a tall, thin woman with leathery skin and frizzy hair too uniformly dark to not be dyed. She wore a blue postal service uniform and stood behind a tiny counter.

I was waiting for Ellie to speak up.

She didn't.

The woman grunted and put her hands on her hips. "Ellie Burke, I know yer not deaf."

I looked down at Ellie. Her shoulders were curled in as if she were trying to make herself as small as possible.

"They're service dogs," I said from behind her, my voice slightly sharp.

Ellie flinched.

I pushed her the half dozen feet to the counter.

The postal worker's face morphed to confused, than neutral, then vaguely apologetic. "Sorry, the light was in my eyes. I didn't see their vests."

"Not a problem," I said. "One of the reasons we're in town is so folks can get used to seeing Ellie with her new partner, Nugget."

Still Ellie was silent.

Oh, for crying out loud, Ms. Snark said inside my head.

"And to get a package I think you have for Bruce."

"Uh, yeah." The woman pivoted and pulled a large padded envelope out of a bin. "Here it is."

I chuckled. "Well, I guess we can make room for that, huh?" I gently poked Ellie's shoulder.

She jumped an inch.

"I need a signature." The postal worker tore a green return-receipt postcard loose from the package and tried to hand it and a pen to Ellie.

She didn't reach out for them.

I took them and crouched down beside Ellie. Her faced looked dazed.

"Here, lemme get somethin' for you to write on." The woman grabbed a magazine from a pile of unsorted mail and handed it over the counter. I took it and passed it on to Ellie.

She shook her head, as if waking up from a dream. Taking the pen, she scribbled on the card I placed on top of the magazine in her lap.

I gathered up all of it, magazine, card and pen, and exchanged the pile for the package.

"Thanks." I sketched a wave at the postal worker and turned the chair toward the door.

Ellie said a belated, "Bye, Betty."

"Y'all take care," the woman called after us.

Back out on the sidewalk, Ellie shivered a little. "You can put the package in the pouch back there."

I shoved aside my almost empty duffel bag that hung from one chair handle and noticed a cloth bag stretched across the back of the chair. It held a black sweater, Ellie's wallet and a bottle of water.

I pulled out the sweater and put the package in the bag in its place.

"You want this?" I handed her the sweater.

She took it and slipped her arms into it.

"Is there a coffee shop or some place that has outside seating?" I wasn't up for another encounter with a business owner just yet, but Ellie and I needed to talk.

She pointed to our right. About a block and a half away were a few lime green bistro tables and chairs. I pushed her in that direction, the dogs moving along beside us.

The shop seemed to be a mix of a coffee shop and ice cream parlor. I guess they were trying to hit all the seasons and the multiple needs of their customers as the day progressed from morning caffeine to afternoon treat. A good business plan in a small town like this.

"Let's sit for a few minutes." Not waiting for an answer, I wheeled the chair up to one of the tables. Nugget took up the cover position.

I looped Buddy's leash over the arm of one of the hideous green chairs. "Stay," I said to him, then turned to Ellie. "I'm getting a coffee. You want anything?"

She opened her mouth. A small jet flew low overhead, drowning out her words.

I realized she hadn't actually spoken. Her eyes had gone wide and she clapped her hands over her ears. Then she squeezed her eyes shut and started rocking back and forth.

Nugget shoved her head onto Ellie's lap. When she ignored her, the dog nudged her elbow.

One hand dropped to Nugget's head. The other covered Ellie's face. "I'm sorry," she whispered.

"No apologies needed," I said in a low, gentle voice. "Focus on the dog. It will help you get grounded."

After about thirty seconds, Ellie lowered the hand from her eyes and looked around. She waved her hand in the air. "Were you going to get a drink?"

Her voice sounded much stronger.

"Yes, you want anything?"

"No. We... um, I'll stick to water."

I retrieved her water bottle for her and went into the shop for my coffee.

When I came out a few minutes later, cup in hand, a woman about Ellie's age was standing next to Nugget, her hand on the dog's head, scratching her ears.

Nugget turned worried eyes toward me. Her body was hunched up, her tail tucked under her, as if she believed *she'd* done something wrong.

I ground my teeth.

Patience, my inner Mom admonished.

"Did you give the dog the release signal?" I asked. I knew I was being rude, ignoring the other woman, but…

Ellie shook her head. "I forgot."

I put the coffee on the table and gave Nugget the release signal, which would hopefully reduce the poor dog's confusion. Then I busied myself with pouring some water into the portable dog dish, to give the two women time to finish their conversation, and me time to find some of that patience.

The woman finally left. Ellie never had introduced us.

I set the dish down on the ground where both dogs could reach it. Then I plopped down in a chair and took a big gulp of coffee.

Which was a mistake. It burned all the way down.

"You okay?" Ellie asked.

I nodded, still trying to fake a neutral expression while my esophagus was on fire.

When the pain eased some, I took a deep breath and managed to muster a calm, sympathetic voice. "Ellie, I know you want to get along with people, but you can't keep letting them mess with her. After a while, you will have a ten-thousand dollar pet, not a service dog."

I was tempted to threaten to take the dog away from her. I still had that option, if I felt she wasn't well suited to having a service dog. But that would mean waiting for Mattie Jones, the director of the agency I trained for, to find another recipient for Nugget, and then training that person. It would be well after the first of the year before I got my training fee.

And as mad as I was, I couldn't bring myself to inflict that wound on Ellie. Today's jumpiness and the flashback were evidence that she really needed the dog, and she'd already started to bond with Nugget.

Ellie nodded, staring at her clasped hands on the table. "I'm sorry. I'll do better."

"Okay. That's all I ask." I blew on my coffee and took a tentative sip. It was just right.

"That was my friend Megan. She said the hurricane is definitely headed for Cuba. They no longer expect it to veer toward the panhandle, but it might edge northward enough to hit the Keys."

"The poor Keys," I said. They got hit with storms way more often than the rest of the state.

She gave me a small smile.

With some degree of equilibrium re-established between us, I asked, "Hey, what was going on earlier? You went kind of little kid on me after my confrontation with Mrs. Warren and when we first went into the post office."

She shook her head slightly. "What do you mean?"

"When that woman, Betty. Is that her name? When she didn't want to let the dogs in."

"She didn't want to let the dogs in?" she echoed.

"Yeah, she got kind of pissy about it, until I pointed out that they were service dogs."

She shook her head again. "I remember saying goodbye to Mrs. Warren, and then I was signing for Bruce's package."

I stared at her.

She dropped her gaze, breaking eye contact. "I get these little blackouts sometimes."

"Are they recent?" I was wondering if they could be related to the sarcopenia or to the PTSD.

But Ellie was shaking her head. "I've had them all my life."

Huh? She'd said it so nonchalantly. Didn't she know that wasn't normal?

CHAPTER SEVEN

"Hey, I could really use a trim." Ellie took the scrunchie off of her pony-tail and ran a hand through her long blonde hair. "My hairdresser's right down the street. Can we see if she can fit me in?"

I stuffed down my curiosity about her strange blackouts. "Sure."

We got our things together and headed on down the sidewalk.

As we passed a storefront, I glanced in the open door. My gaze ran over an aisle of cookies, crackers and granola bars.

My mouth watering, I slowed and looked up. The sign above the door read *Luke's Groceries and Sundries.*

Ellie twisted around in the wheelchair, probably wondering why I had slowed down. She turned her head, following my line of vision to the aisle I'd been eyeballing, across from the snacks. Jars of peanut butter and jelly were lined up on it.

"Luke the third, and his sister run the store now," she said. "His grandfather founded it in the 1960s."

While I appreciated the background information, I was much more interested in the store's contents than its origins. "Hey, can I leave you at the hairdresser's and do a little sightseeing?"

"Sure, but there isn't much to see here, I'm afraid."

Indeed, Ellie's hairdresser had time for a quick haircut. It was a two-chair shop. The occupant of the other chair was flipping through a magazine, her head covered with foil squares.

I stifled a grimace. I'd much rather let the Florida sun provide my red highlights.

I gave Nugget the release signal and told her to lie down. "I'll be back in half an hour then, okay?"

"Sounds good."

I grabbed my duffel bag, and Buddy and I boogied on back to the little store.

It dawned on me that I should've left Buddy with Ellie as well. Technically he's not a service dog, and I shouldn't take him inside establishments unless he was "working" while training, which, at the moment, he was not.

But the young woman behind the counter didn't bat an eye when he trotted in behind me in his service vest. I decided to let it slide. Why complicate things?

"Hi. What can I help you with?" She had a slight Cracker accent and a big smile. Her tallish, broad-shouldered frame was clad in jeans and a smudged white tank top, with the gray straps of a sports bra peeking out on her shoulders, and a kerchief tied around her hair. "Sorry for the scruffy outfit. Today's the day I dust the place, whether it needs it or not."

I grinned. She'd just used one of my mother's lines. "No problem. Can I look around some?"

"Sure, help yourself. Baskets are over there." She pointed with her chin, then grabbed up a large feather duster and stood on tiptoe to brush it across the tops of cans on a high shelf.

I picked up one of the green plastic baskets and made a circuit of the store, piling in a jar of peanut butter, a box of granola bars, and some bananas. I stopped at the small deli counter. I would've loved to get some lunchmeat and cheese, but I had no refrigerator. Then I spotted a double row of hard-boiled eggs. They'd keep off ice for a few days.

The young woman popped around the corner of the counter and donned plastic gloves. "What can I get ya?"

"Four eggs, please."

She plucked them up one at a time, wrapping each in a thin sheet of deli paper. "Say, are you staying out on Haasi Island?"

"Yes. How'd you guess?"

"One, I saw you with Ellie a few minutes ago, and two, Bruce has some strange eating habits, so I can understand why you might want to stock up." She grinned as she handed over the eggs.

I returned the grin. "Hey, what does *Haasi* mean anyway?"

"It's Miccosukee for *sun*. I'm surprised Jack didn't tell you that."

"Why?"

"'Cause he's Miccosukee and proud of it."

I nodded. There were quite a few Native-American tribes in Florida, not just the Seminoles that everyone associated with the state.

The young woman came out from behind the counter, and we headed toward the front of the store. "Can ya give Greta a message for me?"

"Sure," I said.

"Tell her the new multi-grain flour Bruce ordered should be in by this afternoon."

"Bruce ordered? But he doesn't eat bread," I blurted out.

She rolled her eyes. "Unless it's made with rye or rice flour. He's convinced they're okay, but not wheat."

"So why does he care about the other flour?"

The young woman's face drooped. Her constant smile faded. "I think he believes he can make Ellie better if he can just find the right diet for her."

"Oh." My heart felt heavy in my chest. Maybe Bruce did really care about his wife. Becky's theory that he was only trying to make the best of a bad situation might have merit.

I tossed my duffel bag onto the counter. "You can put my stuff in here."

～

Bruce must have returned from his trip, because Jack showed up in the bigger boat to pick us up. I hadn't really taken a good look at it before this.

My father had been a bit of a boat *aficionado*, although he could never afford more than a small fishing boat that he kept in the backyard on a trailer.

If I remembered correctly, this boat before me would be called a performance cruiser—a cross between a cabin cruiser and a sport boat. It was about twenty-five feet, a little stunted for a cruiser, and it had a huge outboard motor, also somewhat unusual on a cabin cruiser.

Jack had anchored offshore and puttered over to us in a rubber dingy even smaller than his skiff. It took three trips to get all of us and our paraphernalia onto the boat.

"Hope you ladies don't need to use the head," Jack said. "The door's stuck again."

I hadn't had the need until he mentioned it. Now I was all too aware of that coffee I'd had. I sat down in the cockpit and crossed my legs, gesturing for the dogs to settle at my feet.

Looking around for a distraction, I glanced over at Ellie. She had a glint in her eyes that I hadn't seen before.

"I love boats," she called over the engine noise and the sound of the air rushing past us. We weren't going all that fast, but the day had turned windy. Tiny ripples showed on the surface of the usually placid river.

"Bruce had this one custom-made. Shorter and with less draft than most cabin cruisers, so it could navigate the Salt River." She was grinning from ear to ear, the most enthusiasm she'd shown about anything to date. "I actually love anything that moves and has an engine."

Which, of course, was why she'd become an engineer.

I returned her grin, then a strong wave of melancholy washed over me, weighing down my muscles. This woman was only in her early thirties and she'd already had and lost the career of her dreams, going from designing the machines she loved to a wheelchair on an isolated island.

Back at the house, I hauled my stash upstairs, anxious to get to my bathroom.

I had some time before lunch, so I looked up "blackouts while still conscious." Most of the list from my Google search had to do with alcoholic blackouts. Was Bruce right and Ellie was a secret drunk?

Could someone as thin as she was have enough tolerance for alcohol that they could still be functional while drunk enough to black out? That seemed unlikely.

And what about her claim that she'd had these episodes all her life?

Only one result from the search referred to "psychogenic blackouts." I clicked on that link, but it was talking about people who fainted under extreme stress.

Even though Ellie had said she'd had the blackouts all he life, I plugged in "PTSD symptoms."

I knew the list by heart, but I ran my gaze down it anyway. There were some dissociative symptoms, such as feeling unreal and disconnected from others, or having no memory for all or part of the trauma the person had experienced. Blackouts definitely weren't on the list though, and the encounter with Mrs. Warren, while annoying, wasn't anywhere near trauma level.

Something was nagging at the back of my brain, but I couldn't force it out into the light of day. When that happens, I've learned the hard way to leave it alone. The idea will surface when it's good and ready.

Ellie didn't show up for lunch, but Bruce was there. He had already taken something of almost everything on the buffet. I stuck with the wheat bread and tuna paste sandwiches and some fruit salad.

Our conversation was superficial and a bit stilted.

"Hey, thanks for getting that package for me," he said, as if Ellie hadn't had anything to do with it. "It's some new parts for my log splitter. This house doesn't have central heat. So we do it the old-fashioned way, with fireplaces. I want to make sure we've got enough wood to get us through, just in case Pierre veers farther north and we get some of his outer bands."

I was surprised he was worried about firewood. In early November, the weather was still a pleasant seventy to eighty degrees most days. But the nighttime temps were starting to dip below sixty. Still, nothing an extra blanket on your bed couldn't handle.

"It might not bother you or me," Bruce said, "but Ellie's so thin. She gets cold easy."

It spooked me a little that he'd seemed to guess my thoughts, but again I was heartened that he was thinking of his wife's well-being.

Greta entered the room and went over to peruse the sideboard. The only platter that was close to empty was the sandwich one—most of the little triangles were on my plate.

She picked the platter up and turned toward the door.

"Greta." Bruce waved her over to the table. He grabbed up the salt shaker and handed it to her. "Get rid of all these. All the salt Ellie dumps on her food can't be good for her."

Greta pursed her lips but made no reply. She took the shaker from him and left the room.

"Um, excuse me for a moment." I stood and rushed after her.

Nudging around her in the main living area, I murmured, "Sorry, nature calls." I hurried to the doorway leading to the hall, then around the corner and past the powder room. I ran to the kitchen, grabbed the salt shaker from the small table there, and jammed it into my pocket.

The salt didn't help the bland food all that much, but it sometimes made the difference between can't tolerate it and able to choke it down.

I got out of the kitchen just as Greta turned the corner. She gave me a funny look, no doubt wondering how I had used the powder room quite that quickly, but she went on past me.

I smiled to myself. I was craving an egg yolk something fierce, since the only thing Bruce allowed to be served here were egg whites. And now I had salt for my hard-boiled eggs.

I returned to the dining room, hoping the salt-shaker-shaped bulge in my jeans pocket wasn't too obvious.

But Bruce wasn't in his seat.

He was across the room, stooped down next to the sickly potted plant that Ellie used to dispose of her unwanted grapefruit juice.

I expected some comment from him about the plant's poor health, but instead he pulled something from behind the pot and rose to a stand.

He held the object out for me to see.

It was a half-empty vodka bottle.

Not knowing what to say about the hidden liquor bottle, I'd claimed to have a headache and fled to my room. The dogs were happily napping, Nugget in her crate and Buddy curled up beside my bed.

I ate a hard-boiled egg with some of my purloined salt, but I was too distracted to truly enjoy it. I paced the floor for a few minutes. I really wanted to get in some more training today, *and* I really wanted to know what was going on with the hidden vodka bottles.

I opened the dresser drawer I had designated as my pantry and grabbed two granola bars. Maybe something tasty would loosen Ellie's lips.

Telling Buddy to stay, I snapped Nugget's leash onto her collar, and we descended to the second floor. I knocked gently on Ellie's door.

"Come in," filtered through the old, glossy wood.

I stuck my head inside. "I come bearing gifts." Nugget and I slipped in, and I closed the door. Then I pulled the granola bars out from behind my back.

Ellie's eyes lit up. "Are those what I think they are?"

"Yup." I walked toward the bed where she was once again propped up against pillows, her e-reader in her lap.

She licked her lips. "I hope you're planning to share."

I handed one of the bars to her. "I made good use of my time while you were getting your hair cut."

She ate the granola bar slowly, making a show of chewing and savoring, rolling her eyes now and then.

I laughed out loud at her antics, while I sat in the armchair near her bed and ate my own treat. I wished I'd bought more than the one box of them.

"Say, where can a girl get something to drink around here?" I said, trying to sound casual.

"You mean besides grapefruit juice or water?" Her tone was slightly snide. She popped the last bite of the granola bar into her mouth.

"Yeah. I was thinking of something a bit stronger."

She chewed and swallowed. "I wish you'd said something this morning. There's an ABC store down the road, just outside of town. And…" She pointed to the granola wrapper on her lap. "I assume you got these at Luke's."

"Yes."

"He's got a good beer selection, if you don't want anything fancy, and there's a dusty little corner with a few wine bottles."

"Um, vodka was what I had in mind." I watched carefully for her reaction.

Which was minimal. "Gotta get that at the ABC store." Her tone was matter-of-fact.

Then she let out a soft sigh. "We used to have a wine cellar here, some really good vintages too. But Bruce got rid of all the bottles a couple of months ago. Said the sulfites were bad for us."

"Has he always been such a health nut?"

She shrugged. "He's always been into exercise and eating right, but it used to be protein shakes and whole grains, fruits and veggies. In the last few months, he's been reading all these articles. He keeps bringing Greta recipes for stuff that's supposed to be so healthy, but most of it tastes like something between cardboard and I don't know…"

"Library paste," Ms. Snark blurted out before I could intercede.

Ellie snickered. "That's probably the best word for it. Last month, he tried to ban bread from the island. I put my foot down. Greta's breads and rolls are to die for, and sometimes they're the only thing served that I can eat."

I can relate, Ms. Snark said, internally this time, thank heavens.

"Fortunately, he didn't fight me on that, just insisted that we special order our flour to make sure it's pure. But he'll only eat the pumpernickel bread. He's convinced that he's allergic to wheat."

Ms. Snark initiated an eye roll, which I quickly stifled.

I leaned forward in my chair. "Do you like bananas?"

Her eyes lit up again. "I do. Yet another thing Bruce has banned."

"I've got one for you if you do good with the training this afternoon."

She grinned. "Using some behavior modification on me, huh?"

I nodded, grinning back.

Forty-five minutes later, I left Ellie's room satisfied that Nugget was coming along nicely regarding the *Brace* command. I'd had Ellie practice it with her, getting down on the floor and pretending that she had fallen. The dog had spread her legs, stood still, and tolerated Ellie's weight well.

And Ellie had moved from the bed to the open area by her French doors without the wheelchair or any help from me.

I was beginning to see a pattern. Ironically, on days that Ellie ate very little, she actually seemed to be stronger. Which made no sense. This morning, she'd passed on the lovely pancakes, saying her stomach was a little off, and had just had a bowl of fruit salad and tea. And she'd skipped lunch, except for my contraband granola bar.

Yet she'd been able to walk without assistance.

Shaking my head, I went back to my room, Nugget in tow. I flexed my arms, which were aching. My legs were also a bit sore.

I was basically a fit person—training dogs is hardly a sedentary job. But I must have been using muscles, while pushing Ellie's wheelchair around town, that I didn't normally use.

In my room, my bed was like a magnet. It was all I could do to stay upright long enough to freshen the dogs' water bowls and usher Nugget into her crate.

Then I kicked off my shoes and settled onto the bed for a much needed nap.

A soft whining noise woke me. It took me a moment to figure out where I was.

The whining again. I sat partway up and looked around.

Nugget was standing up in her crate, her tail tucked between her legs. Buddy sat by the door to the hallway, a long-suffering expression on his face.

I glanced at my watch. I'd slept almost two hours.

"Okay, I'm coming." I grabbed their leashes.

At the last second, I remembered Ellie's banana. I got one out of my dresser-drawer pantry.

On the second floor, I knocked gently on Ellie's door.

No answer.

I turned the knob and nudged it open a crack. The room was empty.

"Stay," I said to the dogs. I tiptoed into the room and put the banana on her nightstand.

A rustling noise had me spinning around. The balcony doors were open, a soft breeze ruffling the sheer curtains.

The rustling noise again, too loud to be the flimsy curtains.

I moved quietly in that direction. "Hello," I called out. If Ellie was on the balcony, I didn't want to startle her.

No answer.

I stepped out onto the balcony. It was deserted. Maybe the rustling had been a squirrel. A trellis ran alongside, entwined with jasmine vines. It would give squirrels easy access.

As if on cue, the jasmine leaves shook. I walked over to that end of the balcony and looked down.

Movement about ten feet from the house, near the edge of the woods. Something black billowed and a flash of red.

My pulse quickened. I blinked, and whatever it was had disappeared.

A little rattled, I turned to go back into Ellie's room. Something registered in my peripheral vision—small and shiny black, caught between the balcony's railing and the wall it was bolted into.

I pulled the ragged scrap of silky material loose, then scanned the edge of the woods below again. I was supposed to assume I'd just seen the pirate ghost.

But a ghost's clothing doesn't snag and leave solid fragments of cloth behind.

CHAPTER EIGHT

I needed to find Ellie and tell her what I'd discovered, but first things first. The poor dogs had waited long enough.

I took them out back and unhooked their leashes so they could romp in the underbrush near the lanai.

I sat down at the picnic table and tried to figure out why someone would pretend to be a ghost. Were they trying to play a joke on the Burkes? Or was there some darker motive?

Perhaps I needed to figure out who first, and that might tell me the why.

Buddy trotted over and put his chin on my thigh.

"Finished already?" I stroked the soft fur on the top of his head and gently scratched behind his ears.

I hadn't seen anyone in the house when I'd come through it. Even Greta wasn't in the kitchen.

I need to locate people as fast as I can. Before they had time to change out of and hide the pirate costume.

I jumped up, startling Buddy. "Where's Nugget?" I scanned the lanai. The dog was nowhere in sight.

She was only two years old, young enough to still have some of the curiosity of a puppy. Who knew what enticing scent had lured her away?

I gritted my teeth. I really needed to be locating and eliminating ghost impersonator suspects. Then I sighed and headed down a trodden path, calling Nugget's name. Buddy trailed behind me. "Nugget," I yelled again, but there was no answering woof from the woods.

Heart thudding and stomach clenched, I was beating myself up for not paying closer attention to her—there were dozens of ways a dog could get hurt in these woods. A noise registered, the low hum of a motor in the distance. I followed the sound.

It led us to a clearing around a rustic shed. The building was maybe twenty by thirty feet, with the same cypress siding as the house, only unpainted and more weather-worn, and its metal roof was rusty. The large door gaped open. I spotted a stack of firewood inside.

Jack trundled into the clearing, pushing a wheelbarrow loaded with chunks of wood.

"Have you seen Nugget?" I said.

He turned his head and pointed back the way he'd come with his chin. "She's back there, pestering Bruce."

"Thanks." Buddy and I moved off down the trail, behind us the steady thud of firewood being thrown onto the stack in the shed, the humming motor sound ahead and getting louder.

The trail disappeared, replaced by some chopped off underbrush that had been crushed underfoot. It couldn't have been easy for Jack to shove that barrow of heavy wood through here.

Eventually we came to the source of the sound—the gas motor of a tall metal contraption, which I assumed was the log splitter. Nearby, Bruce, wearing safety goggles, was using an axe to knock the bark off a large, round slice of wood that had no doubt come from the fallen live oak tree a few feet away. Other round slices were scattered next to it, and its sawed-off branches had been piled to the side. The exposed wood was already a dark tan. The tree had been lying there, seasoning, for some time.

The axe came down, barely missing Nugget's nose as she thrust it forward, sniffing at the wood. I screamed her name.

I doubt she heard me because I couldn't hear Bruce over the motor. But based on lipreading, I was pretty sure he yelled, "Get back, you stupid mutt."

I gestured for Buddy to stay and ran across the small clearing. I grabbed Nugget's collar and pulled her away.

Bruce jumped a little, then pulled the goggles off his face. "Sorry," he yelled over the noise from the splitter's motor. "I didn't see you."

"But you knew Nugget was there," I yelled. I thought my chest might explode. "You could've killed her."

He had the gall to shrug. "How'd she get away from you?"

My stomach twisted—he was right, she was my responsibility. But the guilt just fueled my anger. "That's beside the point," I screamed. "How could you put her at risk? She's an expensive animal."

"Sorry," he yelled, not sounding like he meant it. "But we've gotta get this wood into the shed, and then Jack needs to go to town for some supplies before nightfall."

I opened my mouth but clamped it shut again. No point in arguing with this man over a ten-thousand-dollar dog. Not when he'd spent at least half a million to customize a cabin cruiser. Nugget's monetary worth would mean very little to him.

And no point in trying to explain the intangible worth of a dog that I had loved, fed, and trained for the last six months. Despite the sob story about his boyhood Labrador, this man was no dog lover.

I pulled Nugget farther away from him and yanked her leash out of my back pocket. Clipping it on, I stormed back toward the house, dogs in tow.

We came upon Jack, trundling the now empty wheelbarrow back toward the fallen tree.

I stopped, blocking the thin path. "How long have you two been at this?"

Jack's eyebrows went up. He dropped the barrow's handles and pulled a grubby piece of cloth from his pocket. "A couple of hours." He wiped his sweaty brow.

"Was Bruce with you the whole time?"

He gave me a funny look. "Yeah. Why?"

I shrugged and went for diversion. "I thought I'd bring you all some water from the house."

Jack cracked a small smile. "That sounds good."

"I'll put it by the shed." I had no intention of getting near Bruce any time soon. I would probably do something I'd regret later.

As the dogs and I squeezed around the wheelbarrow, I said, "When are you going to town?"

Jack grimaced, then his face settled into a frown. "As soon as we have this tree chopped up. Bruce didn't want it to get saturated in the storm and have to wait weeks for it to dry out again." Another grimace. "In about three-quarters of an hour."

It was the longest speech I'd heard him make yet. And what was with all the grimacing and frowning?

"Can I go with you? There's something I meant to get in town this morning that I forgot."

"Sure, but be ready to go. The timin's gonna be tight to get back here before dark." Now a vein was throbbing in his temple.

A lightbulb went off in my head. The translation of Jack's little speech was that Bruce wanted to play with his newly fixed log splitter. Which meant poor Jack would be here well into the evening now, instead of home with his family.

Men and their toys, Ms. Snark commented.

❧

The dogs and I went into the house through the back, the screen door banging behind us.

Greta was in the kitchen, her back against the counter, her hand on her chest. "*Ach*, you startled me."

"Sorry. Hey, I was looking for you a little bit ago. Where were you?"

She shot me a glare. I couldn't blame her. It was a rude question.

"I was cleaning upstairs." She glanced behind her, then took a step to her right.

Funny, I hadn't seen or heard any signs of cleaning, but she could've been dusting inside one of the rooms.

I took a step closer.

"What did you want?" She sidled farther sideways.

"Oh, well," I took another step, "um, I'm going into town again with Jack. Do you need anything?" I leaned to one side to see past her.

She leaned in the same direction to block my view. "I will give him a list. I almost have it ready."

"Oh, okay." I straightened, faked an innocent expression.

She relaxed slightly.

I feinted toward her right and then lunged to her left, and got a good look at what was behind her.

A small plate with a pumpernickel sandwich, a slice of pickle hanging out one end.

Aha, she does have her own stash, Ms. Snark chortled inside.

Greta tried to maneuver into my path again, but I leaned around her and picked up a sandwich half. I sniffed the filling. Liverwurst.

Her face had gone ashen. "Please do not say anything to Bruce," she whispered.

I considered for a moment blackmailing her into sharing, but my inner Mom's face popped up in my mind's eye. She shook her finger at me.

I sighed. "Your secret's safe with me. Where's Ellie?"

"On the front porch, now please get these animals out of my kitchen." She tried to sound tough, but her eyes were still clouded with worry.

Would Bruce fire her for bringing contraband into the house?

"Sure, but I promised the men some water."

Greta pulled two bottles of cold spring water out of the fridge and, avoiding eye contact, handed them to me.

I took the water to the shed, which was currently deserted and set the bottles in plain view by the doors. As the dogs and I walked back to the house, I contemplated the status of my suspect list. Greta seemed unusually nervous, but I had trouble imagining her elderly body climbing around on trellises.

According to Jack, he and Bruce had been together around the time the pirate made his hasty descent, but they weren't always together. Bruce could have slipped away while Jack was at the shed stacking wood. Or vice versa, Jack could have pretended to be stacking while taking a detour to play pirate.

We circled around to the front of the house. Ellie was asleep on a wicker chaise on the porch. Her color was better than I'd seen in days, with some pink in her cheeks.

I moved on around the corner of the house to the trellis that ran up next to Ellie's balcony on the second floor. It was bracketed by two Southern rose bushes.

A large crepe myrtle at the corner of the house would block the view from out front, giving the pirate the ability to move from the woods to the trellises and back without likelihood of detection.

I grabbed the trellis and gave it a good shake. It barely moved— certainly sturdy enough for someone to climb. And some of the jasmine vines were crushed in places where one might insert a toe onto a crosspiece.

I checked the ground under the trellis and rose bushes. Pulling out my phone, I snapped a photo of part of a footprint in the soft soil—what looked like the narrow heel of a boot, or perhaps a woman's flat-heeled shoe. Then I examined the rose bushes.

Black threads were twisted around a thorn. I peeled them loose and put them in my pocket, with the scrap of cloth from the balcony railing.

For now, I needed to get ready to go to town, but later I *really* needed to figure out who the pirate was.

Because a human being pretending to be a ghost scared me far more than an actual ghost did.

Once Buddy and I were settled in the cruiser's cockpit, Jack untied the lines and jumped aboard. When the engine was purring and we were safely out in the middle channel of the river, I said, "If we don't get back until almost dark, can you get home safely in your skiff?"

His face puckered a little. I didn't think he was going to answer, but then he said, "I'll stay over. Bruce is gonna need me tomorrow to close up the hurricane shutters, if it looks like the storm's gonna get close to us."

"What about your family?" I blurted out.

A beat of silence, other than the humming of the engine. The vein in his temple throbbed twice. "My oldest boy will help his mother batten down the house."

"How old is he?"

"Eleven."

I stroked Buddy's head, which was resting on my knee. He hadn't liked the skiff much, but in this bigger boat, he was a happy sailor. "How many kids do you have?"

"Three."

"All boys?"

Another half beat before he responded. "Girl's nine. Younger boy's five. Another on the way."

"Congra–" My words were cut off as he gunned the engine, and the boat flew down a straightaway in the river.

After a few minutes, he slowed for a curve. "I gotta go to the hard-ware store," he yelled over the wind, "get a sturdier latch for the woodshed, and some gas for the back-up generator. Okay if I give you Greta's list for Luke's?"

"Sure."

He dug a folded sheet of paper out of his shorts' pocket and handed it to me, careful not to let it go until I had a good hold on it in the rushing air.

I stuffed it in my jeans' pocket. Which reminded me of what I had taken out of that pocket just before we left the island. The black thread and scrap of cloth were now in an envelope tucked away in my laptop case in my room.

Who was the pirate?

I studied Jack. He was certainly strong enough to climb that trellis and not a particularly heavy man, so it would hold him. But he wasn't very tall.

I'd only caught two quick glimpses of the pirate, yet my impression was of a taller man. But it was only an impression. I glanced down at Jack's feet. He was wearing sneakers now.

But as the pirate, he could've been wearing boots with lifts in them, in order to seem taller and scarier.

Yet, I couldn't see what Jack had to gain by scaring the crap out of Ellie. Did he resent her as a "foreigner" on the island?

"How long have you worked for Bruce?" I yelled over the engine roar. We were again on a straightaway, and he seemed determined to get to town as fast as possible.

"Worked for his daddy, back when Bruce was a teenager."

I nodded. Did that long service to the family mean his loyalties were with Bruce, not Ellie? But he didn't seem to particularly like Bruce.

And why was I assuming that the staff had to be loyal to one or the other of them, as if they were on opposing teams?

That led me to wondering where Greta's loyalty lay.

"How long has Greta worked for them?" I yelled.

"About as long. Came a year after I started." He slowed the engine as the small park and the gravel boat ramp came into view. "You need me to get the dingy out?"

"How close can you get?"

By way of an answer, he flipped two brackets on either side of the giant motor and wrestled it out of the water.

"So that's why it has an outboard." I grinned.

"Yup." He gave me a quick smile back.

I loved how the flash of white teeth lit up his weathered face.

And in that moment, I prayed that he was loyal to Ellie, because my subconscious had put a few pieces together. And I'd come to two conclusions.

One, someone was plotting against Ellie for whatever reason, and two, I liked her, felt protective of her. If there were sides to be taken here, I was on hers.

I also liked Jack, despite his somewhat taciturn nature. I'd prefer to be on the same side as he was.

He had let the boat drift close to the slight incline of the boat ramp. "She's got a flatter bottom than most cabin cruisers, another thing that Bruce had customized."

"She's a beauty. Does she have a name?" I hadn't seen one on its stern.

The corners of Jack's mouth twitched. "Bruce calls her Lucinda Mae, but Ellie dubbed her Bruce's Folly. They've only had her a couple of months."

Oh yeah, there were definitely sides here.

We waded ashore, me holding my duffel bag, with my shoes and socks in it, above my head.

Jack, carrying four empty gas cans, jogged over to a black SUV. He pulled several cloth carrying bags out of its back end and tossed them to me. "See you back here in half an hour."

"Got it."

Fortunately, I keep a couple of towels in my car, for times when the dogs and I get caught in the rain. I used one on Buddy and one on my wet, sandy feet, before donning my socks and sneakers again.

I started the car's engine. Then I sat there for a few precious moments.

I was struggling with the urge to turn the car right instead of left and drive home to Mayfair.

The storm was one of the reasons for the butterflies in my stomach, but mostly they were about this crazy household I'd landed in—fake ghosts, weird food, and Bruce. I couldn't figure him out.

I didn't count Ellie's mercurial moods as part of the craziness. She was my client who had PTSD. I expected the unexpected from her.

She was the deciding factor. I couldn't make myself abandon her to whatever the heck was going on over on Haasi Key.

I put my car in gear and left the parking lot, turning left toward the town of Dahlia.

I engaged my Bluetooth to call Will, my real purpose for accompanying Jack to the mainland, to get a good solid phone signal for a change.

My call went straight to voicemail.

Crapola. That meant one of two things. He was either interrogating some bad guy, or he was about to accost some even badder guy to arrest him.

The latter possibility had the butterflies in my stomach doing the tango.

Will is a seasoned cop. He'll be fine. Will is a seasoned cop. He'll be fine. The butterflies settled down some in response to the mantra, but not completely. Never completely when he was working a case.

I left a message, saying that regretfully I wouldn't be able to leave Nugget with Ellie this weekend. She wasn't ready. I signed off in a breezy voice. No point in worrying him about the craziness, when there was nothing he could do about it half a state away.

I pulled up in front of Luke's Groceries and Sundries.

I hadn't thought to put Buddy's vest on him, but no one was behind the counter to question his presence. I quickly perused the shelves, dropping the items from Greta's list into my basket.

I noted the absence of grapefruit juice on said list and hoped that meant we wouldn't be served that anymore. I was with Ellie now. There is just so much of it one could consume before starting to hate it.

More likely Greta's got a freezer full of frozen concentrate, Ms. Snark grumbled.

Into a second basket, I placed things for myself and Ellie—some more bananas and granola bars. And two six-packs of juice boxes, one cranapple and one cherry-berry. I smiled to myself. Regardless of Greta's plans on the subject, no more grapefruit juice for me.

No one was at the deli counter, so I helped myself to the remaining half dozen hard-boiled eggs.

Then I went looking for a flashlight.

I wasn't all that worried about the storm, but I'd been a Floridian long enough to know you planned for the worst and thanked your lucky stars when it didn't happen.

I apparently wasn't alone in that thinking. There were only two flashlights left on the shelf, and most of the batteries were cleaned out as well. I grabbed one flashlight and two of the three remaining packs of D-batteries.

When I lugged everything to the front counter, there was now someone behind it, her back to me. Broad shoulders, shoulder-length blonde hair with dark streaks in it. From the back, she seemed familiar.

"Did you find everything okay?" she said, turning toward me.

It was the same young woman from earlier in the day, but her hair... Earlier it had been covered.

My heart plummeted into my stomach, as I recognized her from another context.

She was Bruce's lover.

CHAPTER NINE

Crapola, Ms. Snark said inside my head.

The woman smiled. "Hi again."

Bile burned the back of my throat. I swallowed hard.

She placed her palms on the counter and pushed herself up some, so she could lean over and look down at Buddy. "Hey, fella. What's his name?"

"B-Buddy," I stuttered.

"Where's his vest?"

"Um, I forgot it. He's my mentor dog," I babbled. "I train service dogs."

Her eyes lit up. "You must be the woman who's training a dog for Ellie then. Shucks, I should've made that connection earlier." She stuck her hand out. "Real pleased to meet ya. I'm Lucy Barnes, Luke's sister."

Lucy… Lucinda! As in, Lucinda Mae.

"Um, yes, Marcia Banks." I took her hand and gave it a quick shake.

"I'm so glad she's gettin' a dog. She used to be such a cheerful person, and strong as can be, full of energy." Her eyes glazed over a little.

"We used to go over to the island, Luke and me, and the four of us would go swimmin'. But now…" She shook her head.

I resisted the urge to curl my lip in a sneer. "Yeah, well hopefully her new dog will help her. Uh, I couldn't find any nutmeg or dried milk. Greta had them on her list."

"I'll get 'em for you." She trotted off down an aisle.

While she was gone, I worked on maintaining a neutral expression as I arranged Greta's requests on the counter. I hoped I had enough cash to cover all of it.

Lucy came back, a small bottle of nutmeg in one hand and a big box of dried milk in the other. She glanced at the four egg cartons on the counter. "You about cleaned me out on those," she said with a chuckle.

"I think Greta's concerned the storm may get close enough that we can't get ashore for a day or two."

Lucy's lips pressed together. "Um, Greta's a bit of a scaredy-cat when it comes to storms. But then again, she's not the only one who's nervous."

As her almost empty flashlight and battery shelf attested.

"Here lemme have those bags." She started ringing things up. "You want me to put this on Bruce and Ellie's tab?"

Relief loosened my tight muscles some. "Yes, please."

I put my stuff up on the counter as she cleared room. "This is my stash. Oh, and I need a loaf of bread."

"All sold out. Oh, that reminds me, Greta's flour came in. Lemme get it." She trotted off again.

Hmm, I could filch some bread slices from the buffet, as needed.

Despite the shock of coming face to face with Bruce's lover, I smiled a little to myself. If need be, I could easily live off of peanut butter and banana sandwiches—my fave comfort food—and hard-boiled eggs for the next few days.

By the time Buddy and I made it back to the boat ramp, dusk was settling around the trees and palmettos of the small park. I quickly parked my car, as far away from the trees as I could get it this time. I didn't particularly want tree limbs through its windows. I grabbed my duffel and one of the carry bags. "Be right back, boy."

Jack had gotten out the rubber dingy. It was pulled partway up onto the gravel ramp. He took the bags from me and pointed his chin toward my car. "Hurry."

I ran for the car, got Buddy out of the back, grabbed the two other bags and locked up.

It was a tight fit getting all of us and the groceries into the dingy, but I didn't complain. There wasn't time for a second trip.

The floor of the cruiser's cabin was covered with gas cans and two large coolers. Jack tilted his chin toward them. "Dry ice." He took the last two grocery bags from me and stowed them on the bench surrounding the small table.

My stomach felt queasy. Should I be more worried about this storm?

My anxiety must have shone on my face. "Only a precaution," Jack said.

I nodded and stepped around him, headed for the door to the head.

"It's stuck again." He frowned. "Can't find anything wrong with it. I think it must swell sometimes from the humidity."

I helped Jack carry the groceries up the pier and into the house, then Buddy and I bolted for the stairs with our duffle bag of contraband.

But my steps faltered as I moved down the second-floor hallway. A door that was normally closed now stood partway open. My pulse rate kicked up a notch. I drifted that way.

A heavy dark-wood dresser stood just inside the door. The big mirror over it showed the rest of the room—a masculine study with a single bed off to one side. The only light came from a floor lamp in one corner, next to an armchair, and a figure, all in black, sat hunched over in that chair.

My breath caught in my throat. Was this our mystery pirate ghost?

I gestured for Buddy to stay back and inched forward to get a better view of the mirror.

The figure was leaning over his or her lap. Then the head came up, the light glinted off something shiny and a hand swiped across the lower half of a masculine face.

I quickly backed away, waved my hand for Buddy to follow, and fled up the stairs to the third floor.

Once in my own room, I dropped my duffel on the floor and sank into my armchair, processing what I had seen.

My best guess was that Bruce Burke had been crying. The shiny object had looked like a cell phone. But it could've been a hand mirror, and he could've been snorting cocaine.

The dinner bell tinkled while I was still trying to decide what to do, if anything, about what I'd seen. My first instinct was to flee this island and never look back. But that wasn't going to happen tonight.

Leaving Nugget in her crate, I took Buddy downstairs with me. We were the first ones in the dining room.

There was no buffet at night. Greta brought our covered plates in on a trolley, along with a big basket of rolls and a bowl of salad.

The rolls were whole wheat and still warm from the oven. I grabbed one and broke it open, practically inhaling one half of it. It was a little drier than usual but still yummy.

When Greta turned her back to get my plate from the trolley, I snatched two more rolls and, under the table, wrapped them in my napkin.

She removed the cover and swept the plate down in front of me, all in one well-practiced smooth movement.

More dry-looking white fish and plain vegetables with brown rice. My lip curled before I could catch myself.

Greta sniffed softly but otherwise didn't react. She left the covers on the plates she put at Ellie's and Bruce's places.

She left the room, and a few seconds later, I heard the tinkle of the dinner bell again, calling the tardy to the table.

Hmm, what else could I pilfer? I eyed Bruce's bread plate. Surely he wouldn't miss it. He never ate the wheat rolls. The plate joined the wrapped rolls on my lap.

The heavy-handled table knife would be hard to hide, so I slipped the teaspoon next to it off the table and shoved it into my jeans pocket, just as Bruce came into the room.

Ellie joined us a minute later, and she was walking on her own.

Woot. I started to jump up to hug her, and caught myself, remembering the stash on my lap. I settled for a big grin instead.

She returned it and almost flounced to her seat at the table. Grabbing the salad bowl, she placed a healthy serving on her salad plate, doused it with the oil and vinegar dressing and took a big bite.

"How are you tonight, Brucey baby?" she asked around the spinach and butter lettuce in her mouth.

He narrowed his eyes at her and shoveled fish into his mouth.

I took a small bite of rice. Either I was getting used to the bland food, or Greta had done something different to it tonight.

"Try the rice," I said. "It's good."

She complied and nodded as she chewed. "Not bad."

I took another bite of rice. Ah, that's what the nutmeg was for. Greta had added it to the rice.

Ellie looked around. "Hey, where's the salt shaker?"

"I had Greta get rid of it," Bruce said. "You don't need all that salt."

Ellie's face turned red. "You did what?" she said through clenched teeth.

I'd taken a bite of fish in the meantime. It was saltier than usual. "Mix the fish with the veggies," I suggested.

The tension in the room didn't ease all that much, but at least an explosion was averted.

Ellie tried my idea, and once again nodded as she chewed. "I like having you around."

"Thanks." *I think*, I added internally. I didn't particularly like being around these two.

By himself, Bruce was barely tolerable. By herself, Ellie was fine, although a bit of a roller coaster ride—sometimes in a good mood, sometimes borderline outrageous, other times neutral, and sometimes depressed and/or childlike.

But together these two were like the oil and vinegar I was pouring on my salad. Still, I had to dawdle until they were both gone, so I could exit with my stash.

Fortunately, they didn't want to be around each other either. Bruce scarfed down his fish, veggies and rice and, nodding at me, left the room.

Ellie pulled another roll from the basket. "Is it me or are these not as good as usual?"

"It's not you. Greta had me get dried milk this afternoon. That might be what she had to use in these."

Ellie shook her head, dropping the roll back in the basket. "You got any more granola bars?"

I smirked at her. "Maybe."

She grinned back. "Let's go."

"After you." I hid the plate, the rolls balanced on top, behind my back as we paraded out of the room. Warm breath on my fingers told me Buddy was sniffing at the plate.

"No, boy," I whispered.

Ellie was slow going up the stairs, but she made it.

I held my breath, hoping that no one would come along and see my weird little stash, bouncing along like a tail. Especially Greta. Jack would probably ignore it. Bruce might too. But not the sharp-eyed and equally sharp-tongued housekeeper.

My arm and leg muscles ached, and a twinge of pain darted across my upper back. I grimaced. All the scurrying around to get supplies and such had distracted me for a while, but now I was excruciatingly aware of my sore body again.

I hoped I wasn't coming down with the flu.

After taking the dogs out back for a few minutes, then delivering a granola bar to Ellie, all I wanted to do was curl up in my bed and sleep. But not before emailing Will. I climbed into bed with my laptop.

He had emailed me, twice.

As I read the subject line of the top one, my grin quickly faded.

Storm prediction changed, get out of there NOW.

Wait, that was his second email. His earlier one was labeled *Storm Update*. I clicked on that one first. It was matter-of-fact, relaying that the storm was now definitely expected to intensify and the cold front, which was supposed to push it farther south, was a weak one. There was a possibility the hurricane would punch right through it.

The message ended with, *Keep a close eye on this thing and get out of there if the prediction gets any worse.*

I clicked on the more recent email, time-stamped only twenty minutes ago, as we were sitting down to dinner.

Okay, he wasn't totally freaking out, but the tone of this one was a little more desperate. He'd attached a screenshot from the Weather Channel's website. The potential cone for where Pierre would make landfall now reached almost to Citrus County.

We would definitely get the outer bands, maybe worse. Still, this house was solid. It had stood for decades and had weathered many a storm.

I went to the Weather Channel site myself. The cone had not shifted any farther. Landfall was expected in the wee hours of Friday morning, which meant the storm had picked up speed.

I checked my phone, to see if Will had texted me. If he had, the texts hadn't gotten through. The phone's charge was low.

First rule of thumb with impending storms—make sure all electronic devices are fully charged. I got up and plugged in both my laptop and the phone. Then I returned to the bed and pulled the computer back onto my lap.

My insides were jittery, more so than the news about the storm's movements merited. I still had tomorrow to get off this island and inland to Mayfair, well out of the hurricane's path. For a moment, I thought I might lose my dinner. I took a deep breath and willed my queasy stomach to settle down.

My fingers poised over the keyboard, I contemplated how to respond.

At an earlier point in our relationship, I would've been pissed at Will's demanding tone, insisting that I leave now. But I knew he was just worried because he loved me.

I started typing.

Pressure in my chest and behind my eyes stilled my fingers. *Oh, Will.* My throat hurt.

I'm not gonna cry!

I stared at my screen. So far I had, *Hey there, Sorry I didn't see your emails sooner.*

I forced my shaky fingers to start typing again.

Hate this crappy cell service here. Did you get my message?

I'll get up early and check the weather report. If it's looking bad, I'll leave right away.

As I said in my message, I'm not comfortable leaving Nugget yet with Ellie. Long story.

I paused, not sure what to say next. Then the words kind of flowed out of my fingertips of their own volition.

Even if Pierre is behaving himself tomorrow, I think I'll leave late afternoon with both dogs to come home through the weekend. We need a break.

I wasn't quite sure who *we* referred to. Ellie? Nugget? Me? Maybe all of the above. Definitely me.

Sorry about the romantic weekend getaway. I'll make it up to you. Love, Marcia

A reply popped up in my inbox less than thirty seconds later.

Not worried about the romantic weekend. Just want you safe. You can't get out of there tonight?

I shook my head.

Sweetheart, the only access to this island is by boat, along a winding river. Not safe in the dark.

I wasn't about to tell him of Jack's and my semi-frantic supply run to town, racing to beat nightfall.

Once I check the weather in the a.m., I'll find a spot with a decent signal and call you. I'll be okay. Stop worrying.

I hit *Send.*

Only a few seconds' delay this time.

I hate this. I want to get in my truck and drive over there now.

I shook my head again. My chest hurt.

Don't. You'll only end up sleeping in your truck. I can't get to the mainland until morning anyway.

I hesitated. Did I want to let Will dictate how I handled this situation?

Crapola. I hated my blinkety-blank trust issues. He wasn't trying to control me. He was worried sick.

I'll leave in the morning regardless if that will make you feel better, I added to the email, then hit *Send.*

Fifteen seconds ticked by.

It will. Are you mad?

I blinked back tears.

No. Miss you so much. I added a <3.

Five seconds this time.

Me too. Love you. Sleep tight.

Love you too. Don't let the bed bugs bite.

One of my motherisms.

I breathed out the air I hadn't realized I'd been holding in and looked up.

Nugget was standing in her crate. Buddy had rested his chin on the side of the bed. They had picked up on my tension.

I let out a half-hearted chuckle. "Well, that's a first," I told them. "I just had a lovers' spat, kissed and made up, all online." Well, it wasn't really a lover's spat, because for once, I'd had time to think and recognize where my own issues were getting in the way.

Maybe Will and I should discuss all touchy subjects via email. I chuckled again to myself.

"Looks like we're leaving in the morning," I said out loud.

I glanced around the room, assessing what needed to be packed in the morning. The space that had seemed cozy earlier now felt cluttered and oppressive.

Like the air pressure around me was off.

CHAPTER TEN

My growling stomach and full bladder woke me in the middle of the night.

I shuffled to the bathroom, then opened the pantry dresser drawer. Eyes only half open, I peeled a hard-boiled egg and liberally sprinkled it with salt. It tasted sooo good, the egg yolk rich and soothing on my tongue.

Savoring the afterglow, I stumbled back to bed.

I jolted to a sitting position, heart stuttering in my chest.

The clanging of metal, coming from outside.

I jumped out of bed and hurried to the doors to my balcony. I saw nothing unusual through the glass. It was barely dawn, the sky still a dark gray. I opened the doors and stepped out.

The tops of the palm trees and live oaks around the house were swaying. The scene was mostly shades of black and gray, the sun not high enough yet to bring out the colors in the landscape.

I took a step to the left to see the river through an opening between the trees. The water was agitated as it lapped against the pylons of the pier. The dense air practically dripped with humidity.

A gust of wind rocked me back on my heels.

We were about to get a thunderstorm, probably spawned by the storm to our south. I strained to remember which side of a hurricane tended to have tornadoes. I was pretty sure it was the backside, which in this case would be the southwestern side. We were to its northeast, so we should be okay.

I blew out a small sigh.

Something clanged against the balcony railing.

I gasped and jumped back, ready to slam the doors closed.

If that's our pirate, he's not being very subtle, Ms. Snark commented.

I hesitated. She was right. Curiosity won out, although I kept my hands on the edges of the doors, ready to close them quickly if need be.

A head popped up between the railing uprights. I gasped again before Jack's identity registered.

"Sorry. Didn't mean to startle you." He climbed up another ladder rung and swung a leg over the railing, the tool belt he wore making the movement awkward. His flannel shirt, hanging open over a white tee shirt, flapped in the breeze.

"What's going on?" I asked, hugging myself. My blue PJs, covered in pictures of Labradors, were quite modest, but it was still a bit embarrassing. And the breeze was chilly.

"Prepping for the storm."

"I heard clanging metal."

"The storm shutters on the first and second floor windows. This floor doesn't have them, so…" He trailed off as he tied a thick rope onto the railing and signaled someone on the ground, no doubt Bruce.

Jack started hauling on the rope, hand over hand.

After a few seconds, a big flat piece of plywood came into view. Jack tied off the rope and wrestled the wood onto the balcony.

I stepped back into my room, to get out of his way.

"Best close the doors," Jack said. "This won't take long. The wood's predrilled. Then you can go back to bed if you want."

"Isn't this kind of excessive, for a storm so far away?" I heard the slight whine in my voice. I love sunlight. The thought of being in a dark room, day *and* night, made me shudder a little.

I was now very glad we were leaving this morning.

Jack hadn't answered me. He was walking the big piece of wood across the balcony. In another moment, it would be against the door frame, with me on the inside and Jack outside.

"Look, I need to get to Dahlia this morning. When will you be finished with all this?" I waved a hand at the sheet of wood.

Jack stopped moving with it leaned up against one side of the frame, his body only half visible at the other end of it. "Big boat's not runnin'."

My chin dropped. "What happened?"

He shrugged. "Don't know. It was fine last night. Bruce figured we should batten down the house first, while we still can." He tapped the wood. "Another couple of hours and these would be impossible to manage in the wind."

"What? The storm's barely going to brush us."

He shook his head. "It changed course during the night and picked up speed."

A chill ran through me. "Huh?"

"We may get a direct hit, and landfall's been moved up to midnight."

My hand went to my chest. My heart hammered rapidly beneath it. Landfall meant when the eye crossed the coastline, roughly the halfway point. Which meant a whole lot of storm had already happened before then.

"What about your skiff?"

He shook his head again. "Water and wind's already too high for it."

"When's the storm likely to hit here?" I still wasn't willing to concede that *I* would still be here when it hit.

"Early this afternoon, with some thunderstorms running ahead of it."

I stepped farther back into my room. "I've gotta call my fiancé."

"Good luck with that." Jack slammed the wood into place, blocking out the wan morning light.

The room was pitch black. I felt my way back to my bed and turned on the lamp on the table next to it.

Sitting on the edge of the bed, I tried to digest the shift in reality. Nugget stood in her crate, whining softly. Buddy plopped his head into my lap.

I looked down into his trusting eyes. My stomach roiled. Will's panic had been warranted, but I hadn't listened.

And now we were stuck on an island in the path of a hurricane.

I threw on yesterday's clothes, took the dogs out back for a quick bathroom break, then I jumped online.

Citrus County was definitely now inside the cone of possible paths the storm might take as it made landfall, and it had intensified to a Cat-2 hurricane, with winds averaging a hundred miles an hour.

Yikes. My heart raced. Modern buildings, constructed according to Florida's now strict building codes, could handle a Cat-2 storm. This old house? Maybe, maybe not.

The female forecaster on The Weather Channel was way too perky as she described how the cold front, that was supposed to have pushed the storm southward, would now most likely just slow it down. Half of the storm would then remain over the warm waters of the Gulf, keeping it strong.

Wonderful, not only was Pierre going to show up as an uninvited guest, but he was going to overstay his welcome.

"The good news is," said Ms. Perky on my laptop screen, "as the eye makes landfall, wind shear in the upper atmosphere may begin to break the storm up." She gave the camera a big smile, as if she'd just announced that Santa Claus was real.

I dashed off an email to Will, although I doubted he was even awake yet.

Going out to find a decent cell signal. Gotta be one somewhere on this blinking island. Hope you're not tied up with a case and can talk. Love you!

I grabbed my phone and Buddy's leash and headed for the door. Halfway there, I turned back to grab a sweatshirt. "Come on, boy."

I tried the pier first. Only one feeble bar. The ripples on the river had distinct white caps, and the breeze was downright stiff. I pulled on the sweatshirt.

Buddy and I started along the beach for the far side of the island. I stopped every hundred feet or so and checked my phone. The wind gusts grew stronger as we rounded the end of the island, but the bars on the phone did not.

We came out on the Gulf shore and I sucked in air. In the distance was one great big dark and ominous cloud.

On my phone, a third bar flickered on and off. I punched Will's speed dial number.

It only rang once. "Marcia!" He sounded far away.

I choked on the lump in my throat. *Way too far away.*

"Can you hear me?" I yelled into the phone, over the wind and the surf splashing against the shore.

"Yeah," he yelled back. "Where are you?"

"Still on the island. Bruce's boat isn't working."

"What…" His voice was lost to static on the line, but that one word had sounded frantic. Then, "…fixed?"

I guessed at the lost words in between. "He hasn't tried to fix it yet," I shouted over the rising wind. "He and Jack have been securing the windows in the house."

"Is… crazy? …gotta get… there."

"There's no way off this island with our boats," I yelled. "Can you get the Citrus County Sheriff or the Coast Guard or somebody to send a boat for us?"

"I'll try... Buddy and Nugget okay?"

My chest turned all warm and gooey. I loved that he cared about my dogs.

"Yes," I yelled. I took a deep breath and crossed my fingers. No point in him going crazy with worry. "We should be fine, even if we can't get out of here. The house is solid. It's weathered many a storm before this."

A long stretch of static, then, "...love you."

"I love you too," I screamed at the top of my lungs.

My screen went dark. Either Will had disconnected or the call dropped.

A sob surged up from my stomach. My body shook with its force. I would've given anything in that moment to be home, in the middle of the chaos and noise of construction. In Will's arms.

The wind was picking up. Lightning split the darkening sky. A couple of seconds later, a deafening clap of thunder.

Too close. Heart galloping in my chest, I turned and stumbled toward the trees—not the safest place in a thunderstorm, but we could move a lot faster on the solid ground along the edge of the woods. My legs ached and wobbled from the effort of flailing through the sand.

Buddy trotted beside me, also struggling a little as the granules sank away under his feet.

At the tree line, I turned and looked back. The small waves, unusual enough on the West coast of the state, were growing bigger and stronger, no longer gently splashing ashore. They were crashing against the beach, sucking sand away as the water withdrew back into the Gulf.

Movement caught my eye, and an eerie sense of *déjà vu* shuddered through me.

Bruce strode across the wet sand, barely beyond the grasping waves.

His blonde lover ran after him. Bruce stopped and turned. Their arms flailed about. They were arguing.

Lucy suddenly closed the gap between them and threw herself at Bruce. They clung to each other.

Lightning knifed across the sky. Another clap of thunder. They broke apart and, holding hands, ran back the way they'd come.

The sky opened up.

CHAPTER ELEVEN

Buddy and I were both drenched by the time we made it back to the house. We went in through the back door.

Greta stood in the middle of the kitchen. Multiple loaves of bread were laid out on cooling racks along the counter. She sniffed. "What the devil were you doing out in that mess?"

"It wasn't a mess when we left," I snapped back, then regretted my surliness.

She sniffed again. "Breakfast in half an hour."

Buddy and I dripped our way through the main living room and up the two flights of stairs to our room.

I went straight to the bathroom and stripped off my soaked clothing.

Buddy stood in the open bathroom door, eyeing the tub longingly.

I chuckled, despite the dire circumstances we were in. He is one of those rare dogs who loves baths.

"Me first." I jumped in the shower and rinsed off the rain water and at least some of my fear under the hot spray. I dried off and wrapped myself in my warm terrycloth robe.

I gestured toward the tub.

Buddy didn't need a second invitation. He leaped in, and I filled the tub with warm water. I soaped him down with human shampoo, having forgotten to bring his doggy version.

Then I pulled the plug in the tub and turned on the shower.

Startled, he tried to jump out. I blocked his way, laughing.

"Sorry, boy. It's the only way I have to rinse you off." At home, we would be doing this in a galvanized wash tub in the backyard, with a hose handy.

He stood under the spray, a stoic expression on his face. I leaned in and scraped the soapy suds from his fur.

When the water ran clear, I turned the shower off. He shook, further drenching my already damp robe.

I laughed and grabbed a towel from the shelf near the linen closet door. I was still chuckling as I dried him off. Nothing like the antics of a dog to make you forget your worries for a bit.

I dressed and left him and Nugget in the room, happily gnawing on chew sticks.

Ellie and Bruce were already at the table when I arrived in the dining room. Ellie's wheelchair was nowhere around, but the dark circles under her eyes were back.

Bruce's hair was wet from the storm, dripping on the shoulders of his gray tee shirt.

I mumbled a good morning and went to the buffet. The first pleasant surprise was a second covered dish, beside the one with the obligatory egg-white and spinach omelets.

I lifted the lid and discovered steaming oatmeal. Grabbing a bowl, I ladled some of the hot cereal into it. The fragrance of cinnamon and apples teased my nostrils. My stomach growled loudly.

The second pleasant surprise was a dish of butter pats next to the tall stack of wheat toast. I hadn't given much thought to the two pounds of butter I'd gotten yesterday, as part of Greta's list of supplies. I'd assumed she needed them for baking.

I helped myself to two slices of toast and four pats of butter and took my place at the table.

Bruce frowned at the squares of butter piled on top of my toast, but he didn't say anything.

Ellie had passed on the toast this morning, which surprised me considering the rare treat of real butter. She had a bowl of oatmeal and one of fruit salad in front of her.

I glanced again at her oatmeal. A big pool of melted butter sat in the middle. She took a spoonful of the fragrant cereal, noisily slurped it up and then smacked her lips.

"I wanna know where the butter came from," Bruce grumbled.

From the store, Ms. Snark commented internally.

"From the store," Ellie said with a small smirk.

I like this girl, Ms. Snark said.

I hid a smile.

Bruce glared at his wife. "I may need to fire Greta."

"Over my dead body." Her voice was low and tight.

He glared some more.

Her defiant expression morphed into something softer, vaguer. She stared at the bowl in front of her. "Oatmeal," she whispered. It was almost a question, as if she didn't believe she was actually eating the wonderful stuff.

Bruce rolled his eyes. "You're such a child."

He glanced my way and apparently remembered they had a guest. "Sorry. We're a little tense this morning."

I nodded slightly and concentrated on my own oatmeal. It was heavenly. The tiny chunks of apple were fresh. The cinnamon danced on my tongue.

I stifled a happy groan.

"Marcia," Bruce said, "we need to move you downstairs today. There's an old servant's room next to Greta's suite. You can share her bathroom."

A small lump formed in my stomach. "Why?"

"The third floor isn't safe. If a tree comes down on the roof..." He trailed off.

My body tensed. I hadn't thought of that. "What's the room like?"

"I'm afraid it's a lot smaller and not as nice as the suite you have now. But feel free to bring down any of the things from upstairs that will make you more comfortable."

My insides were quivering. The oatmeal had turned to sawdust on my tongue. My mind scrambled to process my reaction.

Being trapped on the island was bad enough, but to give up my sanctuary upstairs...

Tell him no, Ms. Snark egged me on. *It won't be that much safer downstairs, if a tree lands on the house.*

An image of my mother, frowning, popped into my head. But I couldn't tell if she was frowning at Ms. Snark's resistance—that was hardly how a good guest should react. Or was she frowning at Bruce? He certainly wasn't being a great host at the moment.

Or was he? He was thinking of my safety. And the dogs. How could I put them at greater risk?

I imagined us in some cramped first-floor room and the whole house crashing down on top of us, Buddy and Nugget and me buried under three floors worth of debris. My chest tightened. I couldn't breathe.

"Look, I know it's an inconvenience." His tone was somewhere between conciliatory and impatient. "It's not really what you want to do, but–"

Ms. Snark escaped. My shoulders went back. "No, what I want to do is get off this blinkin' island."

Ellie snorted. "Don't we all," she muttered into her fruit bowl.

"Jack's working on the boat now." Bruce's tone wasn't all that hopeful.

He gobbled the last bite of his disgusting omelet and stood, tossing his napkin on the table. "I'll show you the room. It's not so bad, and it'll be convenient for taking the dogs out."

I stared down at my half-eaten oatmeal and the toast I hadn't yet touched, the butter pats slowly melting on top. My stomach was one big knot at the moment, but I had no intention of letting this wonderful food go to waste.

I apologized to my inner Mom and turned Ms. Snark loose.

"I'm not finished eating," she said, in her haughtiest tone, nose in the air.

"Fine." Bruce glared at me, his eyes hard as marbles. "Then Ellie can show you, when you ladies are done *dining.*"

A throat cleared in the doorway.

All heads swiveled that way.

Jack stood there, wet and covered in grease. "That boat ain't goin' nowhere anytime soon. Somebody put sugar in the gas tank."

CHAPTER TWELVE

All eyes were now turned on me.

"What? I sure as heck didn't sabotage the boat. I don't even know where the gas tank is."

"Well, I didn't do it." Bruce crossed his arms over his chest. "And I can't see Ellie going out in the middle of the night to do it."

"Didn't happen last night," Jack said. "Motor's gotta run for a while to work the sugar into its parts. It happened sometime yesterday."

Ms. Snark snorted. "Which opens up the list of folks with opportunity more than a little."

"Is the motor completely ruined?" Ellie asked.

"Naw," Jack said. "Sugar doesn't do as much damage as people assume, but it'll need to be towed to the marina so the system can get a thorough cleaning out."

I groaned. There went that slim hope of getting off the island before the storm hit. I sent up a silent prayer that Will would be able to get someone to us in time.

These people might be comfortable trusting their lives to the solidness of this old house, but I wanted out of here, now more than ever.

Bruce sighed. "Come on," he said to Jack. "Let's get the boat secured."

Once they'd left, Ellie said, "Ready to see the room?"

I looked at the oatmeal in my bowl, now cold and congealed. Grabbing the top piece of toast, I used it to convey the rich butter to my mouth. I chomped down half of it, then stood.

"Yeah." Ready as I was likely to get.

The room was as bad as I'd feared. About six by nine feet, it was barely big enough for the single bed, small dresser and tiny nightstand it contained, plus one straight-backed chair. That was it, no other furniture —not even a rug on the worn wooden floor.

"I'll leave you to get your stuff together," Ellie said. "Greta can help carry things down when you're ready."

My legs hurt from slogging along the sandy beach earlier. I sat down on the edge of the bare mattress. A heaviness settled over me. I wasn't sure if it was too little sleep or depression.

Most likely some of both.

I tried to distract myself with the question of who would put sugar in the boat's gas tank. Anyone from town could've done it. Did the Burkes have enemies in Dahlia?

Had Luke, the grocery store owner, gotten wind of Bruce's affair with his sister?

I had no answers, and the distraction wasn't working. My body still felt like lead, and my brain was ruminating over whether or not I should've gone along with the room switch.

Again, I tried to sort out my intense reaction to it. This room was small and not as comfy, but it was clean. And being close to the back door was an advantage. It's hard to find windows of opportunity to get dogs outside for bathroom breaks during a severe storm. The quicker I could take advantage of a lull, the better.

And I was close to the kitchen. I could swipe more bread to my heart's content.

Still, my body refused to move.

Okay, I'd go along with the switch. It probably would be a bit safer down here. And packing up my stuff was a good idea, so I'd be ready if Will managed to get help to me.

It sounded like a plan, but my body was not cooperating. Instead, my heart raced and my stomach clenched.

The last time I felt this out of control, I filed for divorce. The thought hit me so suddenly and so hard that I almost fell off the edge of the bed.

Out of control. The worst feeling ever. Life is about to run you over and you can't stop it from happening.

God grant me the serenity to accept the things I cannot change. This time it was my late father, the pastor, reciting his favorite prayer inside my head.

Thanks for the reminder, Dad. My heart slowed some, my chest warming. But serenity had never been my strongest suit.

My mind moved to the second line of the prayer, *the courage to change the things that I can.*

It didn't take much courage to pack my stuff, which seemed to be the only thing I could control right now. I pushed myself up off the bed, trudged through the house and up the two flights of stairs to my room… no, not my room anymore.

The door was ajar. I nudged it open. All the lamps, including the floor lamp were turned on, but still there were dark shadows in the corners.

Greta was pulling the comforter off the bed. She turned with a start, then her face softened. "I thought I'd take this down to your new room, and the rug, so it would feel more comfortable."

My eyes suddenly stung. What was with me today, that I felt such pathetic gratitude for a small gesture of kindness?

I swallowed hard. "Thank you, Greta."

"You are welcome. Can the dogs have oatmeal? There is some left from this morning."

"Is there milk in it?"

"No, only water, cinnamon and apples." She took a step closer and lowered her voice. "And a little butter."

I chuckled softly. "That's why it was so good."

She beamed, then her face darkened. "I hate cooking now. Everything is... No wonder she is like a stick." She seemed to be talking to herself more than to me, so I didn't answer.

She shook herself, hugging the comforter against her thin body.

"Yes, the dogs can have some oatmeal," I said, "but not too much. The butter might give them the runs."

"That would not be good right now, *ya*?" She gave me a small smile. "I will get your bed made up down there. Then help you carry your things down. The bathroom of my suite is off my sitting room, so you can come in and use it whenever you need to, even during the night. I will leave my door unlocked."

"Thanks, Greta."

She nodded, scooped up the bedside rug, and left the room.

I put Nugget in her crate. I'd deal with her and the crate later.

I quickly stuffed most of the dog gear and my clothes in the larger duffel, saving the smaller one for my stash of food. I'd carry their bowls and my laptop down separately.

I was in a hurry because it had dawned on me that if Lucy was on the island, she had to have gotten here somehow. If she hadn't left again already, there might be another boat stashed somewhere on the Gulf side of the island.

The sounds of the thunderstorm had abated outside. But there would be more of them as the main storm got closer. I wanted to find Lucy's boat, before the next round of thunderstorms came along.

∾

Buddy and I didn't find a boat. We did find Bruce's love nest.

A small beach house, up on stilts—again, the cypress shingles, but this metal roof was newer, not rusty yet. And the two wide front windows had metal hurricane shutters, like the first two floors of the main house.

They were closed, which meant I could search the beach and the surrounding woods, Buddy trotting to keep up, without fear of being spotted if Lucy was still inside.

No boat. Not even any sign of one being dragged up onto the beach. Of course she could've anchored off shore and swam in, but swimming would be dangerous today. The currents would be running strong in the Gulf. And even an anchored boat might not stay put.

Had there been tracks of a boat being pulled up on the beach, and the waves had washed the evidence away?

I started trudging back toward the main house, wrapping my windbreaker tight around me against the spray and stiffening breeze. Buddy kicked up sand as he chased the seagulls scattered in clumps on the beach.

I felt a little queasy, my mind flashing to the seagulls gathering on the baseball field, outside the classroom windows of my elementary school, on a stormy day. It's never a good sign when seagulls come inland, preferring to stand on land rather than soar on the wind over the water.

My mind went back to chewing on the question of how Lucy got onto the island. Had someone dropped her off? The mysterious Luke maybe? Unlikely.

The most logical conclusion was that she was gone again. She'd arrived on her own boat, they'd had their lovers' tryst, and then she'd returned to the mainland.

But why wouldn't Bruce go with her, if her boat was available? Why would he stay on the island, risking his life?

Cypress walls came into view, and I had my answer. The house. His heritage. He wouldn't leave it.

I shook my head. I never got it when people said they weren't leaving their homes during a major hurricane, despite mandatory evacuations. As if their being there would somehow magically save their roof from being torn off or keep a tree from falling on the house. No, all it did was put their lives in jeopardy, right along with their property.

It must give them some sense of control over the uncontrollable.

Ah, and so my thoughts had gone full circle and come back around to control.

At the house, I hung my jacket on the straight-backed chair in my new room and sat on the bed with my laptop.

No email from Will telling me he had arranged my rescue.

I typed out one to him.

Hope you've found someone with a big enough boat to come get us off this blinking island. These people are crazy.

I moved the cursor to the *send* button but didn't click.

I erased the last sentence and rephrased the first one as a question. *Have you found someone with a big enough boat to get us off this island?*

Then I added: *If not, I'm sure we'll be okay. The house is closed up tight, and we have flashlights and plenty of supplies. Love you!*

I hit *send* and shoved the laptop aside. Buddy was snoozing on the rug. I told him to stay and went in search of Ellie, ostensibly to ask her where she wanted Nugget's crate to go.

Although Nugget would still stay with me for now, there certainly wasn't room for the crate in my new quarters.

I found Ellie in the large living area at the front of the house. I had trouble calling it a living room. It was so massive and sprawling, with multiple sections arranged in cozy configurations of sofas and chairs. Heavy dark wooden end tables, polished to a fine gloss, were scattered among the seating arrangements.

Ellie was curled up at one end of a sofa, with her e-reader.

I settled on the chair across from her. Not knowing how to broach what I really wanted to discuss, I opened with the crate. "Where would you like Nugget's crate set up? There's no space for it in my new room."

She waved a languid hand. "Put it wherever you like."

"Let me rephrase the question. Where would you like it permanently? There's no point in moving it twice." The crate was probably collapsible, but it would still be somewhat of a pain to dismantle and move.

She stared at me for a beat, then blinked. "Where do *you* think it would be best to put it?"

I leaned forward. "Maybe first we need to determine when you're likely to want to crate her. Not at bedtime. You want her by your bed so she can wake you if you have a nightmare."

"Why would I want to crate her at all?" Ellie shuddered a little. "Isn't that like putting her in jail?"

She was hitting on something that was a bit of a controversy in the dog training world, with some folks saying crates were inhumane and others comparing them to dens in the wild. While I was pro-crating, I didn't want to use the latter argument. It wasn't all that valid, since dogs aren't true den animals. Normally, wild dogs only used dens when giving birth and nursing small vulnerable puppies.

My mind flashed to Buddy's bed in the kitchen at home, and how he had taken to hiding under it during the noise and commotion of construction.

"Have you ever seen a dog or cat run and hide, say under the bed, when they are overwhelmed?"

Ellie nodded.

"If crate-training is done properly, that's what the crate feels like to them. A safe place. They're not unhappy in there."

Ellie's eyes were still clouded, her face drawn.

"I've even seen rescue dogs, who were beaten in the past and now are afraid of small spaces, but if they're crate trained with loving patience, they'll go right into their crates, no problem. They feel secure there."

Her face puckered even more. Perhaps I shouldn't have mentioned dogs being abused.

"The crate would mainly be for times when you don't need her to be on duty but you have other people in the house."

"Like Greta and Jack?"

"No, Nugget will get used to them and you can get them to abide by the rules. When you have company over, you should crate her."

"Why?"

I paused, slowly drawing in a deep breath. This discussion wasn't usually quite so difficult. But then most of my clients were men, and they got the your-dog-is-not-a-pet-don't-coddle-them concept much faster.

"Okay, *you* can have an affectionate relationship with your dog, but she is not the family pet and you don't want others confusing her with affection and treats. Only *you* give her treats, no one else, and then only when she is working and has performed well. Members of your household can pet her and interact with her *when* she is off duty. But when she's on duty, they should ignore her. And it's best that guests in your home not interact with her at all."

The pinched look on Ellie's face now seemed more rebellious.

"There need to be clear boundaries," my tone was sharper than I'd intended, but I decided that was okay, "so Nugget doesn't get confused. Otherwise, within six months she will be useless as a service dog. And it'll cost you much more than the original ten-thousand dollars to get her retrained, because we'll have to break bad habits."

Actually, I had no idea what Mattie Jones would charge to retrain a soured dog. I'd never encountered that situation before, although Mattie no doubt had.

I was wishing that Ellie were a scholarship recipient instead of a rich client. With the former, I could make the threat of not allowing them to keep the dog if they weren't going to follow the rules.

"We don't have guests all that often." Ellie's tone was forlorn.

My annoyance evaporated and my throat ached. Her life was so isolated.

In a gentler voice, I said, "Even if you have no other reason to do so, you should crate Nugget a time or two each day, so she's used to the crate being her refuge, a good thing."

"Like when?"

"During meals would be a good time. For one, you don't want her looking for handouts at the table. You've noticed that if I bring Buddy to a meal, he always sits off–"

Ellie threw back her head and laughed. "As if she'd want any of the crap Bruce allows to be served."

I startled a little, but I had to agree. Dogs will eat just about anything, but the food served at the Burkes' table might not entice even a canine's undiscerning palate.

I produced a snicker. "True, but the boundaries still need to be maintained. Otherwise, Nugget will be confused."

"I get it," Ellie said in a matter-of-fact voice.

I pulled back. *What? Suddenly she gets it?*

The niggling feeling of the other day had returned. What was with this lady? Talk about mercurial moods.

For some reason, an image was hovering in the back of my mind, of my favorite grad school professor, pacing the front of the classroom during one of her more animated lectures.

I cleared my throat, stalling for time to figure out what my subconscious was trying to tell me. "That's great. And you need to make sure that everybody else gets it too."

Her face suddenly closed. "What do you mean?" Her tone was sharp, yet wary.

Taken aback, I hesitated. I'd meant others in the household, like Jack and Greta, but the niggly feeling in my brain was stronger now.

I shrugged but didn't answer, hoping she would tell me what she *thought* I'd meant.

She narrowed her eyes. "How'd you figure it out?"

Since I still didn't know what she was talking about, I searched for a noncommittal answer. "I have a psychology background," popped out of my mouth.

Where did that come from?

"Well, then let me properly introduce myself." She shoved the e-reader off her lap and leaned forward, thrusting out her hand. "I'm Lori, spelled L-o-r-i."

CHAPTER THIRTEEN

I trudged up the stairs, still reeling from the conversation I'd just had with Ellie. Correction, with Lori, who also occupied Ellie's body.

No wonder my subconscious had produced the image of that particular professor, during that particular lecture—on Dissociative Identity Disorder.

I dredged up the information from that lecture. Multiple personalities had to form in a person's very early years, when the child's sense of identity is first developing. What horrific trauma must Ellie have suffered as a small child to fragment her personality like that?

Ellie/Lori—and no doubt there were others in there as well, with their own names—had the disorder long before she was traumatized by that plane crash. But her earlier trauma would have made her more at risk for developing PTSD.

Lori had asked if the DID diagnosis would interfere with Ellie being able to keep Nugget. "We're in therapy for it," she'd said.

I'd told her I didn't think it would be a problem, while noting that she hadn't said *me* or even *us* being able to keep the dog. In her mind, Nugget was Ellie's dog.

Did she believe that she, Lori, did not have PTSD? She might be right. In DID, the alternate identities, or alters, could have different physical ailments, and they certainly could have different emotional responses to the same event.

Finally, Lori had answered my original question. "Probably the safest place for the dog, when she's not with Ellie, is in our room." Meaning her bedroom, I assumed. The use of *we, us* and *our* was confusing sometimes.

So I was now pulling myself up the steps to get the crate and Nugget, with a hundred questions swirling in my mind.

One of them, unrelated to Ellie/Lori, was why the devil was I so tired? Yes, I'd been up since very early and it had been an eventful morning, but I shouldn't feel this exhausted.

Maybe I'd take a nap once I had the crate moved, although that would mean missing lunch.

Ms. Snark snorted. *No great loss.*

True. I could snatch some bread later and make a peanut butter and banana sandwich in my room. That thought perked me up.

The door to my old room was closed. As I approached, my ears caught a faint noise. A rustling beyond the door.

I tensed. Was the fake pirate ghost in there? Or was my paranoid imagination in overdrive?

Dang. I still hadn't accomplished my true task when I'd gone looking for Ellie—to tell her that the pirate wasn't really a ghost.

Was that another rustling noise? My heart racing, I told myself that Greta was in there cleaning or something.

Not wanting to startle her, I tapped gently on the door, then slowly turned the knob.

I froze in the doorway. The room was silent, and totally black.

The board over the window. I'd forgotten about it.

I reached a slightly shaky hand into the solid darkness and groped along the wall, searching for the switch for the old-fashioned overhead fixture. I held my breath, heart thundering, expecting someone, or some thing, to grab my arm any second now.

When I found the switch and flipped it, the glaring light hurt my eyes.

I scanned the room and swallowed hard. No sign of any beings, living or dead, except for Nugget in her crate. My heart slowed from a gallop to a trot.

The room had lost its homey feel, with my things no longer scattered about. Even some of the knick-knacks were gone. Had Greta put them away so they wouldn't gather dust with the room unoccupied?

The bed, stripped of its comforter, was still made up with sheets and a blanket. The sharp, coldly precise corners made me think of military barracks.

I crossed to Nugget's crate. What I saw there made me clench my teeth. A glob of oatmeal in the middle of her food bowl.

The dog sat at the other end of the crate, eyeing the bowl longingly.

Good girl, I thought but didn't say... yet. I held up my hand in the *Wait* signal, crouched down, and removed the bowl, putting it on top of the crate.

"Come on out, girl." When she was out of the crate, I wrapped my arms around her neck and praised her. "You're such a good girl."

Then I gave her not one but three treats from my fanny pack. After all, I was trying to make up for the oatmeal.

My dogs are trained to never take anything to eat from anyone but their handler, unless given the okay. Nugget had done exactly what she was supposed to do, but that didn't make me any less angry with Greta.

Fortunately, it took me a few minutes to dismantle and flatten the crate, giving me time to realize the woman didn't know she shouldn't have done that. She'd asked if it was okay for the dogs to have the oatmeal, and I'd said yes.

I'd assumed she'd wait for me to come get it from the kitchen. But she, of course, had assumed it was fine to go ahead and give Nugget some.

Tears of frustration stung my eyes. I had lost all control of the training process, thanks to this blinkety-blank storm. By this point, I would have already gone over the nobody-feeds-Nugget-but-Ellie rule with everyone in her household, if good ole Pierre hadn't turned things upside down and sideways.

I wanted to plop down on the floor and have a good cry. But I didn't.

I wrestled the collapsed crate up on one side and positioned it under my arm, grabbing a cross bar with that hand. "Come on, girl. Let's get this down to Ellie's room."

And then I could take my nap. Maybe if I were a bit more rested, I'd be able to get a better grip on my emotions.

I leaned the crate against the wall out in the hallway and turned back to flip off the light switch.

That's when I spotted the shoes—men's sneakers—under the side of the armchair. Had they been there all along and I hadn't noticed them before?

Ms. Snark snorted. *Greta missed them. She might be human after all.*

I shrugged and turned out the light.

The nap didn't help much. I was still exhausted.

My growling stomach had awakened me. Leaving the dogs in my room, I went in search of a couple pieces of bread to make a peanut butter and banana sandwich.

Greta almost caught me in the act. "Oh good, you are awake. I was about to ring the bell. I am sorry lunch is so late. I have much to prepare."

Crapola. I hadn't missed lunch after all.

I wandered into the dining room. Ellie was already there, at the head of the table, but no Bruce yet. And again, the wheelchair was nowhere to be seen.

I grabbed a plate and loaded it with wheat and tuna triangles. I passed on the bland pasta salad, since there was no salt handy to put on it.

Greta bustled in with a big bowl of fruit salad. She set it down on the sideboard.

Ellie turned toward her. "Could you make some pumpernickel sandwiches with the tuna spread, please?"

Greta's eyes went a little wide, but then the corners of her mouth twitched upward. "Of course."

"I'm not going to be eating wheat bread for a while."

I revised my assumption that the woman at the table was Ellie. The voice was crisp, not timid. More likely Lori.

"But I baked a dozen loaves, to get us through the storm." Now Greta's mouth was turned down.

I raised my hand and gave her a small wave. "I'll eat them up. I love wheat bread."

"*Ya*, okay. I will bake more pumpernickel, but I do not have as much rye flour." The housekeeper hurried out of the room.

I helped myself to some fruit salad and sat down at my usual spot catty-cornered to Ellie's… um, Lori's place.

She had already taken some of the pumpernickel triangles and was scraping the white gunk off of them. "I'm thinking that Brucey may be right about one thing. I might be allergic to wheat, or maybe it's the gluten." She popped a piece of the dark bread into her mouth.

I doubted it was gluten—her symptoms were not consistent with Celiac disease, but I couldn't deny that she was doing better.

"I have noticed," I said, "that the less you have eaten at some meals, the stronger you are later in the day."

She nodded. "And the trend I'm seeing is that when I don't eat the wheat bread, I feel better. And when I do eat it, I feel queasy. That's gotten a lot better now."

Okay, that could be gluten intolerance. Fortunately, I didn't have that problem. I popped my second sandwich triangle into my mouth. Like last night's rolls, the bread seemed drier, but Greta had made the layer of spread thicker.

Quite tasty. I wolfed down a third little sandwich, then leaned in closer. "Look, before Bruce gets here, I need to tell–"

"He and Jack are making a last circuit of the island, making sure everything is battened down, the woodshed and the beach house and all."

I pulled back and blurted out, "You know about the beach house?"

She gave me a funny look. "Of course. Bruce had it built for us, as a present for our first anniversary. We used to go there on the weekends, before his father died."

I was totally confused by the *us, we* and *our* in that statement, but I was more concerned about distracting from my gaffe. I quickly said, "That sounds nice."

It didn't work.

"Why would you think we didn't know about it?"

Heat crept up my cheeks. "Um, I just temporarily forgot that you haven't always had health problems." Of course, that wasn't the main reason for my flushed face.

She frowned but then seemed to let it go. "You were saying something?"

"Oh, yes. Uh, the pirate ghost–"

"I had the weirdest experience with him last night. I woke up suddenly, and the girl ghost was standing inside my balcony doors. They were sitting open, only that couldn't be because they're blocked off now by the hurricane shutters. So *while* I was dreaming it, I thought 'This must be a dream.'"

"But–"

She held up a hand. "The girl's pointing at the door to the hallway, and the pirate bursts in and rushes me, tries to drag me out of bed. I fought him, and then he says, 'Be still, wench, or I will kill your lord.' I assume he meant Bruce."

I still needed to tell her the pirate wasn't really a ghost, but now I was curious.

"Then what happened?"

"Well, I kept fighting, of course, and after a couple of minutes, he gave up and rushed out again. I told myself I must have dreamt it all, but…"

"But what?"

"I turned on the light and the door to the hallway was sitting open. We *always* close it at night."

"But why would you think it was a dream? It was so similar to the other time when he tried to assault you, and the girl ghost has warned you before when he was coming."

She shook her head and looked behind her, as if to make sure no one had entered the room. Leaning in toward me, she whispered, "All that happened to Ellie, not me. I wasn't sure if it was real or not."

So I was right. This was Lori I was talking to.

Greta hurried around the corner with a plate of sandwiches in her hands. She headed for the sideboard.

Lori quickly straightened in her chair. "Bring it here, please."

"Of course." Greta deposited the sandwiches on the table in front of us. "I'm baking fish that I can store on the dry ice that Jack brought back yesterday. We should be fine for a few days, even if we lose electricity."

I felt for the woman, trying to maintain some semblance of normalcy. The times I'd had to weather a power outage during a storm, I'd survived on peanut butter and canned goods, sometimes eating baked beans cold from the can.

I grabbed a pumpernickel sandwich triangle and took a bite. It was really good. I smacked my lips.

Lori grinned, and Greta actually smiled as she bustled out of the room.

With her safely out of earshot, I leaned in again. "Lori, I've gotta tell you something. That pirate is not a ghost."

She froze with a sandwich halfway to her mouth. "Say what?"

I told her about hearing the "ghost" on her balcony, seeing him go into the woods, and then finding the scrap of cloth snagged in the railing and black threads on the rosebush below. I took out my phone and showed her the photo of the heel print.

She put the sandwich in her mouth and chewed slowly, her eyes slightly out of focus. "What does this mean?" She seemed to be saying it more to herself than to me, so I stayed quiet.

"The ghosts are make-believe," she finally said. "Someone, no, two someones are pretending to be ghosts?"

"Uh, I think the girl is really a ghost." I hated to admit that, since I wasn't sure I even believed in ghosts. "But the pirate is a very much alive human being."

I paused, took a deep breath. My stomach was tied in knots. How would she take this next part?

"I've pretty much eliminated Greta. The pirate climbed up and down a trellis. And he was too big to be her, and probably too big to be Jack."

Lori sat perfectly still, her face scrunched up, like maybe she was about to cry.

I braced myself to comfort a woman who's just found out her husband was trying to make her crazy.

Although I hadn't completely eliminated *her* from suspicion. Could one of her other personalities have some motive for pretending to be a ghost? But how could one alter be doing the pirate thing, while another, Ellie or Lori, witnessed it? They may think of themselves as separate entities, but they shared the same body.

But one alter could probably influence another alter's dreams. Had Ellie only dreamt about the pirate?

Then who climbed down that trellis and ran into the woods? Ellie was too small. Or was she? I'd only seen glimpses of a black cape and something red.

Lori threw her head back and burst out laughing, jolting me out of my reverie.

"I've finally got him." Then another peal of laughter. She pointed at me. "You should see your face right now."

I closed my gaping mouth.

This woman could use a lesson from Mom on rudeness, Ms. Snark commented.

Lori's expression became more contemplative. "He's either trying to drive Ellie completely around the bend, or scare us into leaving the island. Or both."

Confused, I said, "But we can't get off the island."

She waved an impatient hand. "Not right now. He wants us to leave permanently. Then he can divorce Ellie without giving her any alimony, because she deserted him."

"But you're all married to him."

"Well, technically, legally." She'd risen her voice some, to be heard over the wind that had begun to howl around the house.

Thunder rumbled in the distance. The next outer band of thunderstorms was upon us.

Lori leaned toward me and dropped her voice again. "Ellie's the one who fell in love with Brucey. His father insisted on a prenuptial. If we initiate a divorce, or leave the island for more than a month–"

"What about when you were deployed?" I blurted out.

She waved a hand again. "There was an exception for that, but I was mainly based at MacDill in Tampa. I came home fairly regularly. But leaving for any other reason was defined as desertion, or if we're unfaithful…"

Her face clouded for a brief moment.

"Then we get nothing. But if he leaves us, he forfeits one third of his assets and has to pay alimony. The bloom of love has long since worn off for him, although he still talks about having children." She shuddered slightly. "Someone to inherit the island. But I think he stays in the marriage mainly to avoid paying the money."

The conversation was veering into too-much-information territory. I squirmed a little in my chair. Hoping to shift the subject to something a little less intimate, I asked, "You didn't get along with your late father-in-law?"

Lori smiled, but her eyes were sad. "Ironically, we did get along fine, once he got to know *me*. We used to talk for hours, about anything and everything—literature, politics, engineering. He was a grand old man."

Tears pooled in her eyes. "He's been gone three years now. I still miss him, and I grew to love this house and the island, as an extension of him, I guess. He–"

A clap of thunder, too close for comfort. We both jerked in our chairs. A loud crack, from the back of the house.

Lori's eyes widened. "That can't be good."

She and I jumped up and rushed toward the back hallway. My heart thundered in my chest.

A long, creaking groan, like a hoard of ghosts were descending upon us, then a series of cracks and crashes and a loud thud that shook the house.

Lori had fallen behind. I ran past the kitchen, where Greta was clutching the edge of the counter top, her face blanched.

The back door flew open. Jack and Bruce were literally blown into the hallway.

Lori passed me where I'd stopped. She zipped around the men and grabbed the door, struggling against the wind to close it. I ran over to help her... and froze in the doorway.

The sky had opened up. Rain belted against the house. I was soaked in seconds.

But I still stared at the disaster in front of me.

At the far end of the house, a huge section had broken off of a live oak tree, splitting the trunk almost to the ground. It had brought down multiple branches and even some small trees with it, but fortunately it had missed the house.

Unfortunately, it was the section of the tree to which the satellite dish was attached.

Our only remaining connection to the mainland lay on the ground, in a tangled mass of branches and wires.

CHAPTER FOURTEEN

I felt sick to my stomach, my chest so tight I had trouble breathing.

Bruce pulled me out of the doorway and slammed the door shut.

Lori turned on him. "You fool." Her voice was low and tense. "I told you to get a tree person out here first, to determine the sturdiest tree, but you couldn't wait to get your new toy hooked up."

Bruce hissed something back that I didn't hear.

Meanwhile Jack was shaking the water off his arms and hands. He strode around the corner into the kitchen and over to the counter. I followed him.

He fiddled with the control on a large black radio. All I could make out was static, but he leaned in, his ear close to its speaker.

Bruce and Lori suddenly stopped bickering. They moved together to the kitchen doorway. Silence reigned, except for the static and mumbling coming from the black box and the sounds of the storm outside.

Jack straightened and turned to us. His face was a stone mask, except for a tiny throbbing in a vein on his temple. "This isn't just some more thunderstorms. It's the real deal. The storm has picked up speed and it's grown. It's half again the width that it was yesterday."

My knees wobbled. Annoyed at my own weakness, I said, "But I thought landfall wasn't until midnight."

"It's been moved up to eleven now," Jack said. "And that's when the eye crosses the coastline. We've got the front side of the storm to survive before then."

My legs suddenly gave out completely. I grabbed for the table near me, to keep from falling to the floor.

Jack was next to me in an instant, sliding a shoulder under my arm to hold me up. His stony face softened some.

"We're gonna be okay, Marcia." It was the first time he'd used my name. He looked up at the ceiling. "This house, she's built sturdy. She'll keep us safe." He spoke of the house as if it were a living thing. "Bruce's father had hurricane anchors installed on the roof trusses," he added.

The constriction in my chest eased. I had such anchors added to my own roof eighteen months ago, when I'd had to replace some of the trusses due to termite damage. The metal plates were bolted to the trusses and the frame of the house, making it much harder for the roof to be blown off.

His words had reassured my brain, but my legs continued to refuse to hold my weight.

"You should probably lie down." Jack half carried me toward my room.

Heat flushed my cheeks. I felt like a fool.

But there was no point in resisting. Because my body was incapable of staying upright.

I had no idea how long I'd laid on my bed, on top of the comforter, staring at the ceiling—my body achy and my stomach queasy.

Long enough for my clothes to dry, while my mind went around in circles.

There was no way to find out for myself what the storm was up to. No way to connect with Will. Helplessness felt like a lead weight on my chest, sinking me farther into the mattress.

A soft whimper. Was it one of the dogs?

Buddy planted his front paws on the side of the bed and nudged me with his nose. The whimper had come from me. He thought I was having a nightmare.

I shook my head. "It's okay, boy."

What's wrong with me? I wasn't usually this big a coward. Nor did my emotions normally make my body weak.

I started to get drifty. Thank heavens. Maybe I could sleep through at least some of the storm.

A loud crack of thunder. The two lamps in the room flickered, then went out.

Crapola!

I sat up partway and fumbled on the nightstand for my flashlight. My hand connected with it and managed to knock it to the floor.

I slid off the bed and landed on Buddy's rump. He yelped and slithered out from under me.

"Sorry, boy," I said into the complete darkness.

For a moment, up was down and down was up, and I had a mini flashback to a few months ago, when I'd been locked in a wine cellar in the dark.

I took a deep breath and placed my hands on the floor to ground myself.

"Buddy?"

A solid weight landed on my thigh. I touched the silky fur of his head.

"Nugget? Where are you, girl?"

A second later, a warm tongue licked the side of my face. It tickled and I giggled a little.

That broke through the fear, and suddenly I was laughing at myself.

I felt around carefully for the flashlight and finally located it under the edge of the bed.

When I turned it on and a small beam of light shone across the room, I let out a sigh. My tense muscles relaxed some.

I had back-up batteries, now stashed in the nightstand drawer. As long as I had light, I would be fine.

The wind whistled outside. The house shook a little, as if putting the lie to my efforts to reassure myself.

The queasiness eased, suddenly replaced by a grumbling sensation. Lunch had been interrupted and my stomach was now realizing the deficit.

I used the bed to pull myself upright. My legs seemed a bit stronger. Flashlight in hand, I ventured across the room to the dresser. I'd designated the top drawer as my kitchen.

I pulled out the small plate, a hard-boiled egg and the salt shaker. Laying the flashlight down so it shone across the surface of the dresser, I peeled the egg and sprinkled it lavishly with the salt. For some reason, this salt was not as potent as most. It took twice as much to get the required result.

I put the salt shaker away, then moved the egg toward my mouth, my eyes half closed, anticipating the rich flavor.

My hand froze. The salt crystals reflected back the flashlight's glare, but there were duller, yellow-white specks on the egg as well. A lot of them.

I raised the egg to just in front of my eyes. Could they be pieces of eggshell?

Licking my finger, I touched one of the dull flecks. It wasn't hard. Not eggshell. It had to have come from the salt shaker.

I sniffed it. No odor. Whatever it was, I'd already eaten plenty of it by now anyway. One more fleck wouldn't matter. I put it on my tongue.

No salty taste.

Egg still in hand, I stumbled over to the straight-backed chair and sat down. A few pieces fell into place. Ellie/Lori started getting a lot better after Bruce had banned salt from the table and she'd passed on the wheat bread for several meals running.

Someone had been slowly poisoning Ellie, doctoring the stuff that they knew Bruce wouldn't touch. And since Bruce had been the one to get rid of the salt, maybe he *wasn't* that someone.

And now the same poison was making me weak. I shuddered.

Knuckles against my door. I jerked in my chair.

"Sorry to disturb you." Greta's voice through the door. "Bruce vants everyone in the dining room for a meetink." Stress had thickened her accent considerably.

I left the egg on the plate on the dresser, grabbed the flashlight and stumbled to the door.

Now paranoid, and for good reason, I took both dogs with me. My flashlight beam on the floor in front of us, we made our way to the dining room. My legs were still somewhat wobbly, but I got there without falling on my face.

Two battery-operated camping lanterns adorned the ends of the sideboard, giving the room an eerie glow.

Bruce stood at the head of the table, next to Ellie's usual chair. She sat across from my seat.

Or was it Lori?

I pointed to the corner and both dogs went over and laid down. Then I sat in my spot and studied the woman across from me in the dim light. Shoulders slumped, face pinched. I was betting it was Ellie. Or somebody else, but not Lori.

Greta and Jack filed in and sat down, Jack beside me, Greta next to Ellie.

The meeting turned out to be about the electricity. Bruce informed us that the main generator had been shorted out by a lightning strike close to its shed.

Say what? I'd been assuming that we got electricity somehow from the mainland, maybe via underground cables. But of course, that would be one heck of a project, to run cables all the way from Dahlia to this outer-most island of the Nature Coast Keys. How silly of me.

"Lucky it didn't blow the gas tank," Jack mumbled beside me.

I flashed him a confused look.

"Big silver thing out back," he said in a low voice.

I had noticed the tank yesterday but had assumed it was fuel oil for a furnace. *Duh.* The house didn't have a furnace.

"So the gas cans yesterday were for the back-up generator?"

Jack nodded. "The main generator and its tank were put a ways from the house on purpose. In case they got hit by lightning. The back-up one's in a small storage room off the kitchen."

Bruce was tapping a finger on the table, his lips pinched together. He cleared his throat. "The back-up generator can only handle so much at once. To keep the food in the refrigerator and freezer from spoiling, I'll turn it on for a half hour at a time, but the lights and the well pump have to be off while it's on. Don't open the fridge door. Everything we should need for the next twenty-four hours is in the coolers in the kitchen, right, Greta?"

"Ya." She was hugging herself, even though the room didn't feel chilly to me.

Was Bruce merely being a good captain of the ship, or was he narcissistic enough to be getting off on the role?

"We'll do half-hour intervals until ten-thirty," he continued, "when the lights will go out for the night."

"Good that you've got a flashlight," Jack said to me. "You got extra batteries?"

I nodded. Bruce glared at him.

Yup, he's enjoying being the big enchilada, Ms. Snark commented.

"In case it gets cold tonight, Jack has laid out fires in your fireplaces."

The one in my small room was about the size of a postage stamp. I doubted it would give off much heat.

But right now, I was kind of sweaty in the stuffy, closed-up house. Or was the poison I'd been sprinkling on my eggs and consuming with my sandwiches causing a fever?

My stomach clenched. What if I became truly ill, stuck on this island with no medical help?

I needed to tell someone about the poison, so they could at least try to help me if I started having convulsions or something.

While Bruce rambled on about how we needed to preserve the batteries in the emergency lights and our flashlights, I studied the faces of those at the table.

Ellie was looking down, plucking at a loose piece of skin by the cuticle of her thumbnail. Was she my best bet?

I glanced sideways at Greta. Her face was white as a sheet.

It would be easy for her to do the poisoning, but I couldn't imagine what motive she would have. Nor could I think of a motive for Jack, although I didn't know either one of them very well.

You can be rather naïve about your clients. Will's voice, from a conversation a few months ago, when he was pointing out that just because they were veterans didn't mean they were all good and trustworthy people.

Still, Ellie was the one I knew the best, and she was the one the poisoner had meant to go after. I was collateral damage.

I lingered when Bruce dismissed the meeting and Greta and Jack rose to leave.

Ellie put a hand on the table to push herself to a stand.

"Um, hang on for a minute. There's something I need to talk to you about."

She dropped back down. "Did you want to try to do some training this afternoon?"

With a start, I realized training was the last thing on my mind. Which was so wrong.

"No actually. This is about something else." I leaned in. "You've been feeling so weak because someone has been poisoning you."

She reared back in her chair and stared at me, her mouth hanging open. "What are you talking about?"

Maybe I shouldn't have been quite so abrupt, but how does one gently introduce the subject that someone near and dear might be trying to kill you?

"When Bruce banished the salt, I stole a shaker from the kitchen before Greta could get rid of it. Today, I realized there's some other substance mixed in with the salt. It might be in the wheat bread as well. The things that Bruce doesn't eat."

She shook her head vehemently. "You're crazy. Bruce wouldn't do something like that."

"I'm not saying it's him. The fact that he got rid of the salt and discouraged you from eating the wheat bread points toward it not being him."

But that could be his way of throwing off suspicion. Maybe he'd devised a different plan for getting rid of Ellie.

"And then there's the pirate ghost who isn't really a ghost–"

"What do you mean?" she asked.

It was my turn to gape at her for a second.

Duh, Ms. Snark said. I resisted the urge to smack my forehead. I'd told Lori, not Ellie, about the pirate.

I repeated what I'd found snagged on the railing and rosebush but held back my observations that the fake ghost probably wasn't Greta or Jack. Well, it could be Jack.

Ellie dropped her head onto her arms on the table and began to sob.

Crapola. Now what was I supposed to do?

I opted for nothing and waited her out.

Gradually the sobs eased, became a soft snuffling. She raised her head and swiped the back of one hand across her wet cheeks. "Why do you assume whatever you found in the salt is poison?"

"Haven't you noticed how I've been getting weaker today?"

She looked away, toward the dogs snoozing in the far corner of the room. "I haven't been arou... I've been sleeping a lot today. I hadn't noticed."

I opened my mouth to protest that she'd been sleeping much less than usual today, then caught myself. "Sleeping" was code for she wasn't out, someone else was.

Lori had been the alter in control of the body most of today.

Ellie shook her head. Her eyes slowly shifted from cloudy with worry and wariness toward clear and sharp.

"Lori?" I said.

After a beat, she smiled. "I thought she'd never let me out. Thanks for saying my name. That helped with the last nudge."

"I considered saying your name sooner, to see if I could get you to come out. But I didn't know how Ellie would react to that."

"She knows we have DID But she's not as far along with 'accepting the diagnosis'," Lori made air quotes. "Part of the problem is that she thinks she's the host alter. But she isn't, I am."

"I thought the host was usually the one who went by the person's given name."

"Key word is *usually*. And that's part of the confusion. Even our therapist isn't convinced yet that I'm the host. And another part is that I let Ellie marry Bruce."

"What do you mean, *let* her marry him?"

Her eyes grew shiny. "Is what I say to you confidential, like with a therapist?"

"Well, I don't know if I could refuse to testify in court, but I consider it confidential."

"The pilot in that crash. I'd had an affair with him, six years ago. I knew he was married but since I didn't particularly want to get married, that didn't matter to me."

She paused, took a deep breath. "But it mattered to him. He broke things off, and I went into a tailspin emotionally. One of the advantages of DID is that you can hide inside when you're hurting and let others deal with the world."

I'd never really thought about DID having advantages, but I guess that could come in handy.

"By the time I realized Ellie was falling for Bruce, it was too late. They were engaged. I thought about trying to sabotage the relationship, or even just flat out telling him about us. But he seemed like a nice guy and he's good in the sack–"

I slapped my hands over my ears. "TMI, Lori."

She snorted. "Sorry."

But then curiosity got the better of me. I lowered my hands. "How'd you even find that out?"

Her mouth turned up in a smirk. "Thought it was too much information. Hmm, how can I put this delicately? Ellie has some *issues* that I don't happen to have. She likes the cuddling, but once things progress beyond a certain point, she backs off and, well…" Lori wiggled her eyebrows up and down.

Heat crept up my cheeks. Curiosity may not always kill you, but it sure can be embarrassing sometimes.

"Anyway," Lori continued, "the pilot and I, we managed to stay friends, and that's the only aspect of the relationship that Ellie lets herself acknowledge. She was closer to him as a friend, even more than I was. I had to keep my guard up to a certain extent." She looked away. "I think that's why his death hit her harder—that, and I'd already done a lot of grieving for him before, when we broke up."

She cleared her throat. "Did you say something about you getting weaker?"

Dang, here we go again, Ms. Snark commented.

I repeated to her my belief that the salt and wheat bread contained something poisonous.

She gave me a sad, half smile. "It did occur to me at one point that you were like my Dorian Gray picture. As you got weaker, I got stronger. But I had no idea it had to do with what we were eating. I'm so sorry."

"Not your fault." At least, I hoped it wasn't some other part of her that was doing this. "But I wanted you to know what's going on. Not only so you can protect yourself, but in case I get sicker. It's possible that when we both stop eating the wheat bread, and with the salt gone, the poisoner will try something different."

"Have you been feeling queasy lately?"

"Yes." I stared at her, then understanding dawned. "You said your stomach had been upset, until you stopped eating the wheat bread."

Lori nodded. "I'd thought it was part of the PTSD and depression Ellie's been going through, but it's gotten better the longer I've been off the salt and wheat bread."

She gave a slight shudder. "I was willing to believe Bruce would play pirate to scare Ellie away, but poison…" She shook her head.

"It may not be him." Again, I repeated the evidence that pointed away from him. Then I sat up straighter in my chair as another twist occurred to me. "Or maybe it was him and he started feeling guilty, and that's why he got rid of–"

"Who's feeling guilty about what?" Bruce came around the corner into the dining room.

We both jolted in our chairs.

But before either of us could offer a cover story, Bruce went off. "What are you doing leaving these lanterns burning, using up the batteries?"

It hadn't even registered that the lights had come on while we'd been talking.

I glanced across the table at Lori. But she wasn't there anymore.

"Sorry," Ellie said, in a soft voice. "I forgot to turn them off."

My only response was a growling stomach.

CHAPTER FIFTEEN

I excused myself, and the dogs and I headed for my room.

On our way, I detoured into the kitchen. Greta sat at the table, clutching a mug of tea in her hands, her face pale.

The wind whistled under the eaves, and something crashed in the woods far away. She flinched.

I suppressed a sigh. I was too weary and she was too jumpy to try to make casual conversation. I blurted out, "Hey, Greta, has Bruce said anything to you recently about eliminating wheat bread?"

She shook her head, but her eyes remained on the small kitchen window, one of the few pieces of glass in the house that wasn't covered. There was nothing to see but water slashing against its surface.

I had no words of wisdom to combat her phobia, so I let her be.

In my room, I stuffed an unsalted egg into my mouth, and ate peanut butter straight from the jar. Hoping the good protein would undo some of the damage from whatever was in the doctored salt and wheat bread, I laid down on my bed.

The dogs curled up, yin and yang, on the bedside rug.

Making sure my flashlight was close by for when the lights went out again, I stared at the ceiling. I felt better about my reaction earlier to the satellite dish coming down. I wasn't being a total wacko coward. Yes, I was upset—we all were—but my physical weakness was from the poison in my system, not my emotions.

So who was poisoning the food and who was masquerading as a pirate ghost? Were they the same person, or not?

We only had four players to choose from. Well maybe not. There were also Ellie's alters.

Another comment by that psychopathology prof popped into my head. *Contrary to what you see on TV and in the movies, people with DID are rarely dangerous to anyone but themselves.*

What had she said about *how* they were dangerous to themselves? Oh yeah, they had a higher than normal suicide rate. Which would make sense, considering all they had been through and all they were dealing with.

But there was something else too. Something about the alters sometimes hating each other and not getting it that they shared the same body. In some cases, one alter had tried to kill another one.

So one of the alters could be poisoning Ellie.

I winced. My brain running around in circles had given me a mild headache.

When the lights went out, I gave up. Rolling over, I took another nap.

Again a knock roused me. "Marcia?"

The lights had come back on while I'd slept. I crossed to the door and opened it.

Greta looked like she'd been watching a horror movie—hair sticking out, face white, eyes wide.

My heart jumped into my throat. "What's happened?"

She shook her head. "They cannot hear the bell upstairs, over the noise." She glanced nervously at a shuttered window across from my doorway. A gust of wind rattled the house.

A trembling hand flew to her chest. She swallowed hard. "Could you go up and tell Ellie and Bruce that dinner is ready? I um, still need to put a few things out."

"Sure." She probably just didn't want to go upstairs, where the sound of the wind whipping around the house would be even louder.

"*Danke.*" She turned and hurried down the hallway to the kitchen, hugging the inside wall as if a monster lurked beyond the blocked-off windows along the other side.

I guess to her, the storm was a monster.

My stomach was still a bit knotted, due to my own low-level anxiety —riding out a hurricane isn't exactly a calming experience. But other than that, I felt better than I had all day.

Taking the dogs with me—this might be the closest they came to getting some exercise for a while—I went upstairs.

I came to Bruce's study first. I faked a cough and stomped my feet louder than necessary as I approached his door, not particularly wanting to catch him doing whatever he'd been doing before.

He was sniffling when he came to the door. "Darn allergies."

November isn't exactly allergy season, Ms. Snark observed internally.

He could be allergic to leaf mold, I countered.

"Dinner's ready," I said out loud and quickly turned away.

Ellie opened her door as I was about to knock. "I thought I heard voices, and this time they weren't in my head." She chuckled at her own joke.

"Lori?"

"Yes." She grabbed my arm and pulled me into her room. "Oh goody, you've got the dogs with you. Are they off duty?"

I nodded.

She closed the door and dropped to her knees to pet Nugget and Buddy. "I've got a question for you."

I assumed she was talking to me, even though she was looking at the dogs. "Okay."

"Do you think Nugget would bark if she were in my room, and the pirate came around?"

I paused for a moment to consider that. "Maybe, but probably not. We intentionally pick dogs that aren't particularly territorial to begin with, and then we train them to ignore those and their protective instincts. They can't be reactive with strangers since you have to take them out in public on a regular basis, and they need to stay focused on your needs and commands, not what others are doing."

"But would she try to protect me if he attacked me?"

I slowly shook my head. "She'd be upset, but most likely she'd just whine. I've actually been trying to undo that earlier training with Buddy, now that he's no longer a true service dog."

And because you seem to constantly be poking around in other people's messes, Will's voice said in my head, *and getting yourself in trouble.*

I ignored him. "The results have been hit or miss."

Lori stroked Nugget's silky ears. The dog's eyes were closed. I wouldn't have been surprised if she'd started purring.

"It wouldn't really help then," Lori's tone was regretful, "to have her in the room with me, but–"

"I agree." I intentionally cut her off, suspecting what she was going to ask next. "She wouldn't be much help, and the pirate might hurt her if he saw her as a threat."

Lori's head jerked up. Her face had gone pale. "I hadn't thought of that. Okay, she stays with you for now."

She turned back to Nugget and scratched her behind one ear. "I guess I'll have to rely on the locked door."

"At least he can't come in through the balcony." I pointed toward her French doors. The glass panes in them were like little mirrors now, with the gray steel of the hurricane shutters behind them.

Another face stared back at me, next to my own image in the glass.

I jumped and whirled around. Nothing was there but empty space.

"What's wrong?" Lori stood up.

"Um, I think I saw the teenage girl, in the glass there. She was standing next to me with a strange expression on her face."

"Strange how?"

"She looked downright fierce."

"She's never been threatening before."

I shook my head. "I don't think she is now, at least not to you and me. She looked more... determined? Maybe to protect you."

Lori gave me a lopsided smile. "Not sure how I feel about that."

I responded with a small smile of my own. "Not sure how I would feel either, in your shoes."

"Tell Greta I'll be down in a minute."

The dogs and I went back to the stairs and descended.

Greta was waiting at the bottom. "Ms. Banks, may I speak to you for a moment?"

"Of course."

She led the way to a far, dim corner of the main room. A dark archway I hadn't noticed before materialized into an opening in the wall. I could barely make out a narrow set of steps leading upward into darkness.

Greta followed my line of vision and waved a dismissive hand. "The old servant stairs." She leaned toward me and lowered her voice. "You asked about the wheat bread. Bruce had me special order some new flour. It's whole grain, but not wheat. Gluten-free mixed grains, it's called. That's what I used to bake all those loaves, and the rolls for dinner tonight. Do you think there is something wrong with that flour?"

"Maybe. Ellie started getting stronger around the time she stopped eating the wheat bread." And when the salt was taken away, which could be the main reason for her improvement. My concerns over the bread could be paranoia. "But that was before you got the new flour."

"You think the old flour was tainted." Her voice sounded slightly skeptical. "But Ellie has been getting weaker for months. I have had many new sacks of flour over that time. Surely, they can't all be tainted."

I didn't say anything. My mind was searching for the right words, but it wasn't finding them.

Greta's eyes went wide. "You don't think…" Her hand flew to her mouth. "The flour, it has been tampered with?"

Her words echoed in the stairwell.

"Shh, keep your voice down. I don't know if it has or not, but better safe than sorry, as my mom would say. Can you just serve the pumpernickel for now? But hang onto that bag of flour. My fiancé's a police detective. I'll have him get it analyzed once we can get off this, um, island."

I'd come very close to dusting off a few cuss words to string in front of *island*, but I'd resisted the temptation.

Greta frowned. "We may run out of the dark bread before we can get to the mainland again."

I shrugged. That was the least of my concerns right now.

"Greta, does Ellie have any enemies that you know of?"

She looked a bit startled. Then a strange expression flitted across her face, too fast for me to read it. "*Nein.* She is a sweet girl. People usually like her."

Usually means not always, Ms. Snark noted.

"This pirate ghost, have you ever seen him?"

Her eyes went wide again. "*Nein, nein.*" She shook her head.

A tad too vigorously perhaps?

"Vhy do you ask about him?" Her accent had thickened again.

Why wouldn't *I ask about him?* Ghosts were certainly a topic that made most people curious.

I opened my mouth, although I wasn't quite sure how to phrase my next question—did she know anyone who'd have a motive to impersonate a ghost?

She shook her head again. "I'm sure he's harmless. I must get the rolls now, before they come down, and put out the rye bread instead." She pivoted and hustled off toward the dining room.

She was coming out again, the basket of wheat rolls in her hand, as I reached the doorway, the dogs trailing behind me. I glanced into the empty room, imagining the rice, vegetables, and white fish, probably even drier than usual, under the covers on the plates.

"Um, I'm not feeling all that great. I'm going to skip dinner."

Greta frowned. "The food, it is not my fault it is so dreadful."

"I know."

She gave me a wan smile and hurried past me.

I was almost to my room when I stopped and turned back. The kitchen was empty. I swiped one of the rolls from the basket on the counter.

In my room, I broke it apart and shone the flashlight on it. It looked like it had quite a few of the same yellowish-white flecks as those in the salt. But with multi-grain flour, there were all kinds of flecks, in different shades from white to brown.

I wrapped it in a tissue and put it in a drawer. *Not* the one that had my food stash.

I fished out a banana from that drawer. While I ate it, I went over my conversation with Greta. She had been awfully quick to jump to the idea of someone tampering with the flour. Was that because she was that someone? Was that whole conversation a fishing expedition to see how much I had figured out? And maybe to throw me off her trail?

Then again, maybe she'd been harboring her own suspicions about the food, and my mentioning the flour earlier had solidified them.

I blew out air. Despite my naps earlier, I was still pretty tired.

The fiercest part of a hurricane was the eye wall, and that would be on us in a few hours. The already noisy storm would get much louder at that point. I should get some sleep now, while I could.

I quickly used Greta's bathroom to wash my face and brush my teeth. Then, with Lori's and my conversation in mind, I levered the straight-backed chair under the doorknob in my room. It didn't have a lock.

I didn't change into PJs though, in case I needed to make a hasty exit from the room. I even left my sneakers on as I laid down on my bed and tried to think positive thoughts. We would survive the storm. And Buddy and I would eventually get off this island and see Will again.

I missed him so badly my chest hurt, and guilt made my stomach clench. Was he okay? My plea for him to come rescue me might have dragged him right into the middle of this storm.

As if on cue, the wind kicked up another notch. The old house groaned and seemed to shudder around me.

Adrenaline shot through my system. Up until that moment, I had bought Bruce's hype and Jack's reassurances that the house was solid and could withstand even a Cat-2 hurricane. Now I wasn't as sure.

Suddenly cold, I pulled the comforter over me. Maybe I should try to get my fireplace going. But if I opened the damper would that change the air pressure in the house? And would that make it susceptible to being pulled apart by the storm?

I knew I was over-reacting, but I'd heard horror stories about leaky garage doors causing the garage roof to blow off in a storm, and then the house roof followed.

Longing for an internet connection that would allow me to look up issues like air pressure in buildings during hurricanes, I drifted in and out of a light sleep.

My last coherent thought was that maybe I shouldn't have let on to Greta about my suspicions regarding the flour. If she was the poisoner, it would be very easy for her to tamper with something else now. Weren't excessive amounts of nutmeg toxic?

A giant loaf of whole grain bread was chasing Ellie and me. Buddy and Nugget attacked the bread and Nugget bit off a big chunk. Suddenly she was growing bigger and bigger, like something out of Alice in Wonderland. And Ellie had somehow disappeared.

A low rumbling noise.

A tractor trailer rolled into the scene, but it was only half the size of the bread loaf and of Nugget. She batted at the truck with a big paw.

It rumbled even louder.

The bread and truck faded. So did giant Nugget.

The rumbling continued in the dark room.

But it wasn't completely dark. A faint light surrounded a filmy figure. The teenager, her wispy dress, half transparent—the darkness showing through it. She faced where I lay on the bed and pointed off to her right.

The rumbling was coming from a dog's throat, most likely Buddy's. Rustling noises registered.

"What are you–" Greta's raised voice, accent thick, coming through the wall.

Then a yelp, cut off abruptly.

Had that come from her room or mine? I fumbled for the flashlight. It wasn't on the nightstand. I finally located its cool, smooth cylinder caught up in the blanket.

I flicked it on.

Both dogs stood by my bed, Nugget looking at me. But Buddy stared at the wall adjoining Greta's room and growled ominously.

Renewed rustling.

I jumped out of bed and wrestled the chair out from under my doorknob.

Then caution overcame impulsiveness. I cracked the door slightly, rather than flinging it open.

The hallway, of course, was pitch black. I shone my flashlight down the hall. It picked up Greta's closed door.

A hint of movement on the edge of the circle of light. I chased the movement with the beam, but it was gone.

Probably my imagination.

Still, I needed to know Greta was okay.

I ran the flashlight beam up and down the hallway. It was completely empty.

I turned back into my room and pointed the flashlight at my rug. "Nugget, stay," I said in a low voice. She entered the circle of light and plopped down on her belly.

"Buddy, come."

He leaned against my knee. I placed one hand on his head, and, with the flashlight in the other, we walked toward Greta's door.

I strained to hear any noises from the blackness around us. But my own blood pounding in my ears and the howling wind outside left me essentially deaf to other sounds.

Wait, then the rustling noises I'd heard had to be pretty loud. Not just someone's clothing as they moved, but maybe feet scuffing on the floor? Had I heard Greta struggling with someone?

Heart now thundering in my chest, I tapped on the door with a knuckle and put my ear to the wood. Nothing from inside.

I knocked louder and called out, "Greta?" No response.

I pointed the flashlight toward the floor so I could see Buddy without blinding him. He stood calmly by my knee, not growling. I ran my hand along his back. The fur wasn't standing up.

Taking a deep breath, I grabbed the door knob and turned it slowly, eased the door open. "Greta?" I nudged it open a little farther, flashed my light around her sitting room. Nothing but furniture.

A faint light glinted back at me through the doorway of the bedroom.

I stepped farther into the suite. "Greta," I called out and heard a panicked edge in my voice.

My feet dragging, I moved to the bedroom doorway, shining the flashlight at the floor. The glinting light was coming from under her bed.

Had she crawled under there, trying to get away from the storm? My heart rate slowed slightly, and the vice around my chest eased.

I stepped into the room, crouched down and shone my own light under the bed, fully expecting to see the older woman's scared face staring back at me.

But there was nothing but bedframe and the chrome casing of an unlit flashlight reflecting my beam.

An icy chill ran through me. I duck-walked back two steps and stood.

Buddy whined beside me.

Every fiber of my being resisted the movement, but I forced myself to lift the flashlight upward.

The circle of light surrounded Greta's head and torso, where she lay on the bed, her eyes closed.

Air whooshed out of my lungs. *She's asleep.*

But even as I thought the words, I knew they were a lie.

She was on top of the covers, her lemony-yellow robe twisted askew.

Not her best color, Ms. Snark quipped, but even she sounded scared.

I focused the beam of light on Greta's chest. It wasn't moving.

CHAPTER SIXTEEN

Chills ran up and down my arms, but I made my fingers probe Greta's neck. No pulse. I held two fingers under her nose. No whispers of air movement.

"Buddy, run." It was an old command, one taught to him two years ago, so he could model it for a dog trainee. I prayed he would remember what it meant. "Run!"

He turned and bolted from the room, barking his head off. He'd remembered. *Run, get help.*

I dropped the flashlight on the bed. Tilting Greta's head back, I pulled her chin down, my mind scrambling to remember details from the CPR course I'd taken half a decade ago.

Pinch her nose. Seal your mouth around hers.

I blew air into her mouth. One, two, three, four, five times.

I positioned the heels of my hands, one on top of the other, at what I hoped was the right spot on her chest and pushed down hard.

How many times? I guessed fifteen, counted them out in my head. Then blew five more breaths into her mouth.

Halfway into the second round of fifteen compressions, the door flew open and someone with a camping lantern rushed in.

Then Jack was beside me, his lantern on the floor, casting eerie shadows around the room.

"You know how to do this?" I gasped out.

"Yes." He readied his hands and I counted out loud.

When I hit fifteen, I stepped aside and he took over. I began blowing air again and again into Greta's mouth. Pausing to catch my own breath between every five.

And praying. *Come on, come on. Breathe! Dear Lord, make her breathe.*

Somewhere along the way, more people and lanterns entered the room.

A hand landed on my shoulder. I looked up into Ellie/Lori's blue eyes. I wasn't sure who was looking back.

But she squeezed my shoulder. "I'll take over."

I backed away until I hit the far wall, slid down it to sit on the floor. Buddy crawled halfway onto my lap. As I wrapped my arms around his neck, I heard somebody sobbing.

Realizing it was me, I swallowed hard.

Bruce had taken over for Jack. "Turn on the lights."

Jack ran from the room.

A couple of minutes later, the overhead light came on.

Ellie's and Bruce's backs blocked my view of Greta, but the shift in their demeanor said it all. The tension in those backs eased, but not in a good way. Shoulders slumped.

Both of them still looking down at their housekeeper, Bruce fumbled blindly for Ellie's hand.

The fact that she didn't turn and fall into his arms had me wondering if it was Lori, not Ellie, who was currently out.

"She must've had a heart attack," Bruce whispered. "The stress of the storm…"

"We did all that we could." The voice was a little choked, but strong. Definitely Lori.

I nudged Buddy aside and managed to stand up on wobbly legs. "We need to leave everything as it is."

They both turned, mouths slightly open. Then Lori's eyes lit with dawning awareness. She nodded slightly.

But Bruce's face hardened. He straightened his spine and opened his mouth.

"Look, I don't have the energy to argue." I suspected Ms. Snark was fueling my words, but I didn't have the energy to suppress her either. "My fiancé is a homicide detective. Trust me, we will be in big trouble if we don't leave everything the way it is."

Bruce's eyes pooled with tears. "But we can't just..." he choked out the words, stopped, started again. "We can't leave her like this."

Something shifted in Lori/Ellie's face. She turned and wrapped her arms around him from the side.

His chest began to heave.

"She's at peace," his wife said gently. "Come on." She maneuvered him toward the door. "The storm can't scare her anymore."

He shuffled his feet like a man going to the gas chamber.

"She's at peace," Ellie repeated.

At least, I was pretty sure it was Ellie now.

Disturbing nothing else, I gathered my flashlight and the three lanterns, and Buddy and I left the room. I closed the door and pointed to the floor in front of it. "Protect."

Buddy laid down right where I pointed.

Ellie spun around, her eyes a little wide. When she let go of Bruce, he continued to shuffle away. "Does Nugget know that command?"

"No."

"Can you teach it to her?"

I sighed. "No."

"Why not?"

I waved a hand in the air. This having to repeat the same discussion twice was frustrating. Then I realized how selfish that was.

On Ellie/Lori's end, it had to be four times as frustrating. No, a hundred times as frustrating.

"I'll explain tomorrow. Take care of Bruce."

She nodded and turned to catch up with him.

I checked on Nugget. She was on the rug, but her head was up, her eyes worried.

"It's okay, girl," I said, in a soothing voice. "Stay."

Still carrying the lanterns, I went down the hall to the kitchen. I turned them off and set them on the table. I was exhausted, but way too wired to sleep again anytime soon.

And I wanted to find and secure that bag of flour.

I searched the pantry, using my flashlight to see into the back corners. No flour.

But I did find a stash of items on one shelf, toward the back, that included three cans of sauerkraut and five bars of Belgium chocolate. More of Greta's contraband.

A lump formed in my throat.

I opened another door and was greeted by a noise like a car engine. I'd found the back-up generator. A quick perusal showed that the room was used mostly to store cleaning and household supplies. Shelves held large packages of paper towels and toilet paper, bottles of floor cleaner and furniture polish, but no food.

I backed up and closed the door. The noise ceased. The walls must be well-soundproofed.

I searched the other cabinets. No flour and, more surprisingly, no loaves of multi-grain bread.

The refrigerator was off. I opened it quickly, scanned inside, then slammed it shut again, before too much cold air could get out. I hadn't seen anything that resembled a bag of flour nor a loaf of bread, but during that quick look I'd spotted a package of sausages all the way in the back, next to a large jar of dill pickles.

I was down on the floor in one corner, pulling pots and pans out of the lowermost cabinet, when the roar of the generator made me jump, banging my head on the edge of the opening.

The lights went out and the roar abruptly stopped. The refrigerator was now humming.

A throat cleared behind me.

I jumped up and whirled around, aiming my flashlight toward the sound.

Jack leaned against the storage room door. "What are you doing?"

I rubbed my sore head. "Looking for something."

"I figured that out. Looking for what?"

None of your beeswax, Ms. Snark and Mom chorused inside my head.

Boy, I really was exhausted if even my inner Mom was becoming rude.

I sighed. "I'll know it when I see it." I wasn't about to trust anyone else in this house with anything.

I leaned over and shoved the pans back into the cabinet helter-skelter. Then I grabbed one of the lanterns from the table and moved into the hallway.

Jack also grabbed a lantern and followed me. "Are you still going to sleep in the room next door?"

I stopped, nodded. I didn't want to, but I had no other choice.

Perhaps Greta's death had been natural, as Bruce assumed, but it was more likely, considering what I had heard, that she had been murdered. I wasn't leaving her and her room unguarded, and I certainly wasn't leaving Buddy back in that hallway by himself.

Jack stepped up beside me. His expression was mournful. "It is good that you are not leaving her alone." He patted my arm and walked away.

∼

I lay on my bed, staring at the ceiling in the semi-dark room. I'd turned the commandeered lantern off, but kept the flashlight on, pointed at the door.

I hadn't propped the chair against it again. If Buddy started barking, I wanted to get to him quickly.

And I really didn't think I'd fall asleep, not with a corpse next door and the storm raging worse than ever outside. Something metallic clanged now every time the wind gusted.

I prayed it wasn't a hurricane shutter come loose, letting air get in around old windows. Would those kinds of gusty drafts be enough to take a roof off? I didn't know the answer to that.

Probably the greater risk was that a tree branch would crash through that exposed window, and then the air gusts would do their thing.

Okay, enough of thinking about all the ways the storm could kill us.

I focused on Will instead, tried to think happy thoughts of being in his arms again. But my stomach clenched and worried butterflies invaded my chest. Was he safe, wherever he was?

He's a resourceful man. He can take care of himself. My mother's voice, trying to reassure.

How would you know? You've never met him, Ms. Snark said.

I know him through Marcia, inner Mom countered, her tone huffy.

I laid there, trying to decide if listening to the bickering voices in my head was preferable to feeling guilty.

Voices in my head. A new wave of guilt tightened my chest and stomach.

I made light of such a thing, intentionally segregating parts of myself —my internalized mother, my conscience that had taken on Will's voice in recent times, and the snarky part of myself that I tried desperately to control.

But Ellie/Lori had to struggle every minute of every day with truly segregated parts of herself—fully formed personalities who vied for time in charge of the common body. Personalities who didn't always know what the others knew. How much energy must go into faking that she knew what was going on, when she didn't?

How had she managed to get a master's degree in aeronautic engineering, to get through the intense training required to be an officer in the Air Force? That seemed downright impossible to me. But she'd done those things. She'd held herself together somehow to make those accomplishments happen.

To clear my mind, I repeated a mantra I'd once used when going through a meditation phase.

I am one with the universe. I am one with the power and the light.

Light seemed to be in short supply right now.

I am one with the universe. I am one with the power.

A giant gust of wind rattled the house. Nope, power didn't feel all that friendly right now either.

I am one with the universe.

I'm bored, Ms. Snark said.

More tight chest and clenched stomach. How could I be complaining of being bored when a dead woman was lying not thirty feet from me?

The muscles in my abdomen and around my rib cage were beginning to hurt from all the clenching.

Hmm, guilt may make crunches obsolete, Ms. Snark commented.

"Oh, shut up," I muttered.

Okay, this was too creepy, lying here so close to a dead woman.

I got up, grabbed my laptop and took it and Nugget out into the hall.

I aimed the flashlight at Greta's door to check on Buddy. He blinked in the bright light. "Sorry, boy." I moved the beam down to the floor in front of him. "Stay, protect."

I went down to the kitchen, still close enough to hear him if he barked a warning that someone was trying to get into Greta's room.

Even though I was eating up precious battery time, I sat at the kitchen table and played solitaire on the computer, trying to get my mind off of things.

My mind had other ideas. As I was finishing up a round, Greta's last utterances replayed in my head.

She'd said the words, "What are you–" in a raised voice. She'd sounded surprised, but not particularly afraid. She knew whoever was in her room. Was it the pirate ghost? Up close, did she recognize who it was?

Or did she already know who it was? Could that be why she'd gotten a bit twitchy when I'd asked about the ghost?

Then there were rustling noises, a scuffle maybe, and a yelp, cut short. The sounds of someone overpowering her?

I pushed the computer aside and propped elbows on the table, my chin in my hands.

I doubted she'd had a heart attack. But there had been no signs of violence in the room or on her body. At least none that I'd seen in the poor lighting.

How did she die? And how the heck had whoever was with her gotten out of her room so quickly? Even in the semi-darkness of the hall, I would have noticed if someone rushed past me. And that hall dead-ended just beyond Greta's door.

Despite the howling of the wind and the sound of rain slashing against the kitchen window, I began to feel drifty.

I should get up and check on Buddy....

The silence woke me.

I was slumped over the kitchen table, my head sideways on my crossed arms. One hand had gone to sleep.

I sat up and a dull pain shot from my shoulder and neck halfway down my spine. I wiped drool from my cheek.

The flashlight had fallen from my hand and rolled across the table. It cast weird shadows of the napkin holder against the wall.

The quiet was eerie. The eye of the storm must be over us. I grabbed the flashlight and pointed it at my wrist watch. It was a little after eleven.

A few droplets pattered against the kitchen window. Water being blown off the trees by a random gust.

I needed to get the dogs outside quick, before the other side of the storm was upon us.

I looked around for Nugget but didn't see her.

Reaching over to one of the abandoned lanterns, I clicked it on. Its soft glow revealed enough of the kitchen to see that Nugget wasn't in the room.

I went to the kitchen doorway and held the lantern high. No dog.

Had Ellie changed her mind and come to get her? Wait, Lori and I'd had that conversation, about how it could be dangerous for the dog to be in the room with her. Greta's death might have spooked Ellie and she assumed Nugget would be at least some protection.

I took a big breath, trying to calm the butterflies in my chest and stomach.

First, I would check my room and Buddy. She might have gone down there to join him.

But Buddy was alone in front of Greta's door.

My door was open. I couldn't remember if I'd closed it or not. I stepped into the room and again held the lantern up. No Nugget.

The lantern was kind of heavy, so I left it on the nightstand. Using my flashlight to light a path, I hurried down the hall again. I was rounding the corner, headed for Ellie's room, when I felt a draft.

I glanced over my shoulder, toward its source.

The back door of the house was sitting ajar.

CHAPTER SEVENTEEN

Heart pounding, I ran for the stairs, yelling Ellie's name.

By the time my foot landed on the top step, she and Bruce had come out of their rooms. Both were fully dressed in rumpled, day-old clothes. She had a flashlight. Bruce held a lantern in his hand.

"Do you have Nugget?" I demanded of Ellie.

She shook her head, eyes wide. "She isn't with you? Where is she?"

"I think she went out the back do–" I broke off as a sob tried to force its way up my throat. "I have to find her, before the other side of the eye gets here."

"Come on," Ellie said, "we'll help you look."

Bruce crossed his arms. "Jack and I need to try to fix the satellite dish. I mean we can't get it back up in the tree, but maybe we can get it reconnected." He raised his voice. "Jack."

"Yo."

I whirled around.

Jack stood at the bottom of the stairs, his hair sticking out, his white tee shirt twisted askew above his jeans.

Ellie stood up straighter and something flashed in her eyes. "Well, I'm helping Marcia find our dog." The strength of her voice and the use of *our* told me Lori was up front.

I turned and ran back down the stairs. "You check the dock and the riverside beach," I yelled to her over my shoulder.

I dashed toward the back hallway, to fetch Nugget's leash.

Buddy whined from his spot. I made a quick decision. Even though it meant Greta's room would be unguarded, I wasn't leaving my dog alone in this house of horrors.

"Come on, boy."

In my room, I grabbed up Buddy's leash… and froze.

Nugget's tan leash should have been right next to his black one on my dresser.

It was gone.

My already galloping heart picked up speed. The plate next to where the leashes had rested was empty. The salted egg was gone as well.

Out in the hallway, Lori accosted me. "Won't she be able to follow her nose home?"

I shook my head. "Rain tamps down the smells. A dog lost after a rain like this is as lost as you or I would be."

She nodded. "I've got the front." She started to pivot away from me.

"Wait."

She turned back.

I swallowed hard, still digesting the implications. "Nugget's leash is missing from my room. Someone may have intentionally taken her outside."

Her eyes went wide. "The pirate?"

My stomach roiled. "Maybe."

She nodded again, then turned and took off for the front of the house.

Out back, I headed for the woodshed first. My sneakers smacked and slid across wet leaves and splashed through puddles, my flashlight beam showing the narrow trail in front of us.

I had Buddy on his leash, terrified that he would somehow disappear into the darkness. He stuck close to my heels.

"Nugget," I called every few seconds, the sound echoed by Ellie's voice, which was growing fainter as I moved away from the house.

An occasional small gust of wind made my heart jump in my chest and my stomach drop. The other side of the eye could be upon us at any moment.

I had no idea how fast the storm was moving at this point. Jack hadn't reported recently on any storm news he'd gleaned from the staticky weather radio, and with the chaos of Greta's death, I hadn't thought to ask.

I also didn't know exactly when the eye had reached shore. So I might have an hour to search or five minutes. Or thirty seconds.

And when the other side of the eye hit, it would be with a vengeance.

A huge expanse of water opened up in front of us on the path. I screeched to a halt, almost going down when my feet slipped on the wet leaves. I didn't dare keep going, not knowing how deep the water was nor what critters, driven from their homes, might be lurking in there. Now was not the time for a close encounter with a gator or a poisonous snake.

I searched the surrounding woods with my flashlight beam, looking for higher ground. To our right seemed the best bet.

I flogged my way through the underbrush, praying I didn't step on something living that might take offense and fight back.

Buddy's leash soon became tangled in palmetto fronds. With a queasy feeling in my gut, I unhooked it from his collar and untangled it, then stuffed it in my pocket. "Heel, boy. Stay close."

After about a hundred feet, I veered back toward where I hoped the path would be.

I almost fell over with relief when I found it. And this section wasn't covered with water. We took off again.

The wall of the woodshed reared up in front of us. Again, I slid to a stop.

"Nugget!" I searched the clearing, and swung the flashlight back and forth, creating arcs of light in the surrounding underbrush. No movement, no dog. Although a few small eyes shone back at me, too close together to be Nugget's.

A shiver ran down my spine.

I searched for and finally found the even fainter path to the spot where Bruce and Jack had been cutting up the tree. I followed it more slowly, glancing back every few seconds to make sure Buddy was still with me.

I knew I'd found that clearing when I stepped in a soggy paste—wet sawdust. Again, I searched the surrounding woods with my light. Again, no dog.

"Nugget," I cried out with all the air in my lungs. "Where are you, girl?"

A faint woof in the distance, followed by a clanging metallic sound.

I called Nugget's name once more, then strained my ears. No more woofs. But there was the clanging again. Ahead and off to my right.

It had to be coming from the beach house. A loose hurricane shutter maybe?

It didn't sound all that far away. If I followed the sound, we would come out on the beach and then could follow it back to the main house.

And if I hadn't imagined the woof and Nugget was on that side of the island, she might hear me better if I called her from the open beach.

I didn't dare give myself time to think about it, or I would chicken out. I forged ahead into the woods, following the clanking sound and calling Nugget's name again and again.

We floundered through the underbrush and fought off clinging vines. It felt like an hour but was probably more like fifteen minutes since we'd left the house. But I wasn't about to take my eyes off of what was in front of me in order to glance at my watch.

How much time had passed didn't matter. What mattered was finding Nugget and getting back to the house as fast as we could.

The clanging was louder. We burst out of the woods, and I pitched forward onto wet sand. I rolled over and looked at my feet. A thick vine was wrapped around one ankle.

I was in the process of freeing myself from it when a huge wiggling clump of wet fur landed on me, and a warm, wet tongue scraped along my cheek.

"Buddy, get off."

Moonlight glinted off of matted reddish hair. Heart soaring, I threw my arms around a muddy, sopping Nugget and hugged her close. "Thank you, Lord," I whispered as she licked my face again.

I nudged her off of me and struggled to get up from the sand. She stood beside me and went into the brace position.

Despite the dire circumstances, I couldn't help smiling. "Good girl!" I used her back to steady myself and staggered to a stand.

She was missing her collar. Did it snag on something and get pulled off? The missing leash. Had someone dog-napped her, and she got away from them by pulling out of her collar?

As I brushed myself off, I scanned my surroundings. My breath caught in my throat, but for the wrong reasons.

The view was truly beautiful, with stars and moonlight sparkling on the dark water, and the silhouette of the beach house about fifty feet away, a sprinkling of palm trees around it.

But what had stopped my breathing was the fact that the stars abruptly stopped as one looked out over the Gulf. They just disappeared into the black of night a ways offshore.

That blackness was the other side of the eye wall.

I froze with indecision for a moment.

A large black rectangle hung from the end of the beach house. It waved gently in the breeze off the Gulf, then clanged against the house. The loose shutter.

Should I take the dogs to the beach house, and pray that it survived the second half of the storm as well as it seemed to have weathered the first half?

I'd dropped the flashlight in the sand when Nugget had pounced on me. It had gone out, but the moonlight reflected off its chrome casing.

I picked it up and looked to my left, the shortest distance to the curve of the southern end of the island. I'd half decided to make a run for the main house, when I spotted something dark on the beach about twenty feet away.

My mind computed the shape, and my insides turned to jello. A large alligator was basking in the moonlight on the sand.

Crapola!

I tore my eyes away from him and looked the other way down the beach. It was much farther to the northern end. We would be exposed on the Gulf beach for too long. And if the storm hit and we were forced to take shelter in the trees—it would be poor shelter but better than exposed beach—we'd be at risk of falling into the sinkhole on that end of the island. Not to mention lightning striking a tree or the wind blowing one over on us.

The beach house it was. I took a step in that direction and froze again.

Movement along the side of the house. A human figure, in profile, silhouetted against the light sparkling on the water, arms moving in front of them.

Fixing the shutter?

Sure enough, when the figure stepped away, the dark rectangle no longer waved in the stiff breeze.

I held perfectly still, the dogs sitting, panting, on either side of me.

The figure rounded the corner of the house and was gone.

"Come on, you two," I said in a low voice. I turned and bolted back toward the woods.

We plunged through the underbrush. A branch smacked me in the face. I shoved it aside.

The moonlight barely filtered between the trees. We were about fifteen feet in, when I stopped. "Wait."

I could vaguely detect the dogs' still silhouettes, Buddy ahead of me, Nugget a few feet to my left.

Heart in my throat, I smacked the side of the flashlight and clicked the button back and forth. Miraculously, it came on, and I blew out air. It'd probably had sand in the switch.

With the help of the flashlight beam, we picked our way gingerly through the jungle of vines and palmettos and other Floridian flora. Buddy nudged forward a bit.

"Take us home, boy," I said, even though I had little hope that he knew where the house was any better than I did.

But he sniffed the lacy fronds of palmetto and trotted off to our left. Occasionally, I spotted a clump of smashed grass or a broken twig hanging from a branch. I hoped they were signs that this was the way we had come as we'd battled our way to the beach. The going did seem a little easier in this direction.

I stopped once and listened for sounds of pursuit. All I could hear were the branches of the live oaks and Southern pines high above us, rustling in the stiffening breeze.

I picked up our pace, my heart stuttered in my chest. The storm would be on us again soon.

To distract myself from that looming reality, I focused on the question of who was at the beach house. Jack and Bruce were supposedly trying to fix the satellite dish, and Ellie was searching the river side of the island.

Was there someone else on the island besides the five of us? Four now, with Greta gone.

Nugget touched her nose to the palm of my dangling hand, as if reassuring herself that I was still there.

I smiled down at her. At least we'd accomplished the goal of finding her.

Had Ellie walked the beach from the dock to the southern end of the island, then heard the banging shutter and went to investigate?

Some of the tension eased in my shoulders. That had to be it.

Maybe she'd decided to stay at the beach house, rather than risk getting caught by the storm before she got back to the main house.

My stomach clenched. Why hadn't I checked out the beach house further, instead of running away?

Buddy stopped moving in front of me. I almost ran into his rump.

I looked up from where I'd been shining the light on the ground in front of us. We were in a clearing, and the outline of the woodshed loomed in front of us.

Who says prayer doesn't work? The second miracle of the night had happened.

And barely in time. The wind in the trees picked up speed, the rustling turning into a howl. The splattering sound of rain and hail galloped toward us from behind.

I ran for the shed and shoved back the shiny new slide bolt Jack had installed yesterday. The door blew open. A quick scan with the flashlight. No apparent invasion by gators or snakes.

I hurried the dogs inside and slammed the door shut. A roar erupted outside as the storm hit full-force. The shed vibrated and I leaned all my weight against the door to keep it closed.

Rain pelted the metal roof, sounding like machine-gun fire.

My heart beat almost as fast, blood throbbing in my ears. I was terrified and relieved at the same time. We'd made it back to a familiar landmark, and we had shelter... of sorts.

Thunder rumbled in the distance, followed by a louder, closer clap.

The wind eased for a moment. I quickly rolled two large logs over against the door and piled several more on top of them. I kept stacking wood until the pile was as tall as I was. Then I added several more logs, for good measure.

I found a couple of the larger slices of tree, unsplit, on top of each other off to one side. I perched on them, and the dogs settled on the floor around me, panting softly.

I knew I should turn the flashlight off, spare the batteries. But I couldn't bring myself to plunge us into total darkness.

Besides, we're not going anywhere until morning anyway. That thought made me shudder. Riding out a hurricane in a woodshed was not my idea of fun. But it sure beat being out in the woods.

After about fifteen minutes, I turned off the flashlight. Better to have it when we really needed it, than not have it at all.

And despite the wind howling around the shed, it was snug. No major drafts that I could detect. If the blustering air couldn't get in, then it would be difficult for critters any bigger than insects to get in.

Or at least, that's what I told myself. "You guys will warn me if anything gets in here, won't you?"

Nugget, who'd laid down on my left foot, shifted her weight some. Numbness in that foot told me it had gone to sleep. Gently tugging it out from under her, I wiggled my toes inside my soggy sneaker.

Buddy's chin landed on my right knee, startling me a little. I stroked his head, both of us soothed by the rhythmic motion.

They say your life flashes before your eyes when you're in peril. Mine was doing a more leisurely scroll across the screen in my mind.

My childhood. Wasn't childhood supposed to be carefree and fun? Mostly I remembered the teasing and the bullying at school because of my weird name. And the stiff, awkward feeling of being on display as the pastor's kid at church or whenever any adults came to the house.

I couldn't wait to grow up.

Things got worse in middle school and then kind of better in high school. At least there I'd had a circle of friends who didn't abuse me. They did tease me though, because I always winced whenever anyone cussed.

Which was a lot. We were teenagers, after all.

But my mother had so deeply ingrained in me an aversion to swearing.

Why hadn't I rebelled against that? Weren't teenagers supposed to be rebellious?

I had to admit to myself that I wasn't being fair when I blamed all that on my mother. Yes, she had taught me those lessons, but I didn't have to keep following them.

The closest I'd ever come to rebellion was moving down here to Florida. Mom had hated the idea.

But I really hadn't done it to rebel. I'd wanted to get away, have a fresh start.

Don't you mean run away? My mother's voice.

Well, yeah, I was running away—from bad memories, bad choices. I noted that the movie in my head had skipped right over the whole courtship and marriage thing with Ted. It had no relevance really, except as an example of those bad choices.

Running from yourself. Mom again, and not a question this time.

I tried to come up with a pithy comeback. Where was Ms. Snark when I needed her?

I *was* much better off down here. I'd made friends, loved the climate —most of the time—and had found what was probably my life calling job-wise. Despite the tedious parts, that I could now pass off to my assistant, I loved the dog training.

And I'd fallen in love with a good man.

So why didn't this latter part of the movie in my head seem happier? Was it because I kept stumbling into bad situations? In the almost five years that I'd lived and worked in Florida, I'd dealt with—I counted them on the fingers that I couldn't see in the total darkness—one, two, three, four, five, six bad situations, some involving murder even, and several had almost led to my own demise.

I might like living in Florida, but it had not been a lucky state for me.

If only all this bad stuff would stop happening, I could relax and really enjoy my good life down here.

My mother showed up at the end of my movie, shaking her head slowly. *Did you hear what you just said, Marcia?*

Technically, I thought it. I didn't say it.

Mom snorted, something she would never do in real life. *Listen to yourself, moaning about adversity. Everybody has adversity. It's part of life.*

True, but their adversity doesn't usually involve one to two dead bodies a year.

This did not bode well. I'd been in this shed less than a half hour, and already I was having conversations with the voices in my head.

Or rather arguments with them.

The nature of the adversity doesn't matter. Apparently, my inner Mom wasn't finished with me.

"I know, I know," I said out loud. "It's what you do about the adversity. Whether it makes you stronger or weaker." I'd almost said, *or it kills you*, but I really didn't want to put that idea out into the universe.

No.

No? Whaddaya mean, no?

What matters the most is what you do with your life in between those times of adversity.

Okaaay... What does that mean?

I waited but she'd gone quiet. Guilt, my old frenemy, tightened my stomach.

What did she mean? I was doing good things with my life, helping veterans by training service dogs for them. And I was engaged, and building a new, well, newish house.

Butterflies fluttered in my chest, but it wasn't the fear that had been a constant companion for the last twenty-four hours. It was excitement, a sense of being on the verge of something. My former counselor's face popped into my head. I knew that expression. It meant, *Come on, you can do this. You can figure this out.*

Why wasn't I happy? I was engaged to Will... The butterfly feeling intensified. I actually leaned forward a little in the darkness, as if leaning toward Jo Ann in her office.

I was engaged *to* him, but was I engaged *with* him? Was I truly engaged in lif–

A blood-curdling scream rent the air, loud enough to penetrate the thick walls of the shed. Loud enough to be heard over the storm.

CHAPTER EIGHTEEN

I jolted and fumbled the flashlight. It slipped from my hands. I lunged in the direction it was moving but felt nothing, until I did a face-plant on the floor. My cheek scraped painfully against the rough wood.

Buddy woofed, a slightly irritated sound.

No, wonder. I'd landed half on him. "Sorry, boy." I wiggled off him and sat up. Feeling around with one hand for the flashlight, I gingerly touched my stinging cheek with the other.

Of course, that made it sting worse, but I gritted my teeth and explored the scrapes for splinters. I didn't find any.

My other hand hit against a smooth, cold, rounded surface. I tried to grab it but only managed to nudge it away. The low rumble of something hard rolling over the floor. I pounced in that direction, and one hand closed around the flashlight.

Blowing out pent-up air, I flipped the switch. Light filled the shed. *Hallelujah!*

That's when it finally registered that the sounds of the storm had diminished. The machine-gun rattle of rain had shifted to a pitter-patter on the roof. And a soft whishing of moving trees had replaced the howl of the wind.

No way was the hurricane over that quickly. But maybe the eye wall hadn't reached us yet. Maybe it was beginning to deteriorate, from that wind shear Ms. Perky had predicted. What had just happened could've been a thunderstorm, a fragment that had broken loose as the eye wall began to fall apart.

I set the flashlight on end, the light flowing up like a mini torchiere lamp. I shifted the firewood away from the door, piece by piece, amazed that it had been enough to keep it closed.

I grabbed the door's handle and pulled. Nothing happened.

I double-checked that the old broken latch wasn't engaged, then dug my heels in and pulled with all my strength, which at this point was not that much. Nothing budged.

Had something blown against the door?

Wait, that wouldn't matter. It opened inward.

I remembered the shiny slide bolt, and my stomach hollowed out.

Someone had locked us in. My legs wobbled. I sank down onto the floor cross-legged.

The flashlight dimmed, and then went bright again. I must've jarred it.

Why would someone lock me and my dogs in a shed? Wait, maybe a branch had blown against the door and hit the slide bolt, knocking it closed.

Possible, but unlikely. However, Bruce or Jack might have come by, looking for me and the dogs, saw the slide bolt undone and shoved it home.

That's probably what happened, I told myself, although I only half believed it.

The other half of my brain was pointing out that someone had most likely murdered Greta. And maybe that same someone was trying to get me out of the way. Had they overheard our discussion about the food and the ghost?

I shook my head. Right now the more important question was not the who or why. It was how to get us out of here, preferably before more storm came our way.

Or whoever did lock us in here comes back.

I heard the sound of my own breathing, fast and hard, and made myself stop, take a long, slow breath. Hyperventilating would not be helpful at the moment.

I focused on how to escape. The thick shed door was sturdy, as was the slide bolt. But what about old cypress shingles?

I shone my light up over the wall. There was no inside wallboard, only the backs of the shingles, and they were most likely nailed in. With pretty heavy-duty nails if they were holding up to a hurricane.

My weary brain cells struggled with the physics. The wind was pushing against the outside of the shingles, holding them more firmly against the upright posts they were nailed to.

That's why it was so dangerous when hurricane-strength winds got inside a structure. The air pressed outward, pushing against the siding, pulling the nails loose, until the walls flew apart.

I could knock a shingle loose from the inside, then reach out and open the slide bolt. But the shed would no longer be secure against the storm. I would be committed to getting us to the house before the eye wall caught up with us.

My stomach roiled. A part of me wanted to stay put until the rest of the storm had blown through. The shed had held up through the first half, so it would likely survive the rest.

But there was the scream. Definitely female, so definitely Ellie/Lori. And it had been too loud to have come from inside the main house.

She didn't know that I'd found Nugget. Had she come out again as the thunderstorm eased up, to look some more, and something happened to her? Like the big gator on the beach. A chill ran through me. He was big enough to take on an adult woman, especially one as slight as Ellie.

Gators didn't usually go after humans, but if she startled him, if he saw her as a threat...

My eyes stung. I'd grown fond of Ellie/Lori—well, Lori really. She could be out there, bleeding, helpless against the storm and easy prey for other displaced and hungry animals.

I picked up a log and tentatively poked the wall with it. Had the shingle bowed out some or was it my imagination?

I hit it harder. It gave a little.

Excitement bubbling in my chest, I found a larger log, but one I could still lift and swing with some force. Using it as a battering ram, I pounded on the shingle closest to the right side of the door, at latch height.

It was definitely loosening. I hit harder, again and again.

My limited energy was fading fast. But the memory of that scream kept me going. There were bobcats in Florida. Did they have any on Haasi Key?

I shuddered and hit the shingle again. One end of it broke loose from the six-by-six door post.

Woohoo! I hit it again. A crack and the old wood snapped in the middle. Half of the shingle fell away into the darkness.

I shoved my arm through the hole and felt around, touched the very end of the slide bolt with my fingertips.

Thunder rumbled in the distance. Cool air blew against my arm outside the shed.

I stood on tiptoes and jammed my shoulder as far through the hole as it would go, praying I wouldn't get stuck. I got one fingertip firmly on the knob of the slide bolt and worked it slowly over. Finally, I could pinch it between two fingers and give a good pull.

It gave with a dull thunk and the nearest door blew inward on a small gust of wind, knocking painfully against my other shoulder.

I worked my arm out of the hole and grabbed up the flashlight. Wait, maybe I could find a weapon of some kind? I examined the pile of kindling. None of the sticks seemed worthy of the label *weapon*. Nor worthy of the effort required to haul them along.

The beam landed on a small pair of pruning shears, hooked over a nail on the door post. They would be next to useless against a gator or bobcat, but they were better than nothing, and they fit in my back pocket.

I headed out the shed door, shining the light in front of me. "Come on," I yelled to the dogs over the rising wind.

Buddy bolted past me, running along the path to the house. I jogged after him as fast as I dared, watching for lumps under the wet leaves that could be a snake or other critter.

Nugget stuck with me, her head an inch or two from my left knee.

Buddy stopped, waiting for us to catch up, then he took off again as we neared him.

Bless his little canine heart. He was showing me the way.

But the path was easily visible now. I glanced up. The moon was peeking out between two clouds.

I careened to a stop next to Buddy who stood on the edge of the giant puddle. The moonlight helped us find the place where we had crashed through the underbrush. We followed the rough pattern of broken palmettos and stomped-down grass and came out again on the path.

A gust of wind chased a cloud across the moon. More rumbling thunder, a bit closer. I moved faster.

I didn't remember this part of the path being so long. Had we taken a wrong turn?

Suddenly, a light shone through the trees, up high. I broke into a full-out run.

It was a floodlight on the back of the house. Bruce had turned the lights on. In that moment, I forgave him all his transgressions.

I bolted for the back door of the house, where Buddy waited, panting. Nugget and I ran past the satellite dish, now leaning up against the base of the big oak tree. I spotted the wires stretched along the ground just in time, barely avoided tripping over them.

Opening the door, I shooed the dogs inside, then slammed it shut, making sure it was latched but not locked. Ellie might still be out there.

I called her name in the quiet house.

No response, not even from one of the men.

"Bruce! Jack!"

I raced through the first and second floors of the house, searching. The new thunderstorm was upon us, the wind howling, the rain sluicing against the walls of the house and rat-tat-tatting on the metal shutters and the roof.

But not quite hurricane force yet, based on the level of noise.

I found no humans.

Where else could they be? Surely not the third floor. It wasn't safe up there.

Could they be keeping vigil in Greta's room, since Buddy and I had abandoned the role of keepers of the corpse?

If so, why hadn't they answered when I called their names?

We went to Greta's suite. I told the dogs to lie down and stay. Then I took a deep breath and opened the door, flipped on the overhead light.

Her sitting room was empty, as was the bathroom. Heart racing, I held my breath and tiptoed into her bedroom, flipping on that switch. Greta lay as we'd left her. But now, in the brighter light, I could make out some bruises on her neck.

She was strangled. My hand flew to my own neck.

I gulped and backed out of the room. I found myself bolting through the suite's door as if the devil were chasing me. Slamming the door shut, I leaned my back against it, took a deep breath and tried to get my heart rate back in the vicinity of normal.

Now what? Ellie was still out in the storm, and apparently Bruce and Jack were looking for her and/or me.

Did I dare go out there to help search? My heart raced again at the thought. The full force of the eye wall might not be here yet, but it couldn't be far away now.

Stay put. Will's voice in my head.

I knew he was right. If we all kept running out into the storm, looking for each other…. My stomach twisted. I knew staying in the house was the logical thing to do, but I felt like a total coward.

Something to my left caught my eye. I glanced that way, toward the end of the hall. A few feet away, a panel I hadn't really noticed before was hanging open. I'd thought it was part of the wall.

I nudged it wider. Dark wooden steps leading upward, the old servants' stairs.

I put my foot on the first step.

Seriously? Ms. Snark said in her snidest tone. *You're gonna be the dumb girl in the horror movie who goes exploring in dark places?*

I put my foot back down on the floor.

A wispy figure materialized on the stairs, a few steps up. The teenage girl ghost.

My heart rate kicked up yet again.

She held her hands out in front of her, palms toward me in a stop gesture, and shook her head.

Okay, I get it. Going up the stairs, bad idea.

I stepped back and almost fell over Nugget, who was hovering right behind me. Buddy, next to her, growled low in his throat.

The girl ghost vanished, and two steps up from where she'd been stood the pirate.

He grinned down at me. "Good evening, Ms. Banks," he said in a deep gravelly voice. "Come join us." He motioned for me to come up the stairs.

My mouth went dry and my body froze. Except for my head, which was shaking a vehement *no*.

"Oh, but I insist." He raised his other arm.

I stared at his fingers. They were long and slender, and wrapped around a small pistol.

CHAPTER NINETEEN

His costume was simple. A loose-fitting white poet's shirt with long billowy sleeves, tight black jeans, shiny boots, and a red kerchief tied around his head. A black eye patch covered one eye, and a bushy black beard and mustache, no doubt fake, hid most of the rest of his face.

He wore no sword or old-fashioned gun at his waist, only the little modern pistol in his hand.

It was scary enough. I tried to swallow. My mouth was too dry.

When he turned sideways, again gesturing for me to come up, I spotted the black cape hanging down his back.

I don't think capes are normal pirate attire, Ms. Snark said.

He was about Jack's height, but broader in the shoulders. Maybe the cape was meant to disguise his build when he was running away. It had fooled me. I'd thought he was taller.

"I'm not going to tell you again." His deep voice broke a little on the last word. "Come up the steps slowly."

Buddy growled and showed some teeth.

"Control your dog." The pirate turned the gun's short barrel toward the dogs.

Heart hammering, I put a hand on Buddy's head. Then I held my palm out for him to touch it with his nose.

A part of my brain had been calculating my odds if I pulled out the pruning shears and lunged for the guy. Now I put that thought aside, for the time being at least. If he succeeded in shooting me, the dogs would be next.

I took two tentative steps up. The dogs, sensing my anxiety, nudged against the back of my knees.

The pirate backed up step by step, until he came to a small landing.

One could keep going up the steps, or go to the left down a narrow corridor that I assumed led to the second-floor hallway.

As I got closer to the head of the first flight, the pirate backed into the corridor.

Old-fashioned candle sconces along its right wall had been converted to electricity at some point. Candelabra bulbs flickered, giving off a weak light. A dark arch-shaped mass materialized partway down on the left wall.

My brain stalled for a second, then realized it was the top of the servant stairs, coming up from the main living area. The labyrinth of poorly lit stairs and corridors would've been confusing under the best of circumstances, which these were not.

The pirate gestured with his gun hand for me to go up the second flight of stairs, to the third floor. Once the dogs and I were past him, he followed.

We walked down an even narrower corridor, with more flickering wall sconces. Blood thrumming in my ears, I tried to come up with a plan, but my mind stubbornly focused on stupid things. Why had I assumed the third floor was vacant?

The corridor ended at a door. The pirate gestured for me to open it.

I stepped out into a familiar bathroom. My old suite. The door I'd assumed was a linen closet was the servants' access to the guest suite via the backstairs and corridor.

Muffled noises and a repetitive thudding sound came from the bedroom. I realized I'd been hearing the sounds in the distance for the last minute or so, but I'd been so focused on the pirate and his little gun, they hadn't fully registered.

The pirate shooed me and the dogs through the bathroom and out into the bedroom. Ellie sat in the armchair in the sitting area, strapped to the chair with duct tape. More tape bound her wrists in front of her and her ankles. But her restraints weren't keeping her from banging her feet against the floor.

And she was yelling through a gag, another red kerchief. It sounded like "Help," but it was muffled and garbled. Her eyes went wide when she saw us. She mumbled something from behind the gag.

The pirate stepped over to her and pulled the gag loose. "Stop yelling or I shoot your dog."

She froze.

I again contemplated the pruning shears, but the little gun was still trained on me, and the pirate's gaze flicked back and forth between me and Ellie.

He gestured toward the bed. "You, lie down and put your hands above your head."

My body tensed.

He snorted. "Don't worry. You're not my type. Now lie down." His voice had turned impatient, rising a little in pitch.

I laid down on the bed.

Buddy growled.

"Lie down," I told the dogs, but I didn't give Buddy the *it's-okay* signal. It wasn't okay, not at all.

They dropped to their bellies, but Buddy's eyes stayed on the pirate as he walked to the head of the bed.

Rough hands yanked my wrists together and wrapped something around them several times, then a tearing sound. He sat me up.

Our eyes met.

His—the one not covered by the patch—was a pale blue, surrounded by long blond lashes.

He must have read the anger and defiance in mine. He pointed his gun at Buddy.

"No!" I gasped.

"Then behave." He put the gun into the back of his waistband and quickly wound tape around my torso, pinning my elbows to my sides.

He nudged my shoulder, and I flopped helplessly back against the pillow. He moved to my feet and wrapped duct tape around my ankles.

I was tempted to kick him in the face when he leaned down and used his teeth to create a notch in the tape so he could tear it. With effort, I resisted the temptation. All it would do was piss him off. I'd still be tied up, and he would still have the gun.

He wrapped more tape around my knees. I now resembled a mummy.

From the remaining roll, he tore off two short pieces of tape and stuck one end of each on the footboard of the bed.

To gag us. And far better than a kerchief would. My mouth went dry.

"Where are Bruce and Jack?" I asked, trying to delay the inevitable.

"The idiots went out searching for you two." The gravel in his voice sounded forced now. "Last I saw of them, they went into the beach house. They'll probably hunker down there for the rest of the storm."

"And if they don't?" The fierce voice told me that Lori was up front. "If they come back and catch you doing whatever you plan to do to us?"

The pirate actually laughed. "Bruce will be grateful."

Lori's mouth dropped open. "What? He's in on this?"

He walked over and stood in front of her chair. "No," he said with a sneer, "but he'll be glad that I've liberated him."

Her face paled and tears pooled in her eyes. "He'd never go along with hurting me," she half-whispered, not sounding all that confident.

Crapola. The shock of Bruce's betrayal must've brought Ellie to the surface. If only I'd told her about his affair.

"What *are* you going to do with us?" I said.

The pirate looked my way with a sneer. "I'd planned to surprise you, but maybe I'll let you contemplate your fate for a while. Once the worst of the storm is over, we're going on a hike to the north end of the island, where you two will take a tragic misstep and plummet to your deaths into the sinkhole." Another laugh.

My blood turned to ice. "What about the dogs?"

"If you two behave, I'll let them live." In two strides, he was at the bed again, grabbing the pieces of tape and slapping one over my mouth.

It caught me with my lips partway open. A section of tape stuck to my front teeth, painfully pinching my lip. "Yow."

It came out muffled, but still Buddy sat up and growled softly.

The pirate whirled and pointed the gun at him. Bile rose in my throat.

"Lie down, boy," Ellie quickly said.

Buddy looked at me.

I nodded, holding my breath. *Do as she says, boy. Please lie down.*

He reluctantly sank to his belly.

Ellie's face hardened. She glared at the pirate, or rather Lori did. "If you put a bullet in any of us, you'll never get away with this. There's nowhere to hide a body on this island that they won't be able to find it. Not even a dog's body."

The pirate snorted. "They're not gonna look that hard for a stupid dog."

"Yes, they will. These are valuable service dogs."

The pirate strode to her and whipped the other piece of tape across her mouth. "Time for you to shut up!" The words ended on a high-pitched screech.

CHAPTER TWENTY

To keep Ellie from banging on the floor again, the pirate shoved her knees up through the circle of her arms, so that her feet were on the edge of the chair and her bound wrists were in front of her legs. Then he wrapped more duct tape around her torso and legs.

How many rolls of that stuff does he have? Ms. Snark asked.

I had no energy to react to her as I stared at Ellie's trussed-up body.

Cackling, the pirate walked to the door. "Y'all behave now." The fake gravel was missing from the deep voice, and a slight Florida Cracker accent broke through. Laughter echoed in the hallway after the door slammed shut.

I flopped my head back against the bed pillow. My body felt heavy as lead.

What to do? The pruning shears in my pocket bit into my backside, reminding me that I was a coward and a fool. I'd had the means to at least put up a fight and I'd let myself be tied up.

To protect the dogs. Yeah, but for how long? Would he make good on his promise and not harm them. He didn't strike me as much of a dog person.

I tried to sigh behind my gag and choked a little on the trapped air. And in the process, the tape popped loose from my front teeth.

I worked my tongue between my teeth and pushed its tip against the tape. *Bleck.* Duct tape glue tastes awful.

I pushed my tongue out harder, and the tape seemed to loosen a bit more.

I turned my head toward Ellie. She was rocking back and forth, as far as her restraints would let her. Was she crying? Having a psychotic break?

She glanced my way. Her face was tight with determination. Apparently neither of the above—she was trying to get the chair rocking. Or maybe stretch the tape?

I moved my jaw and lips opened and closed as far as I could, pushed against the tape with my tongue again. Again, it seemed a little looser, but I couldn't be sure. Tentatively, I said, "Buddy."

What came out was "Bu-du," but he raised his head.

Ellie, I mean Lori, stopped moving. She looked my way again.

"Come here," I said to Buddy. It sounded like "Mm-he."

His head tilted to one side.

I wiggled my butt and managed to get myself over to the edge of the bed. "Come," I said slowly, emphasizing the hard C sound and turning the word into two syllables. Now it sounded like "Kuh-me."

He stood, wagging his tail, and came over to the bed.

My mouth tried to grin, but the tape pulled painfully on my lips.

I wiggled around some more, trying to get onto my side so that the handles of the pruning shears, sticking out of my pocket, would be near his face.

I wiggled a bit too strenuously, and fell off the bed.

The pruning shears' tip jabbed painfully into my flesh. I prayed the storm noises from outside had covered the loud thud I'd made when I landed.

I wiggled back and forth again until I got enough momentum going to roll over partway toward the bed, my back to Buddy. "Go get scissors."

What came out was, "Guh geh sizz-er."

I hoped he'd equate the shears' handles with those of a pair of scissors.

Nothing happened. Had he forgotten the *Go-get* signal. It was another task he'd been taught mainly so he could model it for other dogs-in-training.

I tried again, enunciating more carefully. "Gu ge-teh zizz-erz." I stuck my backside up in the air as best I could.

A warm nose poking around. Then the pruning shears slithered out of my back pocket.

Yes!

More wiggling, squirming and rolling and I was facing Buddy. He gingerly held the shears in his teeth. My hands were bound in a praying position, palms together. I spread my fingers apart and grasped the shears between my palms.

Crapola, this wouldn't work. The cutting part was toward my wrists, the handles sticking out beyond my fingers. I tried to turn them around and almost dropped them.

I was about to succumb to tears, when Nugget nudged my bound knees with her nose.

As best I could, I made a shooing motion with my hands. Buddy moved back, but probably more to avoid being bopped in the head with the shears' handles.

Nugget took his place and sniffed my bound wrists.

I imagined that both dogs were thinking, *What silly new game is this?*

"Brace," I said.

What came out was "Brz," but that was enough. Nugget spread her legs and braced herself.

I squirmed around some, trying to figure out how to get some part of me over her back so I could pull up to a sitting position. Finally, by tightening my stomach muscles, as if doing a crunch, and pulling my torso partway up, I managed to loop my bound wrists over her head.

I bent my knees, as much as the tape would allow, and dug my heels into the carpet. Pushing with my feet and pulling my torso up with the help of the dog, I squirmed my way to a sitting position.

I touched my duct-taped mouth to the top of Nugget's head. "Thank you."

It came out, "Ank ew."

She licked my chin and slithered out from under my arms.

For a moment, I thought I would topple sideways, but the dog stayed beside me. I leaned on her to steady myself.

When I was more firmly balanced, I pointed both index fingers over to where Buddy sat, watching us with anxious eyes. Nugget got the idea. She wagged her tail and trotted over to him.

Struggling not to lose my balance or drop the pruning shears, I wiggled and scooted across the floor until I was in front of Lori's knees, eye level with her bound hands.

She leaned slightly forward.

Teetering precariously on my rump, I stretched my hands up to hers. She nabbed the pruning shears between her fingers.

Hallelujah, now they were facing in the right direction.

I held my breath, raised my bound hands up to her again, and spread my palms as far apart as possible.

Using both of her hands to awkwardly open and close the shears, she slowly cut the tape between my wrists.

I ripped the rest of it off, the skin under it stinging. The action sent me over backward. With a newly freed hand, I plucked at the tape around my torso, found an end and got it started. But there was no way I could unwrap it.

"He," Lori said. I looked up. She was trying to hand me the shears.

Swiveling around like a turtle on its back, I took them from her in one hand. It was awkward as all get out, but I managed to cut the tape at the opposite elbow. The shears were quite sharp, which was good and bad. I tore my tank top and jabbed my arm a couple of times.

But finally I got all the way through. I pulled that arm free, then liberated the other one as well.

My heart had been racing for so long I'd stopped noticing, but now it kicked up another notch. We'd reached the point of no return. If the pirate came back now, before we were completely free, who knew what he would do?

Or she.

While I'd been focused on getting us free, a tiny seed had germinated in the back of my mind. The slender hands and higher-pitched voice when the pirate forgot to fake the gravel...

And who else would have a better motive to do all this than Bruce's lover?

I sat up and went at the tape on Lori's wrists with the shears, then cut the tape that forced her into her fetal position and held her to the chair.

We made eye contact. She nodded slightly. We grasped the ends of each other's gags.

"Un, tu, tree," she said, and we both ripped the tape off.

Fire ignited on my lips and cheeks. I barely managed to swallow a shout of pain.

Lori had clamped both hands over her mouth, somewhat stifling the "Yow," that had erupted from her throat. Her eyes were shiny with tears of pain.

But those eyes were clear, and her shoulders were back. She was still Lori.

I gave her a small sympathetic smile and grabbed up the shears again. I started hacking at the tape around my knees. "Did you recognize the pirate?" I used my task as an excuse to keep my eyes down.

"No."

"I think it was Lucy."

She reared back a little in the chair. "Lucy?"

"Yeah." I glanced up, then went back to work on the tape. "I saw her and Bruce on the beach a couple of times, near the beach house."

"Why would she be on the island?"

"Um, she and Bruce are lovers." I glanced up again.

Lori was shaking her head. "They grew up together, Luke and Lucy and Bruce. They're all just good friends."

"What I saw wasn't just friends, even good friends."

Something shifted in her eyes. Her face softened and she began to cry.

Ellie was back and seemed to have some awareness of what I'd just said.

Grinding my teeth, I pulled the last of the tape off my knees and went to work on my ankles.

Ellie flopped forward, her face in her hands, sobbing.

My heart was pounding, my thoughts beginning to scramble as panic set in. We had to get the rest of the way free before Lucy came back.

"Lori," I said, "please come out. I need your help. Lori."

Ellie's head came up, as I managed to cut through the last section of tape.

"No," Lori's firmer voice. "Call Ria out."

"Ria? Who's that?" I was tugging the rest of the tape loose from my ankles.

"Ria thinks she's an Amazon warrior." There was a hint of a snicker in Lori's voice. Then her face sobered. "I shouldn't mock her. Ria's the one who got us through basic training."

I pushed myself up to my knees in front of her and leaned down to cut the tape on her ankles.

"Ria," I echoed the name, still trying to digest the reality of a third significant alter.

Arms flew up in front of me and hands grabbed my shoulders, shoving me over backward. The pruning shears went flying.

Then Lori or Ria—or whoever the heck she was now—was sitting on me, pinning my chest to the floor.

CHAPTER TWENTY-ONE

"Ria," I gasped out with the little bit of air left in my lungs. "I'm on your side."

She narrowed her eyes at me.

"I'm a friend of Lori's."

Her expression wary, she lifted her weight off of me and tried to stand. With her feet still bound together, she landed on her butt next to me.

I struggled to a sitting position, trying to catch my breath. "We've got to get your feet loose fast, and get out of here. Before the person who tied us up comes back."

She shook her head, looked around. "What the devil is going on? And why are we in the guest suite?"

"Buddy, go get scissors." Then to Ria, I said, "I'll give you the long version later. Short version, someone has been trying to poison you, I mean Ellie... the body. When I figured out what was going on, they got more desperate and kidnapped Ellie, brought her up here and tied her up. They were going to kill you, uh, her, once the storm let up–"

"What storm?"

"We're in the middle of a hurricane."

Ria's eyes widened. "That explains the howling wind."

Buddy trotted over with the pruning shears between his teeth.

I took them and handed them to Ria—with some trepidation. I wasn't sure how I felt about arming her.

"Sorry about sitting on you." She savagely ripped at the tape on her ankles. "When I saw that you had these shears..." She trailed off as she freed herself in record time.

She jumped up and reached down to grab my hand. Hauling me to my feet, she said, "Who are you exactly?"

"You know Ellie was getting a service dog, right? I'm her dog's trainer. Um, Lori told me about the DID."

Ria nodded, then froze for a second when she saw my hand, held out for the shears. With obvious reluctance, she gave them to me.

Jamming them into my back pocket again, I rushed to the door and cracked it open.

Male voices drifted up from below. Bruce and Jack were back. I expelled a sigh of relief, more about Jack than Bruce.

Another voice. It sounded like the pirate's, only not as deep and without the gravel.

Lucy. She was talking to them.

I eased the door closed, turned and grabbed Lori's, um, Ria's hand.

Dang, this is confusing.

"Come on." The dogs followed as we hustled across the room and into the bathroom. Ria must have guessed my agenda. She went right to the door to the servants' corridor.

I got the dogs in after us and closed the door. There were only a few sconces on the walls of this hallway, but it was enough light to tiptoe our way to the top of the stairs.

I stopped there. Whispering, I gave Ria the longer version, leaving out the identity of the pirate for now. I was about to ask if she had any questions, when the lights went out.

Crapola. I crouched down and felt around blindly for the dogs. I trusted Buddy to stay with me, but Nugget, not so much—although perhaps being lost in the storm had cured her wanderlust.

"Come here," I whispered to them. Buddy's big nose touched my palm. By feel, I found and removed his collar, then patted around blindly until I connected with a silky ear. I slipped the collar onto Nugget's neck, pulled Buddy's leash from my pocket and snapped it on.

"Ria, follow us," I said softly.

A small grunt was her answer.

"Go on down, boy."

Buddy led the way as we carefully settled one foot and then the other on each step in the pitch black, narrow stairwell. I tried not to imagine what would happen if one of us made a wrong step.

At the second-floor landing there was a bit of ambient light. I peeked around the corner. An arch of medium gray revealed the top of the servant stairs leading up from the main living area. Rumbling male voices drifted up to us.

I half turned and touched Ria's arm, put Nugget's leash in her hand. "Wait here for a second," I whispered. "Buddy, stay."

Worrying a little that Ria might rebel against me taking charge, I tiptoed along the second-floor passageway and stopped at the top of the steps. The light was dim but steady. Most likely coming from camping lanterns then, not flashlights or candles. I strained to hear what they were saying.

I recognized Bruce's baritone but couldn't make out more than the occasional word. A deeper grunt was probably Jack. And the other voice....

I found the stairs' railing and took three careful steps down.

"How'd you get here anyway?" Jack's voice, annoyed.

"I stowed away, when you made the supply run." Yes, that was definitely the pirate's voice, more an alto than the fake bass.

"The stuck door of the head," Jack said. "You'd locked yourself in there."

A low chuckle. I was pretty sure it didn't come from Jack. He'd sounded pissed.

"*Why'd* you come out here?" Jack's tone left the words, *to get stuck in a hurricane* hanging in the air.

A couple of seconds ticked by with no response.

I imagined the awkward glances Lucy and Bruce were exchanging.

"I, uh, knew Bruce would resist leaving the house," Lucy said. "I wanted to convince him to come back to the mainland, with the rest of y'all."

"But the storm hadn't veered this way yet." Jack wasn't buying it. "We were stocking up just in case, at that point."

And what about the sugar in the gas tank? Ms. Snark asked.

I was pretty sure now that Lucy had committed that act of sabotage, to keep us all on the island so she could get rid of Ellie once and for all.

"Look, that doesn't matter now," Bruce, impatient. "What are we going to do about Ellie and Marcia?"

My heart rate kicked up several notches. Did Bruce know we were supposed to be upstairs, tied up and gagged? Was Jack in on it too? That thought made my stomach lurch.

"We can't go out there now," Lucy said. "The storm's picked up again. We'll end up lost ourselves, and maybe get hurt, or worse. There are places they could've found shelter, the woodshed or the beach house."

I slowly breathed out a soft sigh. The men didn't know we were in the house.

I could imagine what Lucy's plan was. Wait until Bruce and Jack had gone out to look for us. Pretend she was going to search too, then take us to the sinkhole on the north end of the island.

We had to somehow expose her before the storm let up.

But if we just waltzed into the living area and confronted her, would she pull her gun and start shooting? I didn't know how stable she was.

Parading around in a pirate's costume, Ms. Snark commented, *I'd say not very.*

"I can't believe they went looking for that stupid dog," Bruce said.

"When you domesticate an animal," Jack's voice, "you must take responsibility for its safety."

That sounded very Native American, and I agreed. Even if Nugget had been a strange dog, maybe a new one I wasn't yet attached to, I still would've searched for her. She was my responsibility.

"I checked the radio," Jack was saying. "Pierre is breaking up some. Wind shear in the upper atmosphere. It should ease up in a few hours."

Smiling a little—my guess had been right—I backed cautiously up the steps and crept back to Ria and the dogs. Wordlessly, I led them down the back stairs into the inky darkness of the first floor.

Feeling along the wall, I found Greta's door, then moved on to my own. Hands out in front of me, I walked slowly to where the dresser should be. I banged my shin on the edge of the bedframe.

My hands felt along the bed, found the nightstand, then my own purloined lantern sitting on it.

I flipped the switch at the lantern's base, and it gave off a soft glow. Ria and I blew out air in unison.

You don't realize how precious light is until it's gone.

"Close the door," I whispered.

Ria eased it shut.

Gesturing for the dogs to lie down, I perched on the side of the bed. Ria took the straight-backed chair.

"There were three voices," I said, "one of them is the pirate who tied us up. And I think it's a woman. Do you know Lucy from town?"

"They all sounded like men to me."

I narrowed my eyes at her. "You snuck up behind me."

She grinned.

I shook my head. "The slightly higher pitched voice, I think that's Lucy. She and Bruce are having an affair."

Ria's eyebrows shot up. "Oh, yeah. Surprised he has the guts to pull that off."

I frowned at her. "Not the word I would use." To me, having an affair was a rather gutless thing to do.

"Oh, he acts all in charge, and Ellie lets him push her around, up to a point, and then Lori puts him back in his place. He caves pretty fast when she goes after him."

That struck me as a fairly accurate description of the dynamics I'd witnessed so far. I almost felt sorry for Bruce. Almost.

Then something else struck me. "How do you know all this?"

Ria's cheeks pinked a little. "Um, I can sometimes hear Lori's thoughts, or what's happening when she's out. What is it that therapist calls it…"

The term surfaced from the depths of my memory. "Co-consciousness?"

She nodded.

I wondered about the "that therapist." Apparently, Ria wasn't all that engaged in the therapeutic process.

Ria threw her shoulders back and puffed out her chest. "So let's go get this woman. There's two of us and only one of her."

Hmm, I was beginning to see a problem with an alter who believed she was an Amazon warrior but who lived inside a waif-sized body like Ellie's.

"Let's try to think of something else. She has a gun."

That didn't slow Ria down much. "All the more reason to take her by surprise, before she can get it out. And we've got the shears."

I shook my head. Even with two against one, shears against a gun didn't seem like great odds. "We could barricade ourselves in here until morning, but it's one of the first places she'll look, when she realizes we're not still upstairs." I gestured toward the door, "And there's no lock."

I was crashing from the adrenaline rush of fighting to get free upstairs. My body longed to crawl into bed and pretend everything would be okay in the morning.

"We *could* stay here," Ria was saying, "and wait for her to come for us. One of us stays by the door, jumps her when she comes in." She stood, spread her legs and put her hands on her hips. "I'll take the first watch."

I almost laughed out loud at the sight of Ellie's five-four, ninety-five-pound body posed like a Spartan soldier.

When I had control of myself, I said, "As tempting as that plan is…" I stroked the comforter on my bed. "I think we need to be more proactive."

I focused on the sounds of the storm. The wind still howled and the rain still rat-a-tat-tatted loudly on the metal roof three stories up, but maybe it was letting up some.

Had the men succeeded in getting the satellite dish fixed? Would it be able to transmit a signal through the interference of the storm?

"Come on then," Ria said, her voice tense. "Let's find this fake pirate."

"Hang on." Where was my laptop? I looked around the dimly lit room. Dang, I'd left it in the kitchen.

I spotted my cell phone on the nightstand, grabbed it up. I tapped the email icon and prayed. It opened, and I switched it over to connect to the wifi network. Hallelujah, it connected, and the incoming emails were updating.

I scanned through them, skipping the one from my mom, subject line: *WHERE ARE YOU?* And the one from Becky: *Storm coming your way!*

Old news I'm afraid, Beck.

Ah, there was the one from Will that I'd been sure would be there. *Coming to you* was the subject line. I clicked on it.

It froze while loading. I held my breath. Suddenly the text of the message popped up. I blew out air.

"What are you doing?" Ria said impatiently.

"My fiancé's law enforcement." I was skimming the email. "I'm gonna tell him to bring reinforcements."

The gist of Will's message was that he was driving to Dahlia and would find someone with a boat to come out to the island to get us. The time stamp was shortly after we had talked yesterday, or rather had tried to talk through the static.

I hit reply. Nothing happened for a few seconds. Again, I held my breath.

Finally, the reply box popped up. I quickly typed: *Bring local sheriff's deputies. One of the ghosts I told you about is fake. Live person who may have killed the housekeeper. Planning to kill Ellie. Love you!*

I opted not to mention that I was on the fake ghost's hit list too. That would really freak Will out and he might do something reckless.

More reckless than driving toward a hurricane? Ms. Snark asked.

Ignoring her, I hit *send*, prayed, and crossed fingers on both hands to boot. Which made it hard to hang onto the phone.

It seemed to take a month but eventually *your message has been sent* came up. Again, I blew out pent-up air.

Ria was tapping her foot, her arms crossed over her chest.

"I sent him an email. I think it went through." I muted the phone and activated its light. Somewhere along the way, I'd lost my trusty flashlight.

"Okay, let's go already."

I shook my head. "We can't just rush out there without a plan."

Ria scowled at me. "What's your plan then?"

"That's the problem. I don't have one."

CHAPTER TWENTY-TWO

"We don't know where Lucy is," I said. "Or where Bruce or Jack are. We don't want them to get caught in the crossfire."

Ria was still scowling. "Why not? That scumbag Bruce is having an affair."

"Um…" I couldn't think of a good comeback to that. "Well, I don't want Jack to get hurt. He's a good man, with a family." I paused, recalling Ellie's earlier tears. "And Ellie loves Bruce. If she wants to divorce him, that's one thing, but seeing him shot—that wouldn't be good for her already shaky mental health."

Ria snorted. "That sniveling idiot."

"You do get, don't you, that if she goes nuts, you'll be stuck in a mental institution right along with her?"

Ria tilted her head to one side. "Hmm, hadn't thought of that."

"And if she kills herself, you'll be dead too."

"Okay, okay." She held up her hands. "We try to keep Bruce from getting killed."

"Or hurt."

Something hard flashed in her eyes. "I don't know, I might hurt him a little myself."

"And then everybody, including fragile Ellie, will go to jail."

Ria rolled her eyes. "So what do you want to do?"

Crawl under the bed? Ms Snark suggested internally.

Again, I ignored her. "I think we need to do some reconnaissance. Find out where everybody is, then come back here and devise a plan from there."

She pursed her lips. After a beat, she nodded and gestured toward the door.

I turned to Nugget. "Lie down, girl. Stay." She flopped onto her belly on the bedside rug.

I debated for a couple of seconds over taking Buddy with us. My heart said *no*, it wanted him safe. But my head realized that he might be able to help, and Will would be furious if he found out later that I'd gone to confront a potential killer without taking the dog with me for protection.

"Buddy, come." He rose and followed me to the door.

"It's about time," Ria said.

I really, really wanted to try to get Lori up front. But I had to trust that she'd directed me to call out Ria for a reason.

With my phone flashlight pointed down in front of our feet, we slipped out into the hallway. I was surprised Ria let me lead the way, but also relieved. She was less likely to go charging into a room if she was behind me.

We eased our way down the hall. My heart was pounding but my feet dragged, the urge to run back to my room almost overwhelming. My fight or flight response was definitely leaning toward flight right now. The thought even crossed my mind to veer left and go right out the back door and into the storm. For a crazy moment, the indifferent assault by Pierre seemed preferable to the intentional malice of that gun-wielding pirate.

Buddy's side brushed against my knee. *The dogs!* I couldn't let them be harmed. My jaw tightened. I straightened my shoulders and turned the corner of the hallway.

A soft gray glow reached out from the large doorway of the living area. At least one lantern was turned on in there.

"Stay, Buddy," I whispered. He sat down near the wall.

I turned off my phone's flashlight, snuck up to the edge of the doorway, and, heart thudding in my chest, peeked around it.

At first the room seemed empty. I located the blankets and pillow strewn across a sofa against the far right wall. Was that where Jack was sleeping? Except he wasn't there now.

Then a movement near the central stairwell caught my eye, an arm gesturing. A bare arm.

It belonged to Lucy, whose back was to me. The white poet's shirt was gone. She wore a tan tank top, above the black jeans.

She gestured again and I spotted Bruce, standing farther back in the shadows, near the wall.

I turned and found myself nose to nose with Ria.

"Lemme see," she mouthed without making any sound.

I shook my head and held up one finger, indicating she should wait a minute. I gently nudged her back the way we'd come.

I almost tripped over Buddy. I put my hand on his head, then quietly patted my thigh, the *Come* signal. He fell into line behind me.

I kept one hand on the wall as we moved past the powder room, toward the darkness near the kitchen.

Ria stopped, as if about to protest. I grabbed her arm and dragged her the rest of the way around the corner.

I turned on my flashlight again, cupping my hand over it to block most of the light.

"Bruce and Lucy are over by the far wall," I whispered. "If we go up the backstairs, we may be able to hear what they're saying."

"Where's Jack?"

"Not in there, best I could tell."

Ria pivoted and led the way this time. Without hesitation, she opened the panel to the stairs and stepped into the inky blackness.

She knows her way around these corridors and backstairs.

Well, duh, Ms. Snark commented.

I closed the panel behind Buddy and myself, before moving my hand off the light.

We went up to the second-floor landing and turned left into the narrow hallway. I turned out my light and pocketed my phone. The gray arch partway down the hall showed us the head of the steps coming up from the living area.

I crouched down and whispered in Buddy's ear. "Stay, boy."

Every muscle in my body tight, I followed Ria as she tiptoed to the head of the stairs.

"What do you mean?" Bruce's voice.

Lucy's response was garbled. All I caught was "…ran off…"

"They went looking for the dog," Bruce said.

More garbled words, then "…heard them downstairs… crazy… went out again…"

It sounded like Lucy was trying to convince him that we had gone back out into the storm. Did she believe that's what we'd done after we got loose?

Ms. Snark snorted. *You were sorely tempted.*

"We've got to find them." Bruce, sounding worried. "And I'm going to tell her about us."

"…too dangerous… if she leaves… violates the agreement."

"No." Bruce's tone had softened. "I did that, when I was unfaithful." His voice now sounded sad.

A small lump formed in my throat. Again, I felt a little sorry for the guy. But only a little.

"…can't tell her…"

"I can't take the sneaking around anymore," Bruce said.

"…lose all that money…" Lucy's voice dropped lower. I couldn't make out words now.

But I'd heard enough. She wasn't content with breaking up Bruce's marriage. She wanted all of his money for herself.

A grinding sound nearby. I suspected it was Ria's teeth.

"Do you have something long-sleeved with you?" Bruce was saying. "We need to search for them as soon as the storm lets up. You'll get torn to shreds out in the woods in that thing." His tone was now tender.

"Okay, I'll go change." Lucy, coming closer. "So we're ready, when the time comes." Her acting was good. She sounded genuinely concerned.

Ria grabbed my arm, and we scurried back down the hall. I could barely make out Buddy's silhouette near the steps. I patted my thigh and kept going.

Ria moved ahead of me. "We're going up," she whispered. "Lots of places to hide up there." We rounded the corner. She started up the stairs into darkness.

I slowed my steps as I felt my way up behind her, not totally thrilled with this plan. The relative security of my room downstairs called to me. But I wasn't willing to be separated from Ria either. I'd have to trust her instincts here.

The third-floor, back hallway was pitch black. I kept a hand on the wall and slid it along as I took one cautious step after another. Buddy's claws tapped quietly on the wood floor behind me.

A hand grabbed my forearm and yanked me sideways. Another hand clamped over my mouth as I was about to yelp. I scrambled to stay on my feet, my heart ricocheting around in my chest.

Buddy's low growl from beside me.

"Shh." Ria's voice. The hands let go of me, and a door snicked closed behind us.

"We're in one of the old servants' rooms," she whispered.

Sheez, lady, ya could've given some warning, Ms. Snark blustered.

But actually she couldn't have. We didn't know how far behind us Lucy was. She might've heard.

I took a deep breath, trying to calm my pounding heart. I held out my hand about where Buddy's head should be and connected with warm soft fur. A cold nose touched my palm.

"Turn on the light," Ria whispered right next to my ear.

I jumped a little, then whispered back, "It might show under the door."

"Good point. What was she wearing that he was so afraid for her tender skin?"

"A tank top."

Footsteps in the hall. I felt Ria stiffen beside me.

I crouched down next to Buddy. "Shh," I hissed softly in his ear.

The footsteps went on by.

I slowly let out my pent-up breath and stood. "Now what?" I whispered.

My brain answered my own question. Lucy was going to the guest suite, my old room.

Duh. Bruce had known she was on the island even before the storm began. I'd seen them on the beach. But he wouldn't have let her stay in the beach house. The smaller structure, on stilts and facing the Gulf, might not have survived the storm.

That's why he'd moved me to the ground floor, so Lucy could be up here—where it was less likely that anyone would figure out she was in the house.

Something else niggled at the back of my mind. I tried to lasso it and bring it forward, but it skittered away like a spooked horse.

"She's in the guest suite," I whispered to Ria.

"Yes! We've got her cornered. Let's go."

I wasn't feeling quite so eager. An image popped into my mind, of the alligator that had gotten into my house a couple of years ago. He'd been cornered too, and he hadn't taken it well.

My stomach twisted in knots, I followed the rustling sound of Ria moving toward the door.

Out in the hall, I ran into her back where she'd stopped moving. Buddy's nose butted against the back of my left knee.

"Shh," she whispered. "Listen."

I strained my ears but couldn't hear anything except rain pelting onto the metal roof right over our heads.

"What?" I whispered back.

"The pipes rattle," she said near my ear, "when the water's running up here."

I felt her move away and followed tentatively, again using the wall of the narrow passageway to keep me from feeling like I was walking off into space.

This time I ran into Ria's arm, extended out. The soft whoosh of a door opening and a tall gray rectangle appeared to our left. "Main third-floor hall," Ria whispered in my ear.

We stepped through the doorway into the polished wood hallway. Some light filtered up from the first floor.

At the end of the hall, a faint gray line under the guest suite's door. We tiptoed up to it and Ria opened it very slowly. She peeked in, then opened it farther and stepped over the threshold.

Buddy and I followed her into the room. It seemed to be empty. The bathroom door was open, a dim light coming from it. The sound of water running in the sink.

Lucy apparently hadn't gotten the memo about the well pump issue.

The scraps of cut and torn duct tape that we'd left scattered on the floor were gone.

I glanced down at the armchair in front of us. There was barely enough light to make out something tan draped over the hideous purple fabric. The tank top.

Ria had moved across to the nightstand by the bed. She held up something in her hand. I squinted at it.

The gun.

Air whooshed out of my lungs, and a knot or two in my stomach loosened.

Ria dropped her arm and started toward me, making a shooing gesture with the hand not holding the gun.

I pivoted toward the door.

"Bruce?" The light brightened and a shadow fell across the floor.

My head jerked around and my breath caught in my throat.

Lucy stood in the bathroom doorway, a lantern held high in her hand, naked from the waist up.

My mouth fell open. I stared at the broad, bare chest—smooth and flat.

My eyes rose to the face.

The light shining from the side of the lantern glistened on a wet cheek, dotted with blond stubble.

CHAPTER TWENTY-THREE

We all stared at each other for a fraction of a second.

"I guess it was too much to hope that y'all had run off into the storm," the man said.

Ria lifted her arms, the gun in both hands, leaning slightly forward, legs spread. No doubt the shooting stance she'd learned in basic training.

The man rounded on her, swinging the lantern. A sickening crunch, and she crumpled.

Somebody screamed. I think it was me.

The pistol skittered across the floor, into the shadows.

"Buddy, go get gun!"

Says something about your life that he knows the word gun, Ms. Snark commented.

Not now!

I launched myself at the half-naked man. We went down, but somehow he ended up half on top of me. He grabbed for my throat with one hand.

Heart thundering, I fended him off with an elbow.

I looked around frantically. Where was my dog? The lantern, on its side, cast weird shadows, but offered little illumination.

"Buddy, protect. Jump!"

Buddy pounced out of the darkness, knocking the man against the bedframe. I scrambled out from under him, remembered the shears, and reached for them. They were gone, apparently knocked out of my back pocket during the struggle.

I jumped to my feet, scanning the floor around me.

A groan to my right. My gaze flicked in that direction. Ria was up on her hands and knees, shaking her head.

The door flew open. I whirled around.

Bruce stood in the doorway, holding another lantern. "What the–"

A sigh was halfway out of my mouth when I sensed movement near my leg. I jerked away and looked down.

Another banshee scream. This time, it wasn't me.

The man's arm was stretched toward my ankle, but Ria, still on her knees, had grabbed him. She held him in a headlock, one hand clutching his hair. He screamed again.

Bruce shook himself like a dog waking up from a bad dream. "Ellie, what are you doing? Let Luke go."

"Hang on to him, Ria," I yelled, afraid Bruce's use of Ellie's name would call her out.

I looked around for Buddy. He stood off to the side, the pistol's handle held gingerly between his teeth.

I ran to him and took the gun. "Good boy," I crooned, almost crying with relief.

Ria rose to a stand, her elbow still wrapped around the man's neck. He managed to get his feet under him but was bent over backward in an awkward pose.

"Ellie, let him go." Bruce took a step toward them. Even in the poor light, I could make out his anguished expression.

"It's okay," I said. "I've got the gun." I held it out, pointed toward the man, Luke.

Ria let him go and took a step back.

Either Luke hadn't heard me or he didn't care that I was now armed. He rounded on Ria and tried to grab her.

She thrust one hand against his chest, holding him at arm's length. But his arms were longer.

I danced around, trying to get a clear shot, but not sure if I'd be able to pull the trigger. I'd never fired a gun at all before, much less at a human being.

His hands closed around Ria's throat.

I'd reversed the gun and raised the butt in the air to club him, when Ria cocked back her free arm. She slugged him.

He teetered for a moment, a shocked look on his face. Then he fell.

Jack appeared in the doorway, a shotgun in his hands. He nudged Bruce aside and scanned the room. "Y'all okay?"

Bruce didn't seem to hear Ria's and my attempts to explain what was going on. He crouched next to the man.

I gave up for the moment and went searching for the roll of duct tape. It was on the floor next to the nightstand.

Jack apparently had been listening. He came over and handed me his shotgun. "Keep him covered."

I stuffed the small pistol in my pocket, much more confident with a shotgun in my hands. I didn't really know how to shoot it either, but I figured it would be easier to aim.

Jack took the roll of tape and knelt at Luke's feet. He started to wrap tape around his ankles.

Some of what we'd said must have sunk in, because Bruce made no protest.

Ria sidled over to me. "Call Lori out," she whispered. "She handles Bruce better than I do." Her eyes glazed over.

"Lori, Lori," I whispered, praying I didn't get Ellie instead.

Her eyes cleared and her posture shifted oh so slightly.

"Lori?"

She nodded, taking in the scene in front of us. "Who knocked him out?" She kept her voice low.

"You did. You, uh, Ria punched him."

She gave me a lopsided grin. "Really? Go, Ria."

"Why did you want her out?" I whispered.

Lori waved a hand in the air. "I'll explain later."

Jack was finishing up securing Luke's wrists with the tape.

"Um," I said, "he needs to be guarded too. We were tied up with the tape, and we got loose."

Jack tilted his head in a single nod, then held out his hand for the shotgun.

I gratefully relinquished it. My limbs, now that the adrenaline was subsiding, felt like lead.

Lori stepped over and put a hand on Bruce's shoulder.

He covered her hand with his. "I know we need to talk, but…"

She nodded. "Marcia and I will be in the kitchen."

We went down the main stairs and through the dimly lit living area. Lori picked up one of the lanterns from an end table. "I'm gonna switch the fridge off and turn the blinkety-blank lights on."

I smiled at her. I'd told her the first time we'd met that I didn't like cussing, not something I necessarily said to most clients, but I'd figured a woman might understand.

And she'd remembered.

"I'll get Nugget." I turned on my phone flashlight, and Buddy and I headed for my room.

I opened the door and shone the light at the floor, so as not to blind Nugget.

She jumped up and trotted over to me. I snickered. The expression on her face was just like the one my brother used to have, when he'd been busy playing and had waited too long, then tried to cross his legs while racing for the bathroom.

"Not yet, girl. Hopefully the storm will let up soon." Did Lori/Ellie have something we could use as piddle pads? We might have to let the dogs go inside.

That's when two things struck me. One, I was now putting Lori's name first, acknowledging that yes, she seemed to be the host alter. And two, she'd remembered about the cussing.

Which meant the person I'd met and liked during those first two meetings, when I'd described the process and then brought Nugget for her approval, was Lori. Although, now that I thought about it, there had been a few moments when a gentler, more timid persona had been present —Ellie.

The lights came on in my room. I blew out a sigh and turned off my phone flashlight.

In the kitchen, Lori had set out wineglasses. "I thought a glass was in order." She brought a bottle of white wine and a corkscrew to the table.

"Didn't Bruce get rid of all the wine?"

Lori wiggled her eyebrows. "Greta wasn't the only one with a stash."

I gave her a small smile. "Only *one* glass?"

"That's all I can have. After two, it's harder for me to stay out front, and one of my alters is a bit of a lush."

Aha, Ms. Snark said inside.

"Does she like vodka, by any chance?"

"No. Why do you ask?" Lori expertly popped the cork and poured the wine.

A couple more pieces fell into place. I sat down and grabbed my glass. Wine never tasted quite so good.

"I think Luke was also trying to convince Bruce that you were a drunk. He was hiding empty vodka bottles around the house for him to find."

"Ah, and I was blaming those on poor Greta."

"Hey, how's your head?" I asked.

"What? Why?"

I touched the side of my head, above the left temple.

She fingered the same area on her head—where a red lump was forming—and winced. "What happened?"

"Luke whacked you, I mean Ria, with a lantern. It doesn't hurt?"

"Only tender to the touch, so it can't be too bad." She chuckled. "You wouldn't believe how many times I've woken up in the morning with bruises or cuts that I have no idea how they happened."

Oh, I could believe that, but I had trouble imagining what it would be like to live life never quite knowing what someone else, who also lived in your body, had been up to when you weren't around.

The dogs had settled at my feet. Nugget whined softly.

"I've got a treat for them as well," Lori said. "Maybe it will distract them from their full bladders." She held up a long sausage, wrapped in yellow plastic. "From Greta's stash."

"Any onions or garlic in that?"

She read the label. "Nope."

"I have a list of foods I'll give you, what's safe and what isn't for dogs."

She unwrapped the sausage and called the golden retriever over. Nugget looked at me when Lori offered her half the sausage.

"It's okay, girl." Then to Lori, as the dog wolfed down the treat, "Only you should feed her and give her treats, and treats only when she's working and has done well."

I had a flash of *déjà vu*. Had I already told her that? Or maybe it was Ellie I'd told.

"Oh, I shouldn't have given her that?"

"Tonight's an exception."

Buddy had sat up next to my knee. His tail thumped the floor.

I chuckled, and Lori held out the other half of the sausage to me. I took it and gave it to him. "You richly deserve this, boy. You saved me."

Again! Ms. Snark's and Will's voices, in unison.

"What did he do?" Lori asked.

I told her how he'd knocked Luke off of me and picked up the gun.

"You sure you can't teach Nugget those commands?"

I shook my head. "They're not compatible with being a service dog. I can get away with it with Buddy because he's a veteran now. He knows how to behave in public."

I took another sip of wine. "And hopefully you'll never need protection again. Luke will be going to jail for a long time."

"You think so?"

"Yes. I'm pretty sure he killed Greta. She and I were near the servant stairs, talking about the possibility that the wheat flour had been tampered with, and I asked her about any enemies you might have and mentioned the pirate ghost. Luke was already in the house at that point. I think he heard us and started covering his tracks. Despite his claim that Bruce would be happy about what he was doing, I think he knew otherwise. He wanted you dead, but he also wanted Bruce to believe it was an accident, or a natural death due to the sarcopenia."

Lori nodded, her expression grim.

"Hey, why did you have me call Ria out?" I asked. "I mean, she is a fighter, and a good one."

"Ellie and I are... how to describe it? We're closer in the system. We even have co-consciousness some of the time. She was near the surface upstairs earlier, when we were getting loose from the tape. She knows what's going on. But she and Ria are more separate. I figured you didn't need Ellie coming out and bursting into tears in the middle of a tricky situation." She smiled and raised her glass. "Besides, I'm a lover, not a fighter."

I returned the smile. "How does that whole switching thing work anyway?" I'd been dying of curiosity ever since Ria had let her eyes glaze over upstairs.

"If one of us doesn't want to be out any longer, we can step back and let someone else come forward. But there's no guarantee who it will be. It helps if someone else says the alter's name."

"Yes, I got that part. But I didn't know you could initiate a switch."

She nodded, then stared into her wineglass before taking a sip.

"Did you know Bruce was gay?" I said it gently, trying to be supportive, but again I was beyond curious to know the answer.

"I think he's bisexual, and yes, I suspected. You know how guys turn and look when a pretty woman goes by?"

"Yeah."

"Well, he did that with women, but also when a buff man went by."

"What are you going to do?"

Translation, Ms. Snark said. *Are you going to divorce him?*

Lori shrugged and stared into her wineglass. "I don't know. That will partly depend on what he wants to do, and on Ellie." She took a sip of wine. "And we've kept our own secrets from him."

I nodded.

"Either way, I will have my own money from now on. That will be one of my requirements if we stay together. And I'm going to make a sizeable donation to your agency."

"Mattie Jones will be thrilled."

Lori stared into her wineglass again. It was almost empty. "It would've been really easy for Luke to tamper with the salt and flour. We get all our groceries through his store." Her voice was mournful.

I sipped some of my wine, then said in a low voice, "By the way, the bag of flour and all the loaves of bread disappeared from the kitchen around the time Greta died. But I have a salt shaker and one of the dinner rolls made from the new flour. The sheriff can get them tested."

At least I hoped those items were still in my dresser drawers.

My glass was empty. I reached for the bottle. *I* could have another glass. "Speaking of Luke's store, I'm glad Lucy wasn't the pirate. I liked her when I met her at the store the first time, but then I realized her resemblance to Bruce's, um, lover. I'd only seen them from a distance. That's why I thought it was her."

"I'm glad it wasn't her too. She's one of the few people in Dahlia that we're pretty good friends with. Earlier when you told me, and Ellie came out for a few minutes—I think she was almost as upset about the idea of Lucy betraying her as she was about Bruce. Even she hasn't been getting along with him all that well lately."

We'd noticed that, Ms. Snark commented.

I ignored her.

"The name of the boat made me suspicious too," I said.

"Lucinda Mae?" Lori threw her head back and laughed. "That was Bruce's mother's name."

"Oh." I gave her a chagrined smile. "Hey, do you think he had any inkling about what Luke was doing? I mean the pirate stuff."

"No." A voice from the doorway behind me.

I whirled around in my chair.

Bruce stood there, his eyes hollow, his skin ashen under his tan. "I don't know what he was thinking. I'd told him a hundred times that I wasn't going to get a divorce." He stared at Lori. "I love…" his voice choked up. "I *loved* you both. And I still love you."

Lori stood—her body had changed slightly, had softened. Ellie was out. She walked to Bruce and took his hand. "Let's talk."

They left the room.

I looked down at Buddy. "Hope they can work it out."

I swallowed the last of my second glass of wine, and figured I'd better stop there. My head was swimming a bit.

I stood up carefully and went to the pantry. Grabbing two bottles of water, I said, "Come on, kids."

The dogs followed me up to the third floor. I opened the guest room door.

Jack motioned me in. He sat on the ugly purple armchair, the shotgun resting on his knees. Luke still lay where he'd landed when Ria had hit him and Jack had trussed him up. His eyes were open, staring at the ceiling.

"He okay?" I handed a water bottle to Jack.

"He'll survive." He let out a low chuckle. "Physically, that is. Not sure about his ego, after being knocked out by little Ellie."

Luke glanced our way, glared at Jack, and went back to staring at the ceiling.

"Thanks." Jack held up the now opened water bottle in a mock toast, then took a long draw on it.

"My fiancé's law enforcement. I got an email out to him a little while ago. Thank heavens you were able to fix the satellite dish."

He shrugged. "It wasn't damaged, just knocked out of the tree and the wires pulled loose."

"Well, it looked like the email went through. If I know Will, he'll be here as soon as the weather clears enough to navigate the river safely."

Or perhaps not so safely, knowing Will. If he could convince some boat owner to take the risk, he'd make the trip sooner instead of later.

And he gives me a hard time about taking risks.

My chest ached from missing him. I drank some water, trying to wash down the lump that had formed in my throat.

After all I'd been through today, I refused to cry now, especially in front of Luke.

"Did you know about them?" I tilted my head in Luke's direction.

Jack nodded. "They've been together, off and on, since they were teenagers."

The wife is the last to know, Ms. Snark said.

"Was it common knowledge?"

"No, they hid it well in town. The folks around here, the white and black ones that is, wouldn't have accepted them as a couple."

"But you're not bothered by it."

He shook his head. "In my culture, homosexuality is revered. A gay person is thought to have two spirits, one male, one female. And they often have special spiritual powers."

"Do you think Luke has special powers?" I blurted out, surprise bordering on shock in my voice.

Jack snorted. "This one. No."

"Hey, I'm right here, ya know," Luke called across the room.

"Shut up," Jack snapped, "or I'll gag you."

I felt my eyebrows fly up.

Jack gave me a half smile. "My people may revere gay people in general, but this one..." He pointed his chin at Luke. "I've known him since he was thirteen. He was a selfish boy and he has grown into a selfish man."

He took another swig of water. "You know," he said quietly, "there is more than one way for a person to have two or more spirits."

I intentionally raised one eyebrow this time. "You know about that." I also kept my voice down.

He nodded.

"You're very observant."

He shrugged. "They've been married five years. And sadly, I spend more time around them than I do with my own wife and kids."

Speaking of selfish men, Ms. Snark said.

I had to agree that Bruce Burke wasn't going to win any prizes for thoughtfulness.

"Have you heard from your family? Are they safe?"

"Wife emailed me before the storm hit. She was taking the kids inland to her sister's."

"Good." I sipped water. "I think Ellie feels safe around you."

Which meant she might let her guard down with him. Lori had never seriously considered Jack as the culprit when we'd been trying to figure out who the pirate was. I hadn't either, I realized now. I'd kept him on the suspect list because that's what you're supposed to do—never eliminate anyone without hard evidence. Will had taught me that.

Again, the lump in the throat. I swallowed hard.

"Thank you for saying that. I'm honored that she trusts me." Jack paused for a moment. "Now *she* might have special powers."

I grinned at him. "I wouldn't be surprised."

The lack of noise woke me. The whoosh of the wind and bombardment of rain on the roof, that had been our constant companions for hours, were gone.

I threw the covers off and swung my legs around to hop out of bed, then aborted the whole hopping idea. My body was stiff and sore, with multiple scrapes, bruises and cuts from my activities during the last twenty-four hours.

I sucked in air to blow out a sigh, and wrinkled my nose. I was still wearing yesterday's clothes.

I eased off the bed and grabbed my phone from the nightstand to check the time. Seven-fifteen. The sun would be up by now.

The dogs were lying on the rug, heads up, staring at me, a pathetically hopeful look in their eyes.

Okay, dogs first, then a shower and clean clothes.

I moved toward the door. "Come on, you two." On second thought, best not to take Nugget outside without a leash. I grabbed Buddy's from the top of the dresser.

We were barely out the back door when Buddy cocked a leg over a palmetto bush. Nugget and I trotted to the edge of the lanai and she squatted in the wet leaves.

I timed them. They peed for two and a half minutes straight.

When they were done, I praised them for holding it in so long and scratched behind their ears.

A new sound penetrated the still woods.

The puttering of an engine.

I ran for the front of the house, the dogs racing along on either side.

A large cabin cruiser was maneuvering into position across the end of the pier.

No way did that thing come down the river. It was twice the size of Bruce's customized cruiser. They had to have come around from the Gulf side of the island.

Three men stood in the cockpit. One wore a dark green uniform, the color of the majority of the Florida sheriff departments' uniforms. Another jumped onto the pier and wrapped a line around a cleat.

The third man I would know anywhere. He was swiveling his head back and forth, scanning the beach and house. He spotted me and broke into a big grin.

I dropped Nugget's leash and was across the yard and down the pier by the time he had stepped off the boat. I threw myself into his arms, almost knocking us both into the murky river.

He braced himself and hugged me tight.

Now I was crying. "I love you," I managed to get out between small sobs.

"I love you too." He chuckled and took me by the forearms to hold me a bit away from him. He was scanning my body, for injuries no doubt, but his voice was casual.

I knew better. He was good at hiding his feelings in front of others.

"Are you okay?" His eyes were worried. "You look a little…"

"Bruised and battered? I am, but nothing serious." I threw my arms around his neck. "I missed you so much."

Another chuckle. "Does this mean that you *are* eventually going to marry me?"

I knew he was just trying to lighten the mood, more of that emotional cover-up, but I heard the words, "How about tomorrow?" coming out of my mouth.

I realized, in that moment, the decision had been made back in the woodshed last night, when my inner Mom was lecturing me on making the most of the times between adversity.

No more waiting to live, waiting until it was totally safe.

Life is never totally safe.

EPILOGUE

We ended up waiting a week.

Sherie Wells had convinced me to wait for my mother to come down. "You know she'll never forgive you if you don't."

Sherie was around my mother's age—although she didn't look it, with relatively few wrinkles in her mahogany skin and only a couple of silver streaks in her black hair. She was a mother of grown children herself, so I figured she was an authority on the subject.

I also figured that Mom would forgive me, eventually. But why make her unhappy?

Besides, our Christmas plans were in limbo now. I'd brought Nugget back with me. Lori/Ellie had not had sufficient training yet for me to leave the dog with her. And she and Bruce had enough to deal with right now.

Lori had emailed to tell me that they were staying together, for the time being at least. They would try to work things out. And she was slowly recovering her physical stamina.

No more secrets, she'd written. *Bruce is coping surprisingly well with my news. His first comment was, "That explains a lot."*

And he's let go of his nutty food ideas. Apparently, most of that had been coming from Luke. He pretended to Bruce that he was worried about my health and kept telling him about "articles" he'd supposedly read. But he was really trying to keep my diet restricted, so I'd have to eat the bread and put the doctored salt on everything else to make it tolerable.

Turns out what he was putting in both the salt and the flour was a cholesterol medicine that can cause sarcopenia.

And you'll never guess what substance, combined with that medication, really aggravates the symptoms... Wait for it. Grapefruit juice!

Oh, and here's the other ironic twist. Guess what Bruce is allergic to...RYE flour. When he stopped eating pumpernickel bread, his sniffles went away.

Seriously, he isn't a bad guy, and truth be told, I've grown fond of him through the years. And of course, Ellie loves him. Ria still wants to hurt him, but I think we've convinced her that's a bad idea.

She says hi, by the way, as does Ellie. And I can hear your curious brain whirring halfway across the state. How do I know they say hi? We've started a system of emailing each other. They each have their own accounts now, so you may hear from them at some point.

We all miss Greta. The house isn't the same without her.

Guilt had washed over me when I'd read that. I'd wished for probably the ten-thousandth time that Greta and I'd had our conversation about tainted flour and pirate ghosts some place other than by the servant stairs.

But Luke wasn't going to get away with her murder. The Citrus County M.E.'s preliminary report had confirmed that Greta was strangled, and the pattern of bruises matched his long, slender fingers. Plus some of his hair had been found in her room.

Lori had signed off with, *Congratulations on your nuptials. May your marriage work out far better than ours has up to this point.*

Interestingly enough, her words did not send shivers of anxiety through my system, as they once would have.

Every marriage was unique, and each one had the potential to be highly successful or to fail. It was up to Will and me to see that we succeeded.

"Earth to Marcia," Becky said. She and I were both framed in the full-length mirror in front of us, her short dark curls in contrast to my long auburn hair.

She was currently holding that hair on top of my head in a loose bun. "What do you think?"

I shook my head slightly. I couldn't shake it very hard, since she had a solid grip on my hair. "I think I like it better down."

I knew Will liked it better that way.

She let go of the bun. "Then how about this?" She swept some of the hair on both sides back and held it behind my head. "This much back, the rest down." She pulled a few wisps loose around my face. "Whadaya think?"

"Yes, I like that."

"How's the dress?" Becky asked as she worked on tying and pinning the hair back.

I stared at myself in the mirror. She had altered one of her own sundresses, a white one with spaghetti straps and a full knee-length skirt. It had light pink and blue flowers splashed all over it.

She wore another of her sundresses, hers blue with pink flowers.

The images of the two dresses blurred as my eyes filled with tears. "It's perfect," I whispered.

"Now stop that." Becky produced a tissue and dabbed at my eyes. "You're messing up your makeup."

"Are you sure it's too late to elope?"

Becky threw back her head and laughed.

Susanna Mayfair pushed open the bedroom door and stuck her head in. "Y'all about ready?"

Buddy pushed past her knees and bounded into the room. He wore a glittery blue collar for the occasion. Someone—either Becky or Susanna, most likely—had tied a white-rose boutonniere to his collar.

I crouched down to pet him.

"Oh no," Becky cried out. "You're getting dog hairs on the dress."

I grinned up at her. "Now my outfit is complete."

She rolled her eyes.

We picked our way from my old bedroom through the construction dust and debris in the torn-up living room and into the kitchen.

There stood my petite mother, bracketed by tall Sherie Wells on one side and plump Edna Mayfair on the other.

She wore a pale blue suit and a pink blouse and held my bouquet of pink and white roses. Tears pooled in her brown eyes, but she was smiling at me. She'd cut her wavy hair shorter than the last time I'd seen her, and let it go to gray. It suited her.

I smiled back and gave her a hug.

Sherie wore her favorite church outfit, a royal blue suit with a fitted jacket, and a matching pillbox hat. The tailored suit was relatively timeless, but the hat was at least thirty years out of style. On her regal head, however, it looked just right.

Short, round, gray-haired Edna wore one of her iconic muumuus. She'd whipped it up with her sewing machine especially for the occasion —a solid pale blue. No wild colors or crazy looking flowers, for a change. Draped down the front was a long string of pink pearls. I glanced down and grinned. Sequined pink flip-flops completed her outfit.

Wait, she was also wearing pearl clip earrings.

I'd never seen Edna with earrings before. Indeed, I hadn't seen clip earrings since the last time I'd attended my father's church, shortly after my wedding to Ted, when I'd had to endure a seemingly unending supply of little old ladies clasping my hand and saying, "Your father is so proud of you, dear."

My eyes stung. *Wish you were here, Dad.*

I surveyed again my own personal entourage of old ladies and my heart swelled. I was very glad Sherie had talked me into waiting. This was much better than some Justice of the Peace's office in Ocala.

"Your mama's letting Edna and me sit up front with her," Sherie said. "In the family section."

My eyes started watering again.

"Sheez." Becky sprang into action, dabbing my eyes with a fresh tissue.

"Come on," Edna said. "Time to git this show on the road." She was grinning from ear to ear.

The kitchen table had been shoved back against the wall, to make room for Nugget's crate, which would normally be in the front room, where all the construction chaos was now.

I paused by it, resting my hand on top. Nugget wagged her tail and licked my fingers through the bars. It felt like she was giving me her blessing.

My heart swelled again. "Thanks, girl," I whispered. After all this dog had been through with Buddy and me on Haasi Key, it would be harder than usual to let her go.

Then Mom was handing me my bouquet, and Becky was hustling me out the back door and across the yard, to the open gate between the two properties that were now one.

Dexter Mayfair, looking spiffy in a pale blue suit, waited there to escort his Aunt Edna up the aisle.

I peeked around the edge of the opening as the other two ushers led Sherie and my mother to their places up front.

Will's... um, *our* long backyard was full, with almost every resident of Mayfair, Florida in attendance—row after row of white wooden, folding chairs on each side of a grassy aisle.

Becky stepped around me. "Come on, kiddo," she said quietly. "Don't chicken out now."

"No risk of that."

Buddy and I followed her around the back of the rows of guests to the end of the aisle.

Everyone was facing forward, not realizing that the bride had arrived.

Except for my friend Jess Randall, the owner of Mayfair's only diner. She was turned around in one of the aisle seats.

She spotted me and waved, grinning.

The other guests shifted their attention toward the back.

Becky began slowly walking forward, holding her bouquet of pink and blue mums.

I clutched my own flowers in a death grip.

Becky was halfway to the big, new deck that Will had built last year on the back of *our* house. The music—coming from a boom box that Susanna was manning—changed.

Not to the traditional wedding march. Been there, done that, for both of us.

Becky had suggested a contemporary alternative, and now the lilting medley of ukulele and Israel Kamakawiwo'Ole's sweet voice singing *Somewhere Over the Rainbow* floated back to me. I smiled and started up the grassy aisle, Buddy at my left knee.

Becky had reached the deck and climbed the two steps up. She moved to the left, and I locked eyes with my husband-to-be. He stood next to his best man, Becky's husband Andy, both of them in navy blue suits with white-rose boutonnieres.

Will's face lit up, his grin bringing out those sexy dimples of his.

I grinned back. *I do, Will Haines, I do.*

∼

AUTHOR'S NOTES

If you enjoyed this book, please take a moment to leave a short review on the ebook retailer of your choice. Reviews help with sales and sales keep the stories coming. You can readily find the links to these retailers at the *misterio press* bookstore (https://misteriopress.com/bookstore/the-sound-and-the-furry-a-marcia-banks-and-buddy-mystery/).

And don't worry, there *are* going to be more stories in this series. This is not the end for Marcia and Will and Buddy by any means; rather it is a new chapter (no pun intended). The next book in the series, *A Star-Spangled Mayfair*, is a holiday story starring the diner owner, Jess Randall. (All the books in the series are listed in order, as well as the rest of my books, at the end of these Author's Notes.)

Normally I do acknowledgments next, thanking all those folks who helped make the story the best it could be, but this time I'm going to start with a link to Marcia's bridal procession music, *Somewhere Over The Rainbow, by Israel Kamakawiwo'Ole* (https://www.youtube.com/watch?v=fahr069-fzE). I went surfing for other songs, besides the traditional

Wedding March, that young people were using today for their wedding processionals, and I found this delightful medley.

Now for the acknowledgments. Bear with me as I express my gratitude and then I will reward you with some interesting background tidbits.

First, my unending gratitude and love to my good friend, Angi, whose support in the early years of my writing career made all the difference in the world. But for this book in particular, her various areas of expertise—service dog training, psychology, and Native American culture—were indispensable.

Next, I want to give my editor, Marcy Kennedy, a special thank you. She recently complimented me on how far I've come in a relatively short time (six years since she started editing my books) regarding the craft of writing. I may be a fast learner, Marcy, but you are an excellent teacher.

Also, I've been remiss in recent books by failing to mention my wonderful virtual author's assistant, Jennifer Lewis Oliver. Without her support, both logistical and emotional, I would not have been able to produce the volume or quality of stories I have. She takes care of so many little things every day, so I can focus on writing.

And while many authors are introverts, I'm not. Yet writing is a very solitary profession. Jennifer's pretty much daily contact has kept this extravert sane.

Jenn, you are so awesome!

And last but absolutely not least, a big thank you to my beta readers, Angi and Marilyn, and to Kirsten Weiss at *misterio press* who read the earliest version of this story and gave wonderful feedback. And as always, love and gratitude to my husband for his excellent proofreading skills and his eternal patience and support.

(If you noticed any typos, don't blame him. I can't help myself. I tweak things right up until publication day. But do let me know, so I can fix the boo-boos. My email is lambkassandra3@gmail.com)

I do hope that members of the LGBTQ+ community don't get mad at me for making my bad guy a gay man. Certainly being gay does not make anyone evil or unstable. Gay people run the whole gamut of good and bad, sane and not so sane. But feeling that one has to hide an important aspect of one's identity can certainly lead to a lot of frustration and sadness, as is portrayed in Ellie's husband's life here.

The Native American attitude toward gays, as expressed by Jack, is common in many tribes. Gay people are not only accepted but to some degree revered as having two souls and special spiritual powers.

While in some places, I have presented Dissociative Identity Disorder in a somewhat light manner—it is a cozy mystery, after all—I, in no way, want to minimize what folks with this disorder are dealing with. I am quite familiar with it, having treated a couple of dozen clients with the disorder through the years when I was a psychotherapist. While adding some humor, I have made every effort to portray DID, and the challenges it creates, as accurately as possible.

Alters do often exist in clusters, and they may have varying degrees of co-consciousness, especially as the healing process progresses. The person hearing the voices of other alters in their head is one of the reasons why this disorder is often confused with schizophrenia, which is a totally different, biologically-based thought disorder.

The average number of alters co-existing in someone with DID is ten. But this number is skewed somewhat by the rarer cases where there are over a hundred alters. In Lori/Ellie/Ria's case, there are at least three others besides them—the "lush" Lori mentions plus at least two child alters. Indeed, child and teenage alters are usually more common than adult ones, because the child alter often gets stuck in their development at the time of the trauma that caused them to split off in the first place. That splitting off allows the child to cope and continue putting one foot in front of the other. They can face their abuser over the breakfast table, because the abuse that happened the previous night happened to alter Joey, not the host alter, Petey, who's eating his cereal.

That is what DID is, an elaborate coping mechanism developed to allow a child to survive horrible abuse, usually of varying kinds and coming from more than one abuser. Unfortunately, that coping mechanism becomes problematic in adulthood.

Also unfortunately, there are very few courses available, even at the graduate school level, regarding this and other trauma-related disorders. I taught a whole unit on these disorders to my undergraduate abnormal psychology students. But sadly, the vast majority of psychologists are not as aware of the intricacies of these disorders as they should be.

On a slightly lighter subject… while trying to be true to reality with DID, I have taken considerable literary license where sarcopenia is concerned. It is real, and it is a disease of the elderly. Certain cholesterol medications can exacerbate it, but most likely wouldn't cause it. And yes, grapefruit juice can increase this exacerbation with some of these drugs.

But it is unlikely that a young adult would develop the disease, even if exposed to high levels of such medications. And the muscle atrophy would most likely not reverse itself when the cholesterol medications were discontinued.

Nor would such a recovery happen as quickly as it does for Ellie/Lori/Ria, and symptoms of sarcopenia would not develop so rapidly in Marcia upon exposure to the cholesterol drugs.

But, ah, literary license is a wonderful thing.

I have not taken such license with the subject of hurricanes (https://www.nhc.noaa.gov/aboutsshws.php), however. While late-season hurricanes are quite rare, they are most likely to develop in the warmer waters of the Gulf of Mexico. And while hurricane season isn't officially over until November 30th, Floridians do tend to stop paying close attention after the end of October, so those occasional late ones can sometimes take us by surprise.

So far, my husband and I have only experienced tropical storm-level intensity (winds up to 74 mph) at our North Central Florida home (built in the 1970s) while we were in residence. But in September of 2017, Hurricane Irma was a Category-3 storm, giving it major hurricane status, when it made landfall at Marco Island, in Southwest Florida.

The predictions of its strength fluctuated as it moved up the state, but when it was predicted to be a Cat-1 storm with Cat-2 gusts by the time it reached our city, we loaded our dog and ourselves into the car and headed north.

While a Cat-2 storm is not considered a "major" hurricane, it can reach wind speeds of a 110 mph (177 km/h). And that is enough to do some serious damage to buildings that are not all that sturdy (and even to some that are).

But the precautions Bruce's father had taken, closing in the foundation and adding hurricane anchors to the roof joists, would make it quite possible for an old but well-built house to survive my fictitious Hurricane Pierre. (By the way, since Irma, we've had our roof inspected and it does have hurricane anchors, so we won't be likely to evacuate for a Cat-1 storm in the future.)

Speaking of fictitious, Haasi Key is a figment of my imagination, but the Nature Coast Keys are quite real. Take a look at a map of Florida and you will see a large cluster of islands, of varying sizes, about midway up the Gulf coast of the state. The town of Dahlia is also fictitious but is very loosely based on the real town of Ozello, Florida (https://www.nature-coaster.com/discover-ozello-the-nature-coast-keys/). However, all of the townspeople in this book are totally made-up characters, as are the businesses mentioned. And the tiny post office is modeled after others I have seen in Florida small towns.

The small park where Marcia leaves her car is modeled on the real Ozello Park, which is indeed little more than a small parking area and a sand and gravel slope down to the water where folks can launch their boats.

And now, a synopsis of the next story in the series, *A Star-Spangled Mayfair*:

Marcia Banks and her octogenarian friend, Edna Mayfair—matriarch of Mayfair, Florida, population 306—are thrilled when the fiancé of the Mayfair Diner's owner volunteers to host a 4th of July extravaganza at their farm. The local Chamber of Commerce has been trying their best to attract more tourists to the Central Florida town.

But the introverted diner owner, Jess Randall, is not so thrilled. She moved to the farm in the first place to get away from the nosy-neighbor nature of a small town. Plus, she tearfully confides to her friend Marcia, she's scared to death of fireworks.

The fireworks do indeed turn out to be deadly. When Jess's fiancé is found with a Roman candle through his chest, Jess becomes the prime suspect, since her only alibi is that she was hiding in a closet covering her ears.

Was the death an accident or was it murder? And is Jess a killer? Marcia and her new husband, Will Haines, come down on opposite sides of that question—with Will agreeing with the detectives on the case. When Jess is arrested, Marcia feels compelled to investigate to clear her friend, but considering what she finds, Jess may or may not thank her.

OTHER BOOKS by KASSANDRA LAMB

The Kate Huntington Mystery Series:
MULTIPLE MOTIVES
ILL-TIMED ENTANGLEMENTS
FAMILY FALLACIES
CELEBRITY STATUS
COLLATERAL CASUALTIES
ZERO HERO
FATAL FORTY-EIGHT

SUICIDAL SUSPICIONS
ANXIETY ATTACK
POLICE PROTECTION

~~

The Kate on Vacation Novellas:
An Unsaintly Season in St. Augustine
Cruel Capers on the Caribbean
Ten-Gallon Tensions in Texas
Missing on Maui

~~

The Marcia Banks and Buddy Mysteries:
To Kill A Labrador
Arsenic and Young Lacy
The Call of the Woof
A Mayfair Christmas Carol
Patches in the Rye
The Legend of Sleepy Mayfair
The Sound and the Furry
A Star-Spangled Mayfair
(coming Summer, 2019)

~~

Unintended Consequences
Romantic Suspense Stories:
(written under the pen name, Jessica Dale)
Payback
Backlash
Backfire
(coming 2019)

ABOUT THE AUTHOR

Kassandra Lamb has never been able to decide which she loves more, psychology or writing. In college, she realized that writers need a day job in order to eat, so she studied psychology. After a career as a psychotherapist and college professor, she is now retired and can pursue her passion for writing.

She spends most of her time in an alternate universe with her characters. The portal to that universe, aka her computer, is located in Florida, where her husband and dog catch occasional glimpses of her.

Kass has completed ten full-length novels in the Kate Huntington Mystery series (about a psychotherapist/amateur sleuth and set in her native Maryland), plus four Kate on Vacation novellas. She is also the author of the Marcia Banks and Buddy cozy mystery series, about a service dog trainer and her sidekick and mentor dog, Buddy. There are five novels and two novellas out in that series, which is set in central Florida. A third novella is due out in the summer of 2019, and another novel in 2020.

To read and see more about Kassandra and her books, you can go to https://kassandralamb.com. Be sure to sign up for the newsletter there to get a heads up about new releases, plus special offers and bonuses for subscribers.

Kass's e-mail is lambkassandra3@gmail.com and she loves hearing from readers! She's also on Facebook (https://www.facebook.com/kassandralambauthor) and Goodreads (http://www.goodreads.com/author/show/5624939.Kassandra_Lamb) and hangs out some on Twitter @KassandraLamb. And she blogs about psychological topics and other random things at https://misteriopress.com.

Kassandra also writes romantic suspense under the pen name of Jessica Dale (https://darkardorpublications.com/jessicas-books/).

Please check out these other great *misterio press* series:

Karma's ABitch: Pet Psychic Mysteries
by Shannon Esposito

Multiple Motives: Kate Huntington Mysteries
by Kassandra Lamb

Maui Widow Waltz: Islands of Aloha Mysteries
by JoAnn Bassett

The Metaphysical Detective: Riga Hayworth ParanormalMysteries
by Kirsten Weiss

Dangerous and Unseemly: Concordia Wells Historical Mysteries
by K.B. Owen

Murder, Honey: Carol Sabala Mysteries
by Vinnie Hansen

Blogging is Murder: Digital Detective Cozy Mysteries
by Gilian Baker

To Kill ALabrador: Marcia Banks and Buddy Cozy Mysteries
by Kassandra Lamb

Steam and Sensibility: Sensibility Grey SteampunkMysteries
by Kirsten Weiss

Never Sleep: Chronicles of a Lady Detective HistoricalMysteries
by K.B. Owen

Bound: Witches of Doyle Cozy Mysteries
by Kirsten Weiss

At Wits'End Cozy Mysteries
by Kirsten Weiss

Payback: Unintended Consequences Romantic Suspense
by Jessica Dale

Plus even more great mysteries/thrillers in the misterio press bookstore (https://misteriopress.com/bookstore/).

Made in the USA
Middletown, DE
15 August 2019